MAN *TO* MAN

JACKSON GREGORY

1st WORLD
LIBRARY
Literary Society

Man to Man

Jackson Gregory

© 1st World Library, 2007
PO Box 2211
Fairfield, IA 52556
www.1stworldlibrary.com
First Edition

LCCN: 2007901811

Softcover ISBN: 978-1-4218-4278-3
Hardcover ISBN: 978-1-4218-4180-9
eBook ISBN: 978-1-4218-4376-6

Purchase *"Man to Man"*
as a traditional bound book at:
www.1stWorldLibrary.com/purchase.asp?ISBN=978-1-4218-4278-3

1st World Library is a literary, educational organization
dedicated to:

- Creating a free internet library of downloadable ebooks

- Hosting writing competitions and offering book
publishing scholarships.

Interested in more 1st World Library books?
contact: literacy@1stworldlibrary.com
Check us out at: www.1stworldlibrary.com

1st World Library Literary Society

Giving Back to the World

"If you want to work on the core problem, it's early school literacy."

- James Barksdale, former CEO of Netscape

"No skill is more crucial to the future of a child, or to a democratic and prosperous society, than literacy."

- Los Angeles Times

Literacy... means far more than learning how to read and write... The aim is to transmit... knowledge and promote social participation."

- UNESCO

"Literacy is not a luxury, it is a right and a responsibility. If our world is to meet the challenges of the twenty-first century we must harness the energy and creativity of all our citizens."

- President Bill Clinton

"Parents should be encouraged to read to their children, and teachers should be equipped with all available techniques for teaching literacy, so the varying needs and capacities of individual kids can be taken into account."

- Hugh Mackay

CONTENTS

CHAPTER I

STEVE DIVES INTO DEEP WATERS

Steve Packard's pulses quickened and a bright eagerness came into his eyes as he rode deeper into the pine-timbered mountains. To-day he was on the last lap of a delectable journey. Three days ago he had ridden out of the sun-baked town of San Juan; three months had passed since he had sailed out of a South Sea port.

Far down there, foregathering with sailor men in a dirty water-front boarding-house, he had grown suddenly and even tenderly reminiscent of a cleaner land which he had roamed as a boy. He stared back across the departed years as many a man has looked from just some such resort as Black Jack's boarding-house, a little wistfully withal. Abruptly throwing down his unplayed hand and forfeiting his ante in a card game, he had gotten up and taken ship back across the Pacific. The house of Packard might have spelled its name with the seven letters of the word "impulse."

Late to-night or early to-morrow he would go down the trail into Packard's Grab, the valley which had been his grandfather's and, because of a burst of reckless generosity on the part of the old man, Steve's father's also. But never Steve's, pondered the man on the horse; word of his father's death had come to him five months ago and with it word of

Phil Packard's speculations and sweeping losses.

But never had money's coming and money's going been a serious concern of Steve Packard; and now his anticipation was sufficiently keen. The world was his; he had no need of a legal paper to state that the small fragment of the world known as Ranch Number Ten belonged to him. He could ride upon it again, perhaps find one like old Bill Royce, the foreman, left. And then he could go on until he came to the other Packard ranch where his grandfather had lived and still might be living.

After all of this—Well, there were many sunny beaches here and there along the seven seas where he had still to lie and sun himself. Now it was a pure joy to note how the boles of pine and cedar pointed straight toward the clear, cloudless blue; how the little streams trickled through their worn courses; how the quail scurried to their brushy retreats; how the sunlight splashed warm and golden through the branches; how valleys widened and narrowed and the thickly timbered ravines made a delightful and tempting coolness upon the mountainsides.

It was an adventure with its own thrill to ride around a bend in the narrow trail and be greeted by an old, well-remembered landmark: a flat-topped boulder where he had lain when a boy, looking up at the sky and thrilling to the whispered promises of life; or a pool where he had fished or swum; or a tree he had climbed or from whose branches he had shot a gray squirrel. A wagon-road which he might have taken he abandoned for a trail which better suited his present fancy since it led with closer intimacy into the woods.

It was late afternoon when he came to the gentle rise which gave first glint of the little lake so like a blue jewel set in the dusty green of the wooded slopes. As he rose in his stirrups

Jackson Gregory

to gaze down a vista through the tree-trunks, he saw the bright, vivid blue of a cloak.

"Now, there's a woman," thought Packard without enthusiasm. "The woods were quite well enough alone without her. As I suppose Eden was. But along she comes just the same. And of course she must pick out the one dangerous spot on the whole lake shore to display herself on."

For he knew how, just yonder where the blue cloak caught the sunlight, there was a sheer bank and how the lapping water had cut into it, gouging it out year after year so that the loose soil above was always ready to crumble and spill into the lake. The wearer of the bright garment stirred and stood up, her back still toward him.

"Young girl, most likely," he hazarded an opinion.

Though she was too far from him to be at all certain, he had sensed something of youth's own in the very quality of her gesture.

Then suddenly he clapped his spurs to his horse's sides and went racing down the slope toward the spot where an instant ago she had made such a gay contrast to dull verdure and gray boulders. For he had glimpsed the quick flash of an up-thrown arm, had heard a low cry, had guessed rather than seen through the low underbrush her young body falling.

As he threw himself from his horse's back, his spur caught in the blue cloak which had dropped from her shoulders; he kicked at it savagely. He jerked off his boots, poised a moment looking down upon the disturbed surface of the water which had closed over her head, made out the sweep of an arm under the widening circles, and dived straight down.

And so deep down under water they met for the first time, Steve Packard with a sense of annoyance that was almost outright irritation, the girl struggling frantically as his right arm closed tight about her. A quick suspicion came to him that she had not fallen but had thrown herself downward in some passionate quarrel with life; that she wanted to die and would give him scant thanks for the rescue.

This thought was followed by the other that in her access of terror she was doing what the drowning person always does—losing her head, threatening to bind his arms with her own and drag him down with her.

Struggling half blindly and all silently they rose a little toward the surface. Packard tightened his grip about her body, managed to imprison one of her arms against her side, beat at the water with his free hand, and so, just as his lungs seemed ready to burst, he brought his nostrils into the air.

He drew in a great breath and struck out mightily for the shore, seeking a less precipitous bank at the head of a little cove. As he did so, he noted how her struggles had suddenly given over, how she floated quietly with him, her free arm even aiding in their progress.

A little later he crawled out of the clear, cold water to a pebbly beach, drawing her after him.

And now he understood that his destiny and his own headlong nature had again made a consummate fool of him. The same knowledge was offered him freely in a pair of gray eyes which fairly blazed at him. No gratitude there of a maiden heroically succored in the hour of her supreme distress; just the leaping anger of a girl with a temper like hot fire who had been rudely handled by a stranger.

Her scanty little bathing-suit, bright blue like the discarded cloak, the red rubber cap binding the bronze hair—she must have donned the ridiculous thing with incredible swiftness while he batted an eye—might have been utterly becoming in other eyes than those of Steve Packard. Now that they merely told him that he was a blundering ass, he was conscious solely of a desire to pick her up and shake her.

"Gee!" she panted at him with an angry scornfulness which made him wince. "You're about the freshest proposition I ever came across!"

Later, perhaps, he would admit that she was undeniably and most amazingly pretty; that the curves of her little white body were delightfully perfect; that she had made an armful that at another time would have put sheer delirium into a man's blood.

Just now he knew only that in his moment of nothing less than stupidity he had angered her and that his own anger though more unreasonable was scarcely less heated; that he had made and still made but a sorry spectacle; that he was sopping wet and cold and would be shivering in a moment like a freezing dog.

"Why did you want to yell like a Comanche Indian when you went in?" he demanded rudely, offering the only defense he could put mind or tongue to. "A man would naturally suppose that you were falling."

"You didn't suppose any such thing!" she retorted sharply. "You saw me dive; if you had the brains of a scared rabbit, you'd know that when a girl had gone to the trouble to climb into a bathing-suit and then jumped into the water she wanted a swim. And to be left alone," she added scathingly.

Packard felt the afternoon breeze through the wet garments

which stuck so close to him, and shivered.

"If you think," he said, as sharply as she had spoken, "that I just jumped into that infernal ice-pond, clothes and all, for the pure joy of making your charming acquaintance in some ten feet of water, all I can say is that you are by no means lacking a full appreciation of your own attractiveness."

She opened her eyes widely at him, lying at his feet where he had deposited her. She had not offered to rise. But now she sat up, drawing her knees into the circle of her clasped arms, tilting her head back as she stared up at him.

"You've got your nerve, Mr. Man," she informed him coolly. "Any time that you think I'll stand for a fool man jumping in and spoiling my fun for me and then scolding me on top of it, you've got another good-sized think coming. And take it from me, you'll last a good deal longer in this neck of the woods if you 'tend to your own business after this and keep your paws off other folks' affairs. Get me that time?"

"I get you all right," grunted Packard. "And I find your gratitude to a man who has just risked his life for you quite touching."

"Gratitude? Bah!" she told him, leaping suddenly to her feet. "Risked your life for me, did you?" She laughed jeeringly at that. "Why, you big lummox, I could have yanked you out as easy as turn a somersault if you started to drown. And now suppose you hammer the trail while it's open."

He bestowed upon her a glance whose purpose was to wither her. It failed miserably, partly because she was patently not the sort to be withered by a look from a mere man, and partly because a violent and inopportune shiver shook him from head to foot.

Until now there had been only bright anger in the girl's eyes. Suddenly the light there changed; what had begun as a sniff at him altered without warning into a highly amused giggle.

"Golly, Mr. Man," she taunted him. "You're sure some swell picture as you stand there, hand on hip and popping your eyes out at me! Like a king in a story-book, only he'd just got a ducking and was trying to stare the other fellow down. Which is one thing you can't do with me."

Her eyes had the adorable trick of seeming to crinkle to a mirth which would have been an extremely pleasant pheno-menon to witness had she been laughing with him instead of at him. As matters stood, Packard was quite prepared to dislike her heartily.

"I'd add to your kind information that the trail is open at both ends," he told her significantly. "I'm going to find a sunny spot and dry my clothes. No objection, I suppose?"

He clambered up the bank and made his way to the spot whence he had dived after her, bent on retrieving his boots and spurs. Her eyes followed him interestedly. He ignored her and set about extricating a spur rowel from the fabric of the bright blue cloak. Her voice floated up to him then, demanding:

"What in the world are you up to now? Not going to swipe my clothes, are you?"

"I'd have the right," he called back over his shoulder, "if I happened to need a makeshift dressing-gown. As it is, however, I am trying to get my spur out of the thing."

"You great big brute!" she wailed at him, and here she came running along the bank. "You just dare to tear my cloak and I'll hound you out of the country for it! I drove forty miles to get it and this is the first time I ever wore it. Stupid!" And she jerked both the garment and the spur from him.

The lining was silken, of a deep, rich, golden hue. And already it was torn, although but the tiniest bit in the world, by one of the sharp spikes. Her temper, however, ever ready it seemed, flared out again; the crinkling merriment went from her eyes, leaving no trace; the color warmed in her cheeks as she cried:

"You're just like all of the rest of your breed, big and awkward, crowding in where you don't belong, messing up the face of the earth, spoiling things right and left. I wonder if the good Lord Himself knows what he made men for, anyway!"

The offending spur, detached by her quick fingers, described a bright arc in the late sunlight, flew far out, dipped in a little leaping spurt of spray, and went down quietly in the lake.

"Go jump in and get that, if you are so keen on saving things," she mocked him. "There's only, about fifteen feet of water to dig through."

"You little devil!" he said.

For the spur with its companion had cost him twenty dollars down on the Mexican border ten days ago and he had set much store by it.

"Little devil, am I?" she retorted readily. "You'll know it if you don't keep on your side of the road. Look at that tear! Just look at it!"

She had stepped quite close to him, holding out the cloak, her eyes lifted defiantly to his. He put out a sudden hand and laid it on her wet shoulder. She opened her eyes widely again at the new look in his. But even so her regard was utterly fearless.

"Young lady," he said sternly, "so help me God, I've got the biggest notion in the world to take you across my knee and give you the spanking of your life. If I did crowd in where I don't belong, as you so sweetly put it, it was at least to do you a kindness. Another time I'd know better; I'd sooner do a favor for a wildcat."

"Take your dirty paws off of me," she cried, wrenching away from him. "And—spank me, would you?" The fire leaped higher in her eyes, the red in her cheeks gave place to an angrier white. "If you ever so much as dare touch me again—"

She broke off, panting. Packard laughed at her.

"You'd try to scratch me, I suppose," he jeered; "and then, after the fashion of your own sweet sex when you don't have the strength to put a thing across, you'd most likely cry!"

"I'd blow your ugly head off your shoulders with a shotgun," she concluded briefly.

And despite the extravagance of the words it was borne in upon Packard's understanding that she meant just exactly what she said.

He was getting colder all the time and knew that in a moment his teeth would chatter. So a second time he turned his back on her, gathered up his horse's reins, and moved away, seeking a spot in the woods where he could get dry and sun his clothes. And since Packard rage comes swiftly and more often than not goes the same way, within five minutes over a comforting cigarette he was grinning widely, seeing in a flash all of the humor of the situation which had successfully concealed itself from him until now.

"And I don't blame her so much, after all," he chuckled. "Taking a nice, lonely dive, to have a fool of a man grab her all of a sudden when she was enjoying herself half a dozen feet under water! It's enough to stir up a good healthy temper. Which, by the Lord, she has!"

CHAPTER II

MISS BLUE CLOAK KNOWS WHEN SHE'S BEAT

Half an hour later, his clothing wrung out and sun-dried after a fashion, Packard dressed, swung up into the saddle, and turned back into the trail. And through the trees, where their rugged trunks made an open vista, he saw not two hundred yards away the gay spot of color made by the blue cloak. So she was still here, lingering down the road that wound about the lake's shores, when already he had fancied her far on her way. He wondered for the first time where that way led?

He drew rein among the pines, waiting in his turn for her to go on. The blue cloak did not move. He leaned to one side to see better, peering around a low-flung cedar bough. His trail here led to the road; he must pass her unless she went on soon.

Beside the vivid hue of her cloak the sunlight streaming through the forest showed him another bright, gay color, a streak of red which through the underbrush he was at first at a loss to account for. He would have said that she was seated in a low-bodied, red wagon, were it not that if such had been the case he must have seen the horses.

"An automobile!" he guessed.

He rode on a score of steps and stopped again. Sure enough, there she sat at the steering-wheel of a long, rakish touring-car, the slump of her shoulders vaguely hinting at despair and perhaps a stalled engine. His grin widened joyously. He touched his horse with his one spur, assumed an expression of vast indifference, and rode on. She jerked up her head, looked about at him swiftly, gave him her shoulder again.

He rode into the road and came on with tantalizing slowness, knowing that she would want to turn again and guessing that she would conquer the impulse. A few paces behind her he stopped again, rolling a fresh cigarette and seeming, as he had been before the meeting, the most leisurely man in the world.

He saw her lean forward, busied with ignition and starter; he fancied that the little breeze brought to him the faintest of guarded exclamations.

"The blamed old thing won't go," chuckled Packard with vast satisfaction. "Some car, too. Boyd-Merril Twin Eight, latest model. And dollars to doughnuts I know just what's wrong—and she doesn't!"

She ignored him with such a perfect unconsciousness of his presence in the same world with her that he was moved to a keen admiration.

"I'll bet her face is as red as a beet, just the same," was his cheerful thought. "And right here, Steve Packard, is where you don't 'crowd in' until you're called on."

She straightened up, sitting very erect, her two hands tense upon the useless wheel. He noted the poise of her head and found in it something almost queenly. For a moment they were both very still, he watching and feeling his sense pervaded by the glowing sensation that all was right with the world, she holding her face averted and keeping her thoughts to herself.

Presently she got out and lifted the hood, looking in upon the engine, despairing. But did not glance toward him. Then she closed the hood and returned to her seat, once more attempting to get some sort of response from the starting system. Packard felt himself fairly beaming all over.

"I may be a low-lived dog and a deep-dyed villain besides," he was frank to admit to himself. "But right now I'm having the time of my life. And I wouldn't bet two bits which way she's going to jump next, either—never having met just her type before."

"Well?" she said abruptly.

She hadn't moved, hadn't so much as turned her head to look at him. If she had done so just then perhaps Packard's extremely good-humored smile, a contented, eminently satisfied smile, would not have warmed her to him.

"Speak to me?" he asked innocently.

"I did. Simply because there's nobody else to speak to. Don't happen to know anything about motor-cars, do you?"

It was all very icily enunciated, but had no noticeably freezing effect upon the man's mood.

"I sure do," he told her cheerfully. "Know 'em from front bumper to tail-lamp. Yours is a Boyd-Merril, Twin Eight, this year's model. Fox-Whiting starting and lighting system. Great little car, too, if you ask me."

"What I was going to ask you," came the cool little voice,

more haughtily than ever, "was not what you think of the car but if you—if you happened to know how to make the miserable thing go."

"Sure," he replied to the back of her head, with all of his former pleasant manner. "Pull out the ignition button; push down the starter pedal with your right foot; throw out the clutch with your left; put her into low; let in your clutch slowly; give her a little—"

"Smarty!" He had counted upon some such interruption, and chuckled when it came. "I know all that."

"Then why don't you do it?" he queried innocently. "You're right square in my way, the road's narrow, and I've got to be moving on."

"I don't do it," she informed that portion of the world which lay immediately in front of her slightly elevated nose, "because it won't work. I pulled out the ignition button and—and nothing happened. Then I tried to force down the starter pedal and the crazy thing won't go down."

"I see," said Packard interestedly. "Don't know a whole lot about cars, do you?"

"The world wasn't made overnight," she said tartly. "I've had this pesky thing a month. Do you know what's the matter?"

He took his time in replying. He was so long about it, in fact, that Miss Blue Cloak stirred uneasily and finally shot him a questioning look over her shoulder, just to make sure, he suspected, that he hadn't slipped away and left her.

"Well?" she asked again.

"Speak to me?" he repeated himself, pretending to start from a deep abstraction. "Oh, do I know what's the matter? Sure!"

She waited a reasonable length of time for him to go on. He, secure in the sense of his own mastery of the situation, waited for her. Between them they allowed it to grow very quiet there in the wood by the lake shore. He saw her glance furtively at the lowering sun.

"If you do know," she said finally and somewhat faintly, but as frigidly as ever, "will you tell me or won't you?"

"Why," he said, as though he had not thought of it, "I don't know. If I were really sure that I was needed. You know it's mighty hard telling these days when you stumble upon a damsel in distress whether a stranger's aid is welcome or not. If there's one thing I won't do it's shove myself forward when I'm not wanted."

"You're a nasty animal!" she cried hotly.

"For all I know," he resumed in an untroubled tone, "the end of your journey may be just around the bend, about a hundred yards off. And if I plunged in to be of assistance I might be suspected of being a fresh guy."

"It's half a dozen miles to the ranch-house," she condescended to tell him. "And it's going to get dark in no time. And if you want to know, Mr. Smarty, that's as close as I've ever come or ever will come to asking anything of any man that ever lived."

He could have sat there until dark just for the sheer joy of teasing her, making her pay a little for her recent treatment of him. But there was a note of finality in her voice which did not escape him; in another moment she would jump down and go on on foot and he knew it. So at last he rode up to the car, dismounted, and lifted the hood.

"Ignition," he ordered her.

She pulled out the little button again. His eyes upon hers, his grin frank and unconcealed, he took a stone from the road and with it tapped gently upon the shaft running from the pump. Immediately there came that little hissing sound she had waited for.

"Starter," he commanded.

And now her foot upon the pedal achieved the desired results; the engine responded, humming pleasantly. He closed the hood and stood back eying her with a mingling of amusement and triumph. Her face reddened slowly. And then, startling him with its unheralded unexpectedness, a gay peal of laughter from her made quite another girl of her, a dimpling, radiant, altogether adorable and desirable creature.

"Oh, I know when I'm beat!" she cried frankly. "You've put one across on me to-day, Mr. Man. And since you meant well all along and were just simply the blunderheaded man God made you, I guess I have been a little cat. Good luck to you and a worth-while trail to ride."

She blew him a friendly kiss from her brown finger-tips, bent over her wheel, and took the first turn in the road at a swiftly acquired speed which left Steve Packard behind in dust and growing wonderment.

"And she's been driving only a month," was his softly whistled comment. "Reckless little devil!"

Then, in his turn cocking a speculative eye at the sun in the west, he rode on, following in the track made by the spinning automobile tires.

CHAPTER III

NEWS OF A LEGACY

When Packard came to a forking of the roads he stopped and hesitated. The automobile tracks led to the left; he was tempted to follow them. And it was his way in the matter of such impulses to yield to temptation. But in this case he finally decided that common sense if not downright wisdom pointed in the other direction.

So, albeit a bit reluctantly, he swerved to the right.

"We'll see you some other time, though, Miss Blue Cloak," he pondered. "For I have a notion it would be good sport knowing you."

An hour later he made out a lighted window, seen and lost through the trees. Conscious of a man's-sized appetite he galloped up the long lane, turned in at a gate sagging wearily upon its hinges, and rode to the door of the lighted house. The first glance showed him that it was a long, low, rambling affair resembling in dejectedness the drooping gate. An untidy sort of man in shirt-sleeves and smoking a pipe came to the door, kicking into silence his half-dozen dogs.

"What's the chance of something to eat and a place to sleep

in the barn?" asked Packard.

The rancher waved his pipe widely.

"Help yourself, stranger," he answered, in a voice meant to be hospitable but which through long habit had acquired an unpleasantly sullen tone. "You'll find the sleeping all right, but when it comes to something to eat you can take it from me you'll find damn' poor picking. Get down, feed your horse, and come in."

When he entered the house Packard was conscious of an oddly bare and cheerless atmosphere which at first he was at a loss to explain. For the room was large, amply furnished, cheerfully lighted by a crackling fire of dry sticks in the big rock fireplace, and a lamp swung from the ceiling. What the matter was dawned on him gradually: time was when this chamber had been richly, even exquisitely, furnished and appointed. Now it presented rather a dejected spectacle of faded splendor, not entirely unlike a fine gentleman of the old school fallen among bad companions and into tattered ill repute.

The untidy host, more untidy than ever here in the full light, dragged his slippered feet across the threadbare carpet to a corner cupboard, from which he took a bottle and two glasses.

"We can have a drink anyhow," he said in that dubious tone which so harmonized both with himself and his sitting-room. "After which we'll see what's to eat. Terry fired the cook last week and there's been small feasting since."

Packard accepted a moderate drink, the rancher filled his own glass generously, and they drank standing. This ceremony briefly performed and chairs dragged comfortably up to the fireplace, Packard's host called out loudly:

"Hi, Terry! There's a man here wants something to eat. Anything left?"

"If he's hungry," came the cool answer from a room somewhere toward the other end of the long house, "why can't he forage for himself? Wants me to bring his rations in there and feed it to him, I suppose!"

Packard lifted his eyebrows humorously.

"Is that Terry?" he asked.

"That's Terry," grumbled the rancher. "She's in the kitchen now. And if I was you, pardner, and had a real hankering for grub I'd mosey right along in there while there's something left." His eye roved to the bottle on the chimney-piece and dropped to the fire. "I'll trail you in a minute."

Here was invitation sufficient, and Packard rose swiftly, went out through the door at the end of the room, passed through an untidy chamber which no doubt had been intended originally as a dining-room, and so came into lamplight again and the presence of Miss Blue Cloak.

He made her a bow and smiled in upon her cheerfully. She, perched on an oilcloth-covered table, her booted feet swinging, a thick sandwich in one hand and a steaming cup of coffee in the other, took time to look him up and down seriously and to swallow before she answered his bow with a quick, bird-like nod.

"Don't mind me," she said briefly, having swallowed again. "Dig in and help yourself."

On the table beside her were bread, butter, a very dry and black-looking roast, and a blacker but more tempting coffee-pot.

"I didn't follow you on purpose," said Packard. "Back there where the roads forked I saw that you had turned to the left, so I turned to the right."

"All roads lead to Rome," she said around the corner of the big sandwich. "Anyway, it's all right. I guess I owe you a square meal and a night's lodging for being on the job when my car stalled."

"Not to mention for diving into the lake after you," amended Packard.

"I *wouldn't* mention it if I were you," she retorted. "Seeing that you just made a fool of yourself that time."

She openly sniffed the air as he stepped by her reaching out for butcher-knife and roast. "So you are dad's kind, are you? Hitting the booze every show you get. The Lord deliver me from his chief blunder. Meaning a man."

"He probably will," grinned Packard genially. "And as for turning up your nose at a fellow for taking a drop o' kindness with a hospitable host, why, that's all nonsense, you know."

Terry kicked her high heels impudently and vouchsafed him no further answer beyond that easy gesture. Packard made his own sandwich, found the salt, poured a tin cup of coffee.

"The sugar's over there." She jerked her head toward a shelf on which, after some searching among a lot of empty and nearly empty cans, Packard found it. "That's all there is and precious little left; help yourself but don't forget breakfast comes in the morning."

"This is the old Slade place, isn't it?" Packard asked.

"It was, about the time the big wall was building in China. Where've you been the last couple of hundred years? It's the Temple place now."

"Then you're Miss Temple?"

"Teresa Arriega for my mother, Temple for my dad," she told him in the quick, bright way which already he found characteristic of her. "Terry for myself, if you say it quick."

He had suspected from the beginning that there was Southern blood of some strain in her. Now he studied her frankly, and, just to try her out, said carelessly:

"If you weren't so tanned you'd be quite fair; your eyes are gray too. Blue-gray when you smile, dark gray when you are angry; and yet you say your mother was Mexican—"

"Mexican, your foot!" she flared out at him, her trim little body stiffening perceptibly, her chin proudly lifted. "The Arriegas were pure-blooded Castilian, I'd have you understand. There's no mongrel about me."

He drowned his satisfied chuckle with a draft of coffee.

"I'm looking for a job," he said abruptly. "Happen to know of any of the cattle outfits around here that are short-handed?"

"Men are scarce right now," she answered. "A good cattle-hand is as hard to locate as a dodo bird. You could get a job anywhere if you're worth your salt."

"I was thinking," said Packard, "of moseying on to Ranch Number Ten. There's a man I used to know—Bill Royce, his name is. Foreman, isn't he?"

"So you know Bill Royce?" countered Terry. "Well, that's something in your favor. He's a good scout."

"Then he is still foreman?"

"I didn't say so! No, he isn't. And I guess he'll never be foreman of that outfit or any other again. He's blind."

Old Bill Royce blind! Here was a shock, and Packard sat back and stared at her speechlessly. Somehow this was incredible, unthinkable, nothing short. The old cattle-man who had been the hero of his boyhood, who had taught him to shoot and ride and swim, who had been so vital and so quick and keen of eye—blind?

"What happened to him?" asked Packard presently.

"Suppose you ask him," she retorted. "If you know him so well. He is still with the outfit. A man named Blenham is the foreman now. He's old Packard's right-hand bower, you know."

"But Phil Packard is dead. And—"

"And old 'Hell-Fire' Packard, Phil Packard's father, never will die. He's just naturally too low-down mean; the devil himself wouldn't have him."

"Terry!" came the voice of the untidy man, meant to be remonstrative but chiefly noteworthy for a newly acquired thickness of utterance.

Terry's eyes sparkled and a hot flush came into her cheeks.

"Leave me alone, will you, pa?" she cried sharply. "I don't owe old Packard anything; no, nor Blenham either. You can walk easy all you like, but I'm blamed if I've got to. If you'd smash your cursed old bottle on their heads and take a brace we'd come alive yet."

"Remember we have a guest with us," grumbled Temple from his place by the sitting-room fire.

"Oh, shoot!" exclaimed the girl impatiently. Reaching out for a second sandwich she stabbed the kitchen-knife viciously into the roast. "I've a notion to pack up and clear out and let the cut-throat crowd clean you to the last copper and pick your bones into the bargain. When did you ever get anywhere by taking your hat off and side-stepping for a Packard? If you're so all-fired strong for remembering, why don't you try to remember how it feels to stand on two feet like a man instead of crawling on your belly like a worm!"

"My dear!" expostulated Temple.

Terry sniffed and paid no further attention to him.

"Dad was all man once," she said without lowering her voice, making clearer than ever that Miss Terry Temple had a way of speaking straight out what lay in her mind, caring not at all who heard. "I'm hoping that some day he'll come back. A real man was dad, a man's man. But that was before the Packards broke him and stepped on him and kicked him out of the trail. And, believe me, the Packards, though they ought to be hung to the first tree, are men just the same!"

"So I have heard," admitted the youngest of the defamed house. "You group them altogether? They're all the same then?"

"Phil Packard's dead," she retorted. "So we'll let him go at that. Old Hell-Fire Packard, his father, is the biggest lawbreaker out of jail. He's the only one left, and from the looks of things he'll keep on living and making trouble another hundred years."

"There was another Packard, wasn't there?" he insisted. "Phil Packard's son, the old man's grandson?"

"Never knew him," said Terry. "A scamp and a scalawag and a tomfool, though, if you want to know. If he wasn't, he'd have stuck on the job instead of messing around in the dirty ports of the seven seas while his old thief of a grandfather stole his heritage from him."

"How's that?" he asked sharply. "How do you mean 'stole' it from him?"

"The same way he gobbles up everything else he wants. Ranch Number Ten ought to belong to the fool boy now, oughtn't it? And here's old Packard's pet dog Blenham running the outfit in old Packard's interests just the same as if it was his already. Set a thief to rob a thief," she concluded briefly.

Steve Packard sat bolt upright in his chair.

"I wouldn't mind getting the straight of this," he told her quietly. "I thought that Philip Packard had sold the outfit to his father before his death."

"He didn't sell it to anybody. He mortgaged it right up to the hilt to the old man. Then he up and died. Of course everything he left, amounting mostly to a pile of debts, went to his good-for-nothing son."

A light which she could not understand, eager and bright, shone in young Packard's eyes. If what she told him were true, then the old home ranch, while commonly looked upon as belonging already to his grandfather, was the property legally of Steve Packard. And Blenham—yes, and old Bill Royce—were taking his pay. Suddenly infinite possibilities stretched out before him.

"Come alive!" laughed Terry. "We were talking about your finding a job. There's one open here for you; first to teach me all you know about the insides of my car; second— What's the matter? Gone to sleep?"

He started. He had been thinking about Blenham and Bill Royce. As Terry continued to stare wonderingly at him he smiled.

"If you don't mind," he said non-committally, "we'll forget about the job for a spell. I left some stuff back at the Packard ranch that belongs to me. I'm going back for it in the morning. Maybe I'll go to work there after all."

She shrugged distastefully.

"It's a free country," she said curtly. "Only I can't see your play. That is, if you're a square guy and not a crook, Number Ten size. You've got a chance to go to work here with a white crowd; if you want to tie up with that ornery bunch it's up to you."

"I'll look them over," he said thoughtfully.

"All right; go to it!" she cried with sudden heat. "I said it was a free country, didn't I? Only you can burn this in your next wheat-straw: once you go to riding herd with that gang you needn't come around here again. And you can take Blenham a message for me: Phil Packard knifed dad and double-crossed him and made him pretty nearly what he is now; old Hell-Fire Packard finished the job. But just the same, the Temple Ranch is still on the map and Terry Temple had rather scrap a scoundrel to the finish than shake hands with one. And one of these days dad's going to come alive yet; you'll see."

"I believe," he said as much to himself as to her, "that I'll have to have a word with old man Packard."

She stared at him incredulously. Then she put her head back and laughed in high amusement.

"Nobody'd miss guessing that you had your nerve with you, Mr. Lanky Stranger," she cried mirthfully. "But when it comes to tackling Hell-Fire Packard with a mouthful of fool questions—Look here; who are you anyway?"

"Nobody much," he answered quietly and just a trifle bitterly. "Tom Fool you named me a while ago. Or, if you prefer, Steve Packard."

She flipped from her place on the table to stand erect, twin spots of red leaping into her cheeks, startling him with the manner in which all mirth fled from her eyes, which narrowed and grew hard.

"That would mean old Hell-Fire's grandson?" she asked sharply.

He merely nodded, watching her speculatively. Her head went still higher. Packard heard her father rise hurriedly and shuffle across the floor toward the kitchen.

"You're a worthy chip off the old stump," Terry was saying contemptuously. "You're a darned sneak!"

"Terry!" admonished Temple warningly.

Her stiff little figure remained motionless a moment, never an eyelid stirring. Then she whirled and went out of the room, banging a door after her.

"She's high-strung, Mr. Packard," said Temple, slow and heavy and a bit uncertain in his articulation. "High-strung, like her mother. And at times apt to be unreasonable. Come in with me and have a drink, and we'll talk things over."

Packard hesitated. Then he turned and followed his host back to the fireplace. Suddenly he found himself without further enthusiasm for conversation.

CHAPTER IV

TERRY BEFORE BREAKFAST

A gay young voice singing somewhere through the dawn awoke Steve Packard and informed him that Terry was up and about. He lay still a moment, listening. He remembered the song, which, by the way, he had not heard for a good many years, the ballad of a cowboy sick and lonely in a big city, yearning for the open country. At times when Terry's humming was smothered by the walls of the house, Packard's memory strove for the words which his ears failed to catch. And more often than not the words, retrieved from oblivion, were less than worth the effort; no poet had builded the chant, which, rather, grown to goodly proportions of perhaps a hundred verses, had resulted from a natural evolution like a modern Odyssey, or some sprawling vine which was what it was because of its environment. But while lines were faulty and rhymes were bad, and the composition never rose above the commonplace, and often enough sank below it, the ballad was sincere and meant much to those who sang it. Its pictures were homely. Steve, catching certain fragments and seeking others, got such phrases as:

"My bed on dry pine-needles, my camp-fire blazin' bright, The smell of dead leaves burnin' through the big wide-open night," and with moving but silent lips joined Terry in the triumphant refrain:

> "I'm lonesome-sick for the stars through the pines
> An' the bawlin' of herds . . . an' the noise
> Of rocks rattlin' down from a mountain trail . . .
> An' the hills . . . an' my horse . . . an' the boys.
> An' I'd rather hear a kiote howl
> Than be the King of Rome!
> An' when day comes—if day does come—
> By cripes, I'm goin' home!
> . . . Back home! Hear me comin', boys?
> *Yeee*! I said it: 'Comin' home!'"

He sat up in bed. The fragrance of boiling coffee and frying bacon assailed his nostrils pleasurably. Terry's voice had grown silent. Perhaps she was having her breakfast by now? With rather greater haste than the mere call of his morning meal would seem to warrant, he dressed, ran his fingers through his hair by way of completing his toilet, and, going down a hallway, thrust his head in through the kitchen doorway.

"Good morning," he called pleasantly.

Terry was not yet breakfasting. Down on one knee, poking viciously into the fire-box of an extremely old and dilapidated stove, she was seeking, after the time-honored way of her sex, to make the fire burn better. Her face was rosy, flushed prettily with the glow from the blazing oak wood. Packard's eyes brightened as he looked at her, making a comprehensive survey of the trim little form from the top of her bronze hair to the heels of her spick-and-span boots. About her throat, knotted loosely, was a flaming-red silken scarf. The thought struck him that the Temple fortunes, the Temple ranch, the Temple master, all were falling or had already fallen into varying states of decay, and that alone in the wreckage Terry Temple made a gay spot of color, that alone Terry Temple was determined to keep her place in the sun.

Terry, having poked a goodly part of the fire out, made a face at what remained and got to her feet.

"I've been thinking about you," she said.

"Fine!" said Packard. "You can tell me while we have our coffee."

But he did not fail to mark that she had given him no ready smile by way of welcome, that now she regarded him coolly and critically. In her morning attitude there was little to lead him to hope for a free-and-easy chat across a breakfast-table.

"You strike me," said Terry abruptly and emphatically, "as a pretty slick proposition."

"Why so?" asked Packard interestedly.

"Because," said Terry. For a moment he thought that she was going to stop there. But after a thoughtful pause, during which she looked straight at him with eyes which were meant to be merely clear and judicial but which were just faintly troubled, she went on: "Because you're a Packard, to begin with."

"Look here," protested young Packard equably, "I didn't think that of you; honestly, I didn't. How are you and I ever going to get anywhere . . . in the way of being friends, I mean . . . if you start out by blaming me for what my disreputable old scamp of a grandfather does?"

Terry sniffed openly.

"Forget that friendship gag before you think of it, will you?" she said quickly. "Talking nice isn't going to get you anywhere with me and you might as well remember that. It won't buy you anything to start in telling me that I've got pretty eyes or a dimple, and I won't stand one little minute for your pulling any of that girlie-stuff on me. . . . I said, to begin with, you're a Packard. That ought to be enough, the Lord knows! But it's not all."

"First thing," he suggested cheerfully, "are you going to ask me to have breakfast with you?"

"Yes," she answered briefly. "Since you are here and since dad had you stay all night. If you were the devil himself, I'd give you something to eat."

"Being merely the devil's grandson," grinned Packard, "suppose I tuck in and help? I'll set the table while you do the cooking."

"I don't bother setting any table," said Terry as tartly as she knew how. "Besides, the coffee and bacon are both done and that's all the cooking there is. You know where the bread and butter and sugar are. Help yourself. There isn't any milk."

She poured her own coffee, made a sandwich of bacon and bread, and went to sit as he had found her last night, on the table, her feet swinging.

Steve Packard had gone to sleep filled with high hopes last night, and had awakened with a fresh, new zest in life this morning. Like the cowboy in the ballad, he had wanted nothing in the world save to be back on the range, and he had his wish, or would have it fully in a few hours, when he had ridden to Ranch Number Ten. Fully appreciating Terry's prejudices, he had meant to remember that she was "just a kid of a girl, you know," and to banter her out of them. Now he was ready to acknowledge that he had failed to give Terry her due; with a sudden access of irritation it was borne in upon him that if she was fully minded to be stand-offish and unpleasant, he had something more than just a kid of a girl to deal with. Frowning, he sought his tobacco and papers.

"Going to eat?" asked Terry carelessly. "Or not?"

"I don't know . . . yet," he returned, lifting his eyes from his cigarette. "Most certainly not if you don't want me to."

"Ho!" taunted Terry, the bright light of battle in her eyes. "Climbing on your high horse, are you? Well, then, stay there."

Packard lighted his cigarette and returned her look steadily.

"Kid of a girl, nothing!" he told himself. And going back to his epithet of yesterday, "Little wildcat."

"Then," continued the girl evenly, taking up the conversation where it had broken down some time ago, "I'll say what I've got to say. First, because you're a Packard. Next, because it was pretty slick work, that stunt of yours, diving into the lake for me, pretending you didn't know who I was, and grabbing the first chance to get acquainted. Much good it'll do you! Maybe I haven't been through high school and you have fussed around at college; just the same, Mr. Steve Packard, Terry Temple's not your fool or any other man's! And, on top of all of your other nerve, to try and make me think you didn't know you owned your own ranch! And trying to pump me and corkscrewing away at dad when he was full of whiskey. . . . Pah! Your kind of he-animal makes me sick."

"You think," he offered stiffly, "that I'm hand and glove with Blenham? And, perhaps, that I'm taking orders from my grandfather, trying to put one over on you?"

"Thinking's not the right word," she corrected sharply. "I know."

He shrugged. As he did so it struck him that there was nothing else for him to do. She had the trick of utter finality.

"And," she called after him as he turned abruptly to leave the room, "you can tell old Hell Fire for me that maybe he's got the big bulge on the situation right now but that it's bad luck to count your chips until the game is over. There's a come-back left in dad yet, and . . . and if you or your hell-roaring old granddad think you can swallow the Temple outfit whole, like you've done a lot of other outfits . . ."

Packard went out and slammed the door after him.

"Damn the girl!" he muttered angrily.

Terry, sitting on the table, grew very still, ceased the swinging of her feet, and turned to peek cautiously out at him from the kitchen window. Her look was utterly joyous.

"Men are always horrid creatures before they've had their breakfasts," she informed the stillness about her complacently.

CHAPTER V

HOW STEVE PACKARD CAME HOME

Had Steve Packard ridden straightway back to Ranch Number Ten he would have arrived at the ranch headquarters long before noon. But, once out in the still dawn, he rode slowly. His mind, when he could detach it from that irritating Terry Pert, was given over to a searching consideration of those conditions which were beginning to dawn on him.

It was clear that his destiny was offering him a new trail to blaze, one which drew him on with its lure, tempting him with its vague promises. There was nothing to cause surprise in the fact that the ranch was his to have and to hold if he had the skill and the will for the job; nor yet in the other fact that the outfit was mortgaged to his grandfather; nor, again, was it to be wondered at that the old man was already acting as actual owner. For never had the oldest Packard had any use for the subtleties and niceties and confusing technicalities of the law. It was his way to see clearly what he wanted, to make up his mind definitely as to a desired result, and then to go after it the shortest way. And that way had never led yet through the law-courts.

These matters were clear. But as he dwelt upon them they were made complex by other considerations hingeing upon him. Most of all he had to take stock of what lay in his own mind and soul, of all that dwelt behind his present purpose.

Riding back to Ranch Number Ten, saying, "It is mine and I mean to have it," was simple enough. But for him actually to commit himself to the line of action which this step would entail would very obviously connote a distinct departure from the familiar, aimless, responsibility-free career of Steve Packard.

If he once sat into the game he'd want to stick for a showdown; if he started out now bucking old man Packard, he would perhaps wind up in the scrap-heap. It was just as well to think things over before he plunged in—which set him musing upon Terry again.

Swerving from yesterday's path, he followed a new trail leading about the edge of the Temple ranch and into the southeastern borders of Ranch Number Ten. At a logging-camp well up on the slope of the mountains just after he had forded the upper waters of Packard's Creek, he breakfasted on warmed-over coffee and greasy hot cakes.

He opened his eyes interestedly as he watched a gang of timberjacks cutting into a forest of his pines.

"Old man Packard's crowd?" he asked the camp cook.

"Sure thing," was the cook's careless answer. Steve Packard rode on, grown more thoughtful than before. But he directed his course this way and that on a speculative tour of investigation, seeking to see the greater part of the big, sprawling ranch, to note just what had been done, just what was being done, before having his talk with Blenham. And so the first stars were out before he came once more to the home corrals.

While Steve was turning down into Packard's Grab from the foot-hills the men working for Ranch Number Ten, having eaten their supper, were celebrating the end of a hard day's work with tobacco smoke and desultory talk.

There were a dozen of them, clear-eyed, iron-muscled, quick-footed to the last man of them. For wherever Packard pay was taken it went into the pockets of just such as these, purposeful, self-reliant, men's men who could be counted on in a pinch and who, that they might be held in the service which required such as they, were paid a better wage than other ranches offered.

Young, most of them, too, boisterous when upon occasion their hands were idle, devil-may-care scalawags who had earned in many a little cattle town up and down the country their title as "that wild gang of Packard's," prone to headlong ways and yet dependable.

There are such men; Packard knew it and sought them out and held them to him. The oldest man there, saving Bill Royce only, was Blenham the foreman, and Blenham had yet to see his thirty-fifth birthday.

Ten years ago, that is to say before he came into the cattle country and found work for Packard, Blenham had been a sergeant in the regular army, had seen something of service on the border. Now, in his dealings with the men under him, he brought here all that he had learned from a military life.

He held himself aloof, was seldom to be found in the bunk-house, making his quarters in the old ranch-house. He was crisp and final in his orders and successful in exacting swift attention when he spoke and immediate obedience when he ordered.

Few of his men liked him; he knew this as well as another and cared not the snap of his big, blunt fingers. There was remarkably little of the sentimental about Blenham. He was a capable lieutenant for such as the master of the Packard millions, he earned and received his increase in wages every year, he got results.

This evening, however, the man's heavy, studied indifference to all about him was ruffled. During the afternoon something had gone wrong and no one yet, save "Cookie" Wilson, had an inkling of what had plunged the foreman into one of his ill-tempered fits.

To-morrow it would be a ranch topic when Cookie could have had ample time to embroider the thin fabric of his surmise; for it had fallen to the cook's lot to answer the bunk-house telephone when there had been a long-distance message for Blenham—and Wilson recognized old man Packard's voice in a fit of rage.

No doubt the foreman of Ranch Number Ten had "slipped up" somewhere, and his chief, in a very few words and those of a brand not to be misunderstood, had taken him to task. At any rate Cookie was swelling with eager conjecture and Blenham was in an evil mood. All evening his spleen had been rising in his throat, near choking him; now suddenly he spewed it upon Bill Royce.

"Royce!" he burst out abruptly.

The blind man was lying upon the edge of his bunk at the far end of the room, smoking his pipe. He stirred uneasily.

"Well?" he asked. "What is it?"

"Cool old cucumber, ain't you?" jeered Blenham. "Layin' there like a bag of mush while you listen to me. Damn you, when I talk to you, stand up!"

Royce's form stiffened perceptibly and his lips tightened about the stem of his pipe. But before he could shape his rejoinder there came an unexpected voice from one of the four men just beginning a game of pedro under the swinging lamp, a young voice, impudent, clear-toned, almost musical.

"Tell him to go to hell, Bill," was the freely proffered counsel.

Blenham swung about on his heel, his eyes narrowing.

"That you, Barbee?" he demanded sharply.

"Sure it's me," rejoined Barbee with the same cool impudence. And to the man across the table from him, "Deal 'em up, Spots; you an' me is goin' to pry these two bum gamblers loose from their four-bit pieces real *pronto* by the good ol' road of high, low, jack, an' the game. Come ahead, Spots-ol'-Spotty."

Blenham stared a moment, obviously surprised by this attitude taken by young Barbee.

"I'll attend to you when I got nothin' else to do, Barbee," he said shortly. And, giving the whole of his attention again to the man on the bunk, "Royce, I said when I talk to you to stand up!"

To the last man of them, even to young Barbee, who had made his youthful pretense at an all-embracing interest in the cards, they turned to watch Bill Royce and see what he would do.

They saw that Royce lay a moment as he was, stiff and rigid

to his hands and feet, that his face had gone a fiery red which threw the white of the long scar across his nose into bloodless contrast, that the most obvious thing in the world was that for the moment his mind was torn two ways, dual-purposed, perfectly balanced, so that in the grip of his contending passions he was powerless to stir, a picture of impotence, like a man paralyzed.

"Blenham," he said presently without moving, his voice uncertain and thick and ugly, "Blenham—"

"I said it once," cried Blenham sharply, "an' I said it twice. Which ought to be enough, Bill Royce! Hear me?"

They all watched interestedly. Bill Royce moistened his lips and presented his pitiful spectacle of a once-strong man on the verge of yielding to his master, to the man he hated most on earth. A smile came into Blenham's expectant eyes.

The brief silence was perfect until the youthful Barbee broke it, not by speech but by whistling softly, musically, impu-dently. And the air which Barbee selected at this juncture, though not drawn from the classics, served its purpose adequately; the song was a favorite in the range-lands, the refrain simple, profane, and sincere. Translated into words Barbee's merry notes were:

"Oh, I don't give a damn for no damn man that don't give a damn for me!"

Blenham understood and scowled at him; Bill Royce's hesitant soul may have drawn comfort and strength from a sympathy wordlessly expressed. At any rate his reply came suddenly now:

"I've took a good deal off'n you, Blenham," he said quietly. "I'd be glad to take all I could. But a man can't stand everything, no, not even for a absent pal. Like Barbee said, you know where you can go."

Cookie Wilson gasped, his the sole audible comment upon an entirely novel situation. Barbee smiled delightedly. Blenham continued to frown, his scowl subtly altered from fierceness to wonder.

"You'll obey orders," he snapped shortly, "or—"

"I know," replied Royce heavily. "Go to it. All you got to do is fire me."

And now the pure wonder of the moment was that Blenham did not discharge Royce in three words. It was his turn for hesitation, for which there was no explanation forthcoming. Then, gripped by a rage which made him inarticulate,—he whirled upon Barbee.

Yellow-haired Barbee at the table promptly stood up, awaiting no second invitation to that look of Blenham's. Were one staging a morality play and in search of the personification of impertinence, he need look no farther than this cocksure youth. He was just at that age when one is determined that there shall be no mistake about his status in the matters of age and worldly experience; in short, something over twenty-one, when the male of the species takes it as the insult of insults to be misjudged a boy. His hair was short—Barbee always kept it close cropped—but for all that it persisted in curling, seeking to express itself in tight little rings everywhere; his eyes were very blue and very innocent, like a young girl's—and he was, all in all, just about as good-for-nothing a young rogue as you could find in a ten days' ride. Which is saying rather a good deal when it be understood that that ten days' ride may be through the cattle country back of San Juan.

"Goin' to eat me alive?" demanded Barbee lightly, "Or roast me first?"

"For two cents," said Blenham slowly, "I'd forget you're just a kid an' slap your face!"

Barbee swept one of the fifty-cent pieces from the table and tossed it to the foreman.

"You can keep the change out'n that," he said contemptuously.

It was nothing new in the experience of Blenham, could be nothing unforeseen for any ranch foreman, to have his authority called into question, to have a rebellious spirit defy him. If he sought to remain master, the foreman's answer must be always the same. And promptly given.

"Royce," said Blenham, his hesitation passed, "you're fired. Barbee, I'll take you on right now."

Few-worded was Blenham, a trick learned from his master. Across the room Bill Royce had floundered at last to his feet, crying out mightily:

"Hi! None o' that, Blenham. It's my fight, yours an' mine, with Barbee jus' buttin' in where he ain't asked. If you want trouble, take a man your size, full-grown. Blind as I am— and you know the how an' the why of it—I'm ready for you. Yes, ready an' anxious."

Here was diversion and the men in the bunkhouse, drawing back against the walls, taking their chairs with them that there might be room for whatever went forward, gave their interest unstintedly. So completely that they did not hear Steve Packard singing far out in the night as he rode slowly toward the ranch-house:

"An' I'd rather hear a kiote howl
Than be the King of Rome!
An' when day comes—if day does come—
By cripes, I'm goin' home!
Back home! Hear me comin', boys?
Yeee! I said it. Comin' home!"

But in very brief time Steve Packard's loitering pace was exchanged for red-hot haste as the sounds winging outward from the bunk-house met him, stilled his singing, and informed him that men were battling in a fury which must have something of sheer blood-thirst in it. He raced to the closed door, swung down from the saddle, and threw the door open.

He saw Bill Royce being held by two men, fighting at them while he reviled a man whom Steve guessed to be Blenham; he saw Blenham and a curly-haired, blue-eyed boy struggling up and down, striking the savage blows of rage. He came just in time to see Blenham drive a big, brutal fist into the boy's face and to mark how Barbee fell heavily and for a little lay still.

The moment was charged with various emotions, as though with contending electrical currents. Bill Royce, championed by a man he had never so much as seen, had given fully of his gratitude and—they meant the same thing to Bill Royce—of his love; after to-night he'd go to hell for "yellow" Barbee.

Barbee, previsioning defeat at Blenham's hard hand, suffering in his youthful pride, had given birth, deep within him, to an undying hatred. And Blenham, for his own reasons and after his own fashion, was bursting with rage.

"Get up, Barbee," he yelled. "Get up an', so help me—"

"I'm goin' to kill you, Blenham," said Barbee faintly, lifting himself a little, his blue eyes swimming. "With my hands or with a knife or with a gun or anyway; now or to-morrow or some time I'm goin' to kill you."

"They all heard you," Blenham spat out furiously. "You're a fool, Barbee. Goin' to get up? Ever goin' to get up?"

"Turn me loose, boys," muttered Bill Royce. "I've waited long enough; I've stood enough. I been like an ol' woman. Jus' let me an' Blenham finish this."

They had, none of them, so much as noted Steve Packard's entrance. Now, however, he forced them to take stock of him.

"Bill Royce," he said sharply, "keep your shirt on. Barbee, you do the same. Blenham, you talk with me."

"You?" jeered Blenham. "You? Who are you?"

"I'm the man on the job right now," answered Packard crisply. "And from now on, I'm running the Ranch Number Ten, if you want to know. If you want to know anything else, why then you don't happen to be foreman any longer. You're fired! As for foreman under me—my old pardner, Bill Royce, blind or not blind, has his old job back."

Bill Royce grew rigid.

"You ain't—you ain't Stevie come back?" he whispered. "You ain't Stevie!"

With three strides Packard reached him, finding Bill Royce's hand with his.

"Right you are, Bill Royce," he cried warmly as at last his

and Royce's hands locked hard.

"I'm fired, you say!" Blenham was storming, his eyes wide. "Fired? Who says so, I want to know?"

"I say so," returned Packard shortly.

"You?" shouted Blenham. "If you mean ol' man Packard has sent you to take my place just because— It's a lie; I don't believe it."

"This outfit doesn't happen to belong to old man Packard—yet," said Steve coolly. "Does it, Royce?"

"Not by a jugful!" answered the blind man joyously. "An' it never will now, Steve! Not now."

Blenham looked mystified. Rubbing his skinned knuckles he glared from Steve to Royce, then to the other faces, no less puzzled than his own.

"Nobody can fire me but ol' man Packard," he muttered heavily, though his tone was troubled. "Without you got an order from him, all signed an' ready for me to read—"

"What I have," cut in Steve crisply, "is the bulge on the situation, Blenham. Ranch Number Ten doesn't belong to the old man; it is the property of his grandson, whose name is Steve Packard. Which also happens to be my name."

Blenham sneered.

"I don't believe it," he snapped. "Expect me to pull my freight at the say-so of the first stranger that blows in an' invites me to hand him my job?" He laughed into the newcomer's face.

Packard studied him a moment curiously, instinctively aware that the time might come when it would be well to have taken stock correctly of his grandfather's lieutenant. Then, before replying, he looked at the faces of the other men. When he spoke it was to them.

"Boys," he said quietly, "this outfit belongs to me. I am Steve Packard, the son of Philip Packard, who owned Number Ten Ranch and who mortgaged it but did not sell it to his father—my grandfather. I've just got back home; I mean to have what is mine; I am going to pay the mortgage somehow. I haven't jumped in with my sleeves rolled up for trouble either; had Blenham been a white man instead of a brute and a bully he might have kept his job under me. But I guess you all know the sort of life he has been handing Royce here. Bill taught me how to ride and shoot and fight and swim; pretty well everything I know that's worth knowing. Since I was a kid he's been the best friend I ever had. Anything else you boys would like to know?"

Barbee had risen slowly from the floor.

"Packard's son or the devil's," he said quickly, his eyes never leaving Blenham, "I'm with you."

The man whom, over the card-table, Barbee had addressed as Spotty and whose nickname had obviously been gained for him by the peculiar tufts of white hair in a young, tousled head of very dark brown, cleared his throat and so drew all eyes to himself at his side of the room.

"Bill Royce bein' blind, if you could only prove somehow who you are—" he suggested, tone and expression plainly indicating his willingness, even eagerness, to be convinced.

"Even if I can't see him," said Royce, his own voice eager, "I know! An' I can prove it for my part by a couple of little questions—if you boys will take my word for it?"

"Shoot," said Spotty. "No man's called you liar yet, Bill."

"Then, Stevie," said Royce, just a shade of anxiety in his look as his sightless eyes roved here and there, "answer me this: What was the first horse you ever rode?"

"A mare," said Steve. "Black Molly."

"Right!" and Royce's voice rang triumphantly. "Next: Who nailed the board over the door? The ol' cedar board?"

"I did. Just before I went away."

"An'," continued Royce, his voice lowered a trifle, "an' what did you say about it, Stevie? I was to know—"

"Coach him up! Tell him what to say, why don't you?" jeered Blenham.

"I don't think I need to," replied Royce quietly. "Do I, Steve?"

"I was pretty much of a kid then, Bill," said Packard, a half-smile coming into his eyes for the first time, a smile oddly gentle. "I had been reading one of the Arabian Nights tales; that's what put it into my head."

"Go ahead, Steve; go ahead!"

"I said that I was going to seek my fortune up and down the world; that the board above the door would be a sign if all went well with me. That as long as I lived it would be there; if I died it would fall."

There was a little, breathless silence. It was broken by Bill

Royce's joyous laughter as Bill Royce's big hand smote his thigh.

"Right again, Steve! An' the ol' board's still there. Go look at it; it's still there."

Again all eyes sought Blenham. For a moment he stood uncertain, looking about him. Then abruptly he swept up his hat and went out. And Barbee's laughter, like an evil echo of Royce's, followed him.

CHAPTER VI

BANK NOTES AND A BLIND MAN

"He'd as soon set fire to the hay-barns as not," said Royce. "Better watch him, Steve."

And so Steve, stepping outside, watched Blenham, who had gone swiftly toward the ranch-house and who now swung about sharply and stopped dead in his tracks.

"He's up to something, Bill," conceded Packard. And called quietly to Blenham: "Every step you take on this ranch, I'm right along with you, Blenham."

Whereupon Blenham, his hesitation over, turned abruptly and went down to the corral, saddled, and rode away.

On the heels of the irate foreman's wordless departure Steve Packard and Bill Royce went together to the old ranch-house, where, settled comfortably in two big arm-chairs, they talked far into the night. A sharp glance about him as he lighted a lamp on the table showed Packard dust and disuse everywhere excepting the few untidy signs of Blenham's recent occupancy.

An old saddle sprawled loosely upon the living-room floor, littered about with bits of leather and buckles; from a nail hung a rusty, long-rowelled Mexican spur; on the hearth-stone were many cigarette stumps and an occasional cigar-end. An open door showed a tumbled bed, the covers trailing to the floor.

"I'd give a year off my life for a good look at you, Steve," said Royce a trifle wistfully. "Let's see—thirty-five now, ain't you?"

"Right," answered Packard.

"An' big?" asked Royce. "Six foot or better?"

"A shade better. About an inch and a half."

"Not heavy, though? Kind of lean an' long, like Phil Packard before you?"

Packard nodded; then, with Royce's sightless eyes upon him, he said hastily:

"Right again, Bill; kind of lean and long. You'd know me."

"Sure, I would!" cried Royce eagerly. "A man don't change so all-fired much in a dozen years; don't I remember just how you looked when you cut loose to see the world! Ain't made your pile, have you, Steve?"

Packard laughed carelessly.

"I'm lord and master of a good horse, saddle, bridle, and seventy-odd bucks," he said lightly. "Not much of a pile, Bill."

"An' Number Ten Ranch," added Royce quickly.

"And Number Ten Ranch," Packard agreed. "If we can get

away with it."

"Meaning what? How get away with it?"

"It's mortgaged to the hilt, it seems. I don't know for how much yet. The mortgage and a lot of accrued interest has to be paid off. Just how big a job we've got to find out."

"Seen your grandfather yet?"

"No. I should have looked him up, I suppose, before I fired Blenham. But, being made of flesh and blood—"

"I know, I know." And Royce filled his lungs with a big sigh. "Bein' a Packard, you didn't wait all year to get where you was goin'. But there'll be plenty of red tape that can't be cut through; that'll have to be all untangled an' untied. Unless your grandfather'll do the right thing by you an' call all ol' bets off an' give you a free hand an' a fresh start?"

"All of which you rather doubt, eh, Bill?"

Royce nodded gloomily.

"I guess we've gone at things sort of back-end-to," he said regretfully. "You'd ought to have seen him first, hadn't you? An' then you kicked his pet dawg in the slats when you canned Blenham. The old man's right apt to be sore, Steve."

"I shouldn't be surprised," agreed Steve. "Who are the Temples, Bill?"

"Who tol' you about the Temples?" came the quick counter-question.

"Nobody. I stayed at their place last night."

Royce grunted.

"Didn't take you all year to find her, did it?" he offered bluntly.

"Who?" asked Packard in futile innocence.

"Terry Temple. The finest girl this side the pearly gates an' the pretties'. What kind of a man have you growned to be with the women, Steve?"

"No ladies' man, if that's what's worrying you, old pardner. I don't know a dozen girls in the world. I just asked to know about these people because they're right next-door to us and because they're newcomers since my time."

Again Royce grunted, choosing his own explanation of Packard's interest. But, answering the question put to him, he replied briefly:

"That little Terry-girl can have anything I got; her mother was some class, too, they tell me. I dope it up she just died of shame when she come to know what sort she'd picked for a runnin' mate. An' as for him, he's a twisty-minded jelly-fish. He's absolutely no good. An', if I ain't mistaken some considerable, you'll come to know him real well before long. Watch him, Steve."

"Well," said Packard as Royce broke off, sensing that this was not all to be said of Temple; "let's have it. What else about him?"

But Royce shook his head slowly, while his big, thick fingers filled his pipe.

"We ain't got all night to jus' squat here an' gossip about our neighbors," he said presently. "There's other things to be said before things can be done. First rattle, an' to get goin', I'm much obliged for that little bluff you threw Blenham's way about me being your foreman. What you need an' what you got to have is a man with both eyes wide open. Oh, I know, Steve," as Packard started to speak. "You'd offer me the job if both my legs an' arms was gone, too. But it don't go."

"I'm going to need a man right away," argued Steve. "I'll have to do a lot of running around, I suppose, looking up the law, arranging for belated payments, and so forth. I don't want to leave the ranch without a head. You know the men, you know the outfit."

But Royce, though his lips twitched, was firm.

"I don't know the men any too well either," he said. "They're all your grandfather's hirin'. But they're all live an' they all know the game. I won't swear as to how far you can trust any one of 'em; but you'll have to find that out for yourself as we go on."

"Name one of them for me," was Packard's quiet way of accepting his old foreman's ultimatum. "I'll put him on at least temporarily."

"There's Yellow Barbee," suggested Royce. "Somethin' of a kid, maybe kind of wild an' harum-scarum, maybe not worth much. But he ain't a Blenham man an' he did me a good turn."

Already Packard was on his feet, going to the door.

"Barbee!" he shouted. "Oh, Barbee!"

The bunk-house door opened, emitting its stream of light.

"Call me?" came Barbee's cool young voice, impudent now as always.

"Yes, come here a minute, will you?"

Barbee came, his wide hat far back upon his tight little curls, his swagger pronounced, his sweet blue eyes shining softly—his lips battered and bruised and already swelling.

"Come in and shut the door," said Packard.

Barbee entered and stepped across the room to lounge with his elbow on the chimney-piece, looking curiously from Packard to Royce.

"I'm here to run this outfit myself, Barbee," Packard told him while returning the youth's regard steadily. "But I need a foreman to keep things going when I'm obliged to be away. I gave the job to Royce. He won't have it. He suggests you."

Barbee opened his eyes a trifle wider. Also the quick flush running up into his brown cheeks made him look more boyish than ever, giving him almost a cherubic air. But for all that he managed to appear tolerably unmoved, quite as though this were not the first time he had been offered such a position.

"How much is in it?" was what Barbee said, with vast indifference.

Steve hesitated. Then he frowned. And finally he laughed.

"You've got me there," he admitted frankly. "All the money I've got in the world to-night is right here." He spilled the contents of his pocket upon a table. "There's about seventy-five bucks. Unless I can turn a trick somewhere before pay-day all you boys will have to take your pro rata out of that."

Bill Royce shifted nervously in his chair, opened his mouth, then closed it wordlessly. Barbee shrugged elaborately.

"I'll take a chance," he said. "It would be worth it if I lost; jus' to put one across on Blenham."

"All right," and still Packard eyed young Barbee keenly, wondering just how much ability lay hidden under that somewhat unsatisfactory exterior. "You can go back to the boys now and tell them that you're boss when I'm not on hand. Before they go to work in the morning you show up here again and we'll talk a lot of things over."

Barbee ducked his head in token of acquiescence and perhaps to hide the glitter in his eyes, and walked on his heels to the door. Packard's voice arrested him there.

"Just one thing, Barbee: I don't want any trouble started. Not with Blenham or with any of old man Packard's men. I know how you feel, but if you work for me you'll have to let me be the one who starts things. Understand?"

The new foreman paused irresolutely. Then, without turning so that Packard might see his face, and with no spoken reply, he ducked his head again and went out, slamming the door after him.

"I ain't sure he's the right man for the job, Steve," began Royce a trifle anxiously. "An' I ain't sure whether he's square or crooked. But I don't know the rest of the men any better an'—"

"I'll watch him, Bill. And, as I've said already, I'm here to do most of the foreman act myself. We'll give Barbee his chance."

He came back to the table from whose top there winked up at him the few gold and silver coins which spelled his working capital, and stood looking at them quizzically.

"I got a yarn to spin, Stevie," came thoughtfully from Royce with a great puff of smoke. "You better listen in on it now—while we're alone."

Packard returned to his chair, made his own smoke, and said quietly:

"Go to it, Bill. I'm listening."

"Barbee's gone, ain't he? An' the door shut?"

"Yes."

"Then pull up close so's I won't have to talk loud an' I'll get it out of my system: Before your father died he wasn't makin' much money, not as much as he was spendin'. He'd tied into some minin'-stock game that he didn't savvy any too well, an' for a long time all I'd been clearin' here he'd been droppin' outside.

"An' the deeper he got in the hole the wilder he played the game: there was times when I didn't believe he cared a tinker's damn what happened. Whenever he needed any cash all he had to do was soak another plaster on the ranch, borrow again from his father. An' ol' Number Ten is plastered thick now, Steve; right square up to the hilt.

"Well, when Phil Packard died he did it like he'd done everything else, like he had lived, makin' a man think he was in a hurry to get a job over an' done with. Ridin' horseback one week an' the nex' week sendin' for me in there." He jerked his head toward a remote room of the big house. "An' he talked to me then about you."

Packard waited for him to go on, offering no comment. Royce, hunched over in his chair, straightened up a little, shook himself, and continued:

"He had drawed some money out'n the bank, all he had left. I dunno what for, but anyways he had it under his pillow alongside his ol' Colt. An' he give it to me, sayin' he was caught sudden an' unexpected by his death, an' for me to take care of it an' see that you got it when you come back. It was in greenbacks, a little roll no bigger'n your thumb, an' when I counted 'em I near dropped dead. Ten little slips of paper, Steve, an' each good for one thousan' bucks! Ten thousan' dollars did Phil Packard slip me that night not a half-hour before he went over. For you. An' I got 'em for you, Steve; I got 'em safe for you."

His big shoulders rose and fell in a deep sigh; he ran a toil-hardened hand across his forehead. Packard opened his lips as though to speak, but was silent as Royce continued:

"I took the money, Steve, an' went outside for a smoke, an' my hands was shakin' like I was cold! Ten thousan' bucks in my tail pocket! It was a dark night an' I didn't lose nineteen secon's hidin' the wad in a good safe place. Which," slowly, "was the las' time I ever saw it!"

"I thought you said—"

"I got it safe? I have. But I ain't ever seen anything since that night, Steve. The night your dad died, the night I hid the money, was the night I went blind."

"You haven't told me about that yet, Bill," said Packard gently.

"No; but I'm goin' to now. It's part of the yarn I got to spin to-night. Like I said I took the wad—your father had slipped it back in a flat sort of pocketbook—an' went outside. It was night already an' dark. Ten thousan' bucks for me to keep safe for you!"

Again he ran his hand across his forehead.

"I knew where there was a rock in the corner foundation of the house that I could work loose; where if I put the greenbacks they wouldn't spoil if it rained or even if the house burned down. I stuck 'em in there, got the rock back like it was before, made sure nobody saw me, an' went off by myself for a smoke.

"'Cause why did I take that chance? I didn't take no chances at all, I tell you, Steve! How did I know, your father gettin' delirious at the finish which came downright quick, but he'd give the game away? An' on the ranch then there was men that would do mos' anything for ten thousan', give 'em the show.

"Your gran'father had come over an' he had brought Blenham with him an' his mechanic, Guy Little; an' there was a couple of new men in the outfit I'd picked up myself that I knew was tough gents.

"No! I didn't take no chances, seein' the money was yours an' not mine to fool with. I stuck it in the wall an' I sneaked off an' for three hours I squatted there in the dark with my gun in my hand, waitin' an' watchin'. Which was playing as safe as a man could, wasn't it, Steve?"

Packard got up and came to Royce's side, putting his hand gently on the foreman's shoulder.

"It strikes me you've done rather a good deal for me, Bill," he said quite simply.

"Maybe," said Royce thoughtfully. "But no more'n one pardner ought to do for another; no more'n you'd do for me, Stevie. Don't I know you? Give you the chance you'd do as much for me; eh, boy? Well, here's the rest of the story: Your dad was dead: ol' Hell-Fire was blowin' his nose so you'd hear it a mile an' I was feelin' weak an' sick-like, knowin' all of a sudden that Phil Packard had been damn' good to me an' wantin' to tell him so now it was too late. Late an' dark as it was I went down to the bunk-house, tol' the boys to stick aroun' for orders in the mornin', saddled my horse and beat it for a quiet place where I could think. I never wanted to think so much in my life, Steve. Remember the ol' cabin by the big timber over on the east side?"

"The old McKittrick place? Yes."

"Well, I went there to make a fire in the ol' fireplace an' sit an' think things over. But I got to tell you about a feller name of Johnny Mills. You didn't know him; he's workin' for the Brocky Lane outfit now. Well, Johnny was as good a cow-man as you want, but you always had to watch him that he didn't slip off to go quail-huntin'. With a shot-gun he was the best wing-shot I ever heard a man tell about.

"He used to sneak for the McKittrick cabin where he kep' an ol' muzzle-loadin' shot-gun, an' shot quail aroun' them springs up there when he'd ought to be workin'. Then he'd come in an' brag, tellin' how he'd never missed a shot. The boys, jus' to tease Johnny, had gone to the cabin that very day an' drawed his shot out, jus' leavin' the powder alone so Johnny would think he'd missed when he pulled the trigger an' no birdies dropped.

"See what I'm drivin' at? I tied my horse an' started along the little trail through the wild-holly bushes to the cabin.

Somebody was waitin' for me an' give me both barrels square in the face. That's when an' how my lights went out, Steve."

It came as a shock, and Packard paled; Royce had been so long making his explanations and then put the actual catastrophe so baldly that for a moment his hearer sat speechless. Presently—

"Know who did it, Bill?" he asked.

"If I knew—for sure—I'd go get him! But I don't know; not for sure." His big hands clenched until they fairly trembled with their own tenseness. "It's tough to go blind, Steve!"

His hands relaxed; he sat still, staring into that black nothingness which always engulfed him. When he spoke again it was drearily, hopelessly, like a man communing with his own sorrow, oblivious of a listener:

"Yes, it's fair hell to be blind. If there's anything worse I'd like to know what it might be. To be walkin' along in the dark, always in the dark—to stumble an' fall an' hear a man laugh—to pitch head firs' over a box that had been slipped quiet in your way—"

"Blenham did that sort of thing?" demanded Packard sharply.

It would have done Bill Royce good to see the look in his eyes then. Royce nodded.

"Blenham did whatever he could think of," he muttered colorlessly. "An' he could think of a good many things. Just the same—maybe some day—"

"And yet you stayed on, Bill?" when Royce's voice stopped.

"I'd promised your dad I'd be here—with the coin—when you come back. He knew an' I knew you might blow in an' blow out an' never get word unless I was right here all the time. An' ol' man Packard, after I was blind I went to him an' he promised I could stick as long as I just obeyed orders. Which, I've done, no matter what they was.

"But the end's come now; ain't it, Steve, ol' pardner? But to get this tale tol' an' the money in your hands: I didn't know who'd tried to do for me, but I guessed it must have been some one who'd found out somehow about the ten thousan' an' thought I had it on me. When I come to at the cabin an' firs' thing tried to get a chaw of tobacco I foun' my pockets all turned wrong side out. It might have been Johnny Mills himself; he didn't know about the gun bein' fooled with; it might have been Blenham; it might have been Guy Little; it might have been somebody else. But I've thought all along an' I pray God I was right an' that some day I'll know, that it was Blenham."

He rose suddenly.

"Come ahead, Steve," he said, his voice matter of fact as of old. "It's up to you to ride herd on your own simoleons now."

"You've left it in the same place? In the rock foundation-wall?"

"Yes. I couldn't find a safer place."

"And you haven't been back to it all these months?"

"Not until las' Saturday night. It was jus' six months then. I figgered it out I'd make sure once every six months. I went in the middle of the night an' made sure nobody followed me, Steve. Come ahead."

Packard slipped his arm through Royce's and they went side by side. The night was filled with stars; there was no moon. The wall, as they came around the corner of the house, shone palely here and there where a white surface glinted vaguely through the shadows.

"Nobody aroun', is there, Steve?" whispered Royce.

"Nobody," Packard assured him. "Where is it, Bill?"

Royce's hands, groping with the wall, rested at last upon a knob of stone near the base of the foundation. He tugged; the stone, rudely squared, came away, leaving a gaping hole. Royce thrust his hand in, searched briefly, and in a moment brought out a flat wallet clutched tightly.

"Yours, Steve!" he said then, a quick, palpitating note of pure joy in his cry. "Blind as I was, I put it over for you! Here's ten thousan', Steve. An' the chance to get ol' Number Ten back."

Packard was taking the wallet proffered him. Suddenly Royce jerked it back.

"Let me make sure again," he said hastily. "Let me be dead sure I've made good."

He fumbled with the wallet, opened the flap, drew out the contents, a neat pack of folded bank-notes. He counted slowly.

"Ten of 'em," he announced triumphantly as he gave the wallet over to its proper owner.

Packard took them and they went back to the house. The rays of the lamp met them; through the open door, back to the living-room, they walked side by side. The table between them, they sat down. Packard put the wallet down, spread out the ten bank-notes.

"Bill," he said, and there was a queer note in his voice, "Bill, you've gone through hell for me. Don't I know it? And you say I'd do as much for you? Are you sure of it, Bill?"

Royce laughed and rubbed his hands together.

"Dead sure, Stevie," he said.

Packard's eyes dropped to the table. Before him were the ten crisp bank-notes. Each was for one dollar. Ten dollars in all. His heritage, saved to him by Bill Royce.

"Bill, old man," he said slowly, "you've taught me how to play the game. Pray God I can be as white with a pardner as you have been."

And, crumpling the notes with a sudden gesture, he thrust them into his pocket.

CHAPTER VII

THE OLD MOUNTAIN LION COMES DOWN
FROM THE NORTH

It was perhaps eight o'clock, the morning blue, cloudless, and still. Packard had conferred briefly with Barbee; the Ranch Number Ten men had gone about their work. Steve and Bill Royce, riding side by side, had mounted one of the flat, treeless hills in the upper valley and were now sitting silent while Royce fumbled with his pipe and Steve sent a long, eager look down across the open meadow-lands dotted with grazing cattle.

Suddenly their two horses and the other horses browsing in a lower field, jerked up their heads, all ears pricked forward. And yet Steve had heard no sound to mar the perfect serenity of the young day. He turned his head a little, listening.

Then, from some remote distance there floated to him a sound strangely incongruous here in the early stillness, a subdued screech or scream, a wild, clamorous, shrieking noise which for the life of him he could not catalogue.

It was faint because it came across so great a distance and yet it was clear; it was not the throbbing cry of a mountain lion, not the scream of a horse stricken with its death, nothing that he had ever heard, and yet it suggested both of these sounds.

"Bill!" he began.

"I heard it," Royce muttered. "An' I've heard it before! In a minute—"

Royce broke off. The sound, stilled a second, came again, seeming already much closer and more hideous. Steve's horse snorted and plunged; some of the colts in the pasture flung up their heels and fled with streaming manes and tails. Royce calmly filled and lighted his pipe.

Stillness again for perhaps ten or twenty seconds. Steve, about to demand an explanation from his companion, stared as once more came the shrieking noise.

"You can hear the blame thing ten miles," grunted Royce. "It's only about half that far away now. Keep your eye glued on the road across the valley where it comes out'n Blue Bird Canon."

And then Steve understood. Into the clear air across the valley rose a growing cloud of dust; through it, out of the canon's shadows and into the sunlight, shot a glistening automobile, hardly more than a bright streak as it sped along the curving down-grade.

"Terry Temple?" gasped young Packard. Royce merely grunted again.

"Jus' you watch," was all he said.

And, needing no invitation, Packard watched. The motor-car's siren—he had never heard another like it, knew that such a thing would not be tolerated in any of the world's traffic centres—sounded again a long, wailing note which went across the valley in billowing echoes.

Then it grew silent as, with the last of the dangerous curves behind it, the long-bodied roadster swung into the valley. Packard, an experienced driver himself, with his own share of reckless blood, opened his mouth and stared.

It was hard to believe that the big, spinning wheels were on the ground at all; the machine seemed more like an aeroplane content with skimming the earth but hungry for speed. Only the way in which it plunged and lurched and swerved and plunged again testified to highly inflated tires battling with ruts and chuck-holes.

"The fool!" he cried as the car negotiated a turn on two wheels with never a sign of lessened speed. "He'll turn turtle. He's doing sixty miles an hour right now. And on these roads—"

"More likely doin' seventy-five," grunted Royce. "Can do ten better'n that. Out on the highway he's done a clean hundred. That car, my boy—"

"He's going into the ditch!" exclaimed Steve excitedly.

The car, racing on, was already near enough for Steve to make out its two passengers, a man bent over the steering-wheel, another man, or boy, for the figure was small, clinging wildly to his place on the running-board, seeming always in imminent danger of being thrown off.

"He's drunk!" snapped Packard angrily. "Of all blind idiots!"

Another strident blast from the horn, that sent staid old cows scurrying this way and that to get out of the way, and the car swerved from the road and took to the open field, headed straight toward the hill where the two horsemen were. Jerking his horse about, Steve rode down to meet the new arrivals. And then—

"My God! It's my grandfather! He's gone mad, Bill Royce!"

"No madder'n usual," said Royce.

The car came to a sudden stop. The man on the running-board—he had a man's face, keen and sharp-eyed and eager, and the body of a slight boy—jumped down from his place and in a flash disappeared under the engine. The man at the wheel straightened up and got down, stretching his legs. Steve, swinging down from his saddle, and coming forward, measured him with wondering eyes.

And he was a man for men to look at, was old man Packard. Full of years, he was no less full of vigor, hale and stalwart and breathing power. A great white beard, cut square, fell across his full chest; his white mustache was curled upward now as fiercely as fifty years ago when he had been a man for women to look at, too.

He was dressed as Steve had always seen him, in black corduroy breeches, high black boots, broad black hat—a man standing upward of six feet, carrying himself as straight as a ramrod, his chest as powerful as a blacksmith's bellows, the calf of his leg as thick as many a man's thigh; big, hard hands, the fingers twisted by toil; the face weatherbeaten like an old sea captain's, with eyes like the frozen blue of a clear winter sky.

His voice when he spoke boomed out suddenly, deep and rich and hearty.

"Stephen?" he demanded.

Steve said "Yes" and put out his hand, his eyes shining, the surprising realization upon him that he was tremendously glad to see his father's father once more. The old man took the proffered hand into a hard-locked grip and for a moment held it, while, the other hand on his grandson's shoulder, he looked steadily into Steve's eyes.

"What sort of a man have they made of you, boy?" he asked bluntly. "There's the makings of fool, crook an' white man in all of us. What for a man are you?"

Steve flushed a little under the direct, piercing look, but said steadily—

"Not a crook, I hope."

"That's something, if it ain't everything," snorted the old man as, withdrawing his hand, he found and lighted a long stogie. "Blenham tells me you fired him las' night?"

Young Packard nodded, watching his grandfather's face for the first sign of opposition. But just now the old man's face told nothing.

"Thinking of runnin' the outfit yourself, Stephen?" came the next question quietly.

"Yes. I had intended looking in on you in a day or so to talk matters over. I understand that my father left everything to me and that it is pretty heavily mortgaged to you."

"Uhuh. I let Phil have a right smart bit of money on Number Ten firs' an' las', my boy. Don't want to pay it off this mornin', do you?"

Steve laughed.

"I'm broke, Grandy," he said lightly, unconsciously adopting the old title for the man who had made him love him and hate him a score of times. "My working capital, estimated last night, runs about seventy-five dollars. That wouldn't quite turn the trick, would it?"

The old man's eyes narrowed.

"You mean that seventy-five dollars is all you've got to show for twelve years?" he asked sharply.

Again, hardly understanding why, Steve flushed. Was a man to be ashamed that he had not amassed wealth, especially when there had never been in him the sustained desire for gold? He owed no man a cent, he made his own way, he asked no favors—and yet there was a glint of defiance in his eye, a hint of defiance in his tone, when he replied briefly.

"That's all. I haven't measured life in dollars and cents."

"Then you've missed a damn' good measure for it, my son! I ain't sayin' it's the only one, but it'll do firs' class. But you needn't get scared I've gone into the preaching business. . . . An' with that seventy-five dollars you're startin' out to run a big cow outfit like this, are you?"

There was a gleam of mockery in the clear blue eyes which Steve gave no sign of seeing.

"I've got a big job on my hands and I know it," he said quietly. "But I'm going to see it through."

"There's no question about the size of the job! It's life-size, man's size—Number Ten size, if you want to put it that way. It wants a real man to shove it across. Know just how much you're mortgaged for?"

"No. I was going to ask you."

"Close to fifty thousan' dollars, countin' back interest, unpaid. More'n you ever saw in a day, I reckon."

Steve shrugged. This to hide his first inclination to whistle. Fifty thousand—why, he didn't know Number Ten ranch was worth that much money. But it must be worth a good deal more if his grandfather had advanced so much on it.

"It is a nice little pile," he admitted carelessly.

The old man grunted, thrust his hands into his pockets, and drew deeply at his stogie. Steve rolled a cigarette. In the silence falling upon them they could hear the sound of the mechanician's wrench.

"Anything wrong with the car?" asked Steve for the sake of breaking unpleasant silence.

"Not that I know of. He's jus' takin' a peek to make sure, I guess. That's what he's for. He knows I got to get back to my place in a couple of shakes."

Steve smiled; by wagon road his grandfather's ranch home was fifty miles to the northward.

"You won't think of going back before noon."

"Won't I? But I will, though, son; Blenham's sticking aroun', waitin' for my say-so what he'll do nex'." He snapped open a big watch and stared at it a moment with pursed lips. "I'll be back home in jus' one hour an' a half. All I got is fifteen minutes to talk with you this mornin'."

"You mean that you can drive those fifty miles in an hour and a quarter!"

"Have done it in less; if I was in a hurry I'd do it in an hour flat. But allowin' for time out I want fifteen minutes more'n that. And now, if we're goin' to get anywhere—"

He stopped suddenly and stood toying with his big watch passing it back and forth through the loop he made of its heavy chain, his gaze steady and earnest and searching upon his grandson.

"Stephen," he said abruptly, "I ain't playin' any favorites in my ol' age. An' I ain't givin' away big chunks of money hit or miss. You wasn't countin' on anything like that, was you?"

"No, I wasn't," announced Steve quickly. "I remember your old theory; that a man should make his own way unaided, that—"

"That whatever he got he's got to get with his one head an' one set of han's. Now, the things I got to say I'll spit out one at the time: Firs', I'd like to have you come visit me for a spell at my place. Will you do it? To-day, to-morrow, any time you feel like it."

"Yes; I'll be glad to."

"That's good. Nex', not even if you was the right man for the job you can't save this ranch now; it's too late, there's to much to dig up in too short a time. I've got my hooks in deep an' whenever that happens I don't let go. I want you to quit before you get started."

Steve looked his surprise.

"Surely," he said wonderingly, "you don't want me to give you the ranch just because you happen to hold the mortgages on it?"

"Business is business, Stephen," said the old man sternly. "Sometimes, between Packards, business is hell. It'd be that for you. I've started out to get this outfit an' I'd get it. An' doin' it I'd be wastin' my time besides breakin' you all to smithereens. Better drop it."

Steve had hardly expected this. But he answered calmly, even lightly.

"I think I'd like a try at holding it."

"That's two things," old man Packard said crisply. "Number three is this here: Blenham tells, me you've put Royce in as foreman under you?"

"I offered him the place. He could have it yet if he wanted it. But he refused. I've passed the job on to a man named Barbee."

"Barbee!" cried the old man. "Barbee! That yellow canary-bird? Meaning him?"

"Yes," retorted Steve a trifle stiffly. "Anything wrong with him?"

"I didn't roll them fifty miles to talk about jay-birds an' canary-birds an' such," growled his grandfather. "But here's one thing I've got to say: This ranch is goin' to be mine real soon; that's in the cards, face up. It's as good as mine now. I've been runnin' it myself for six months. I want it right, hear me? What do you know about running a big outfit? What does a kid without whiskers like Barbee know about it? Think I want it all run down in the heel when it comes to me? No, sir! I don't. Blenham knows the lay of the land, Blenham knows my ways, Blenham knows how to run things. I want you to put Blenham back on the job!"

Steve bit his lip, holding back a hot reply.

"Grandfather," he said slowly, "suppose we take a little more time in getting squared around? I want to do what's right; I know that you want to do what's fair and square. I am willing to consult you about ranch matters; I'll come to you for advice, if you'll let me; I'll try to keep the ranch up to time and"—with a smile—"in my hands and out of yours. That's a good sporting proposition. But as for Blenham—"

"Put him back as foreman and I'll talk fair with you. I want Blenham back here, Stephen. Understand that?"

"And," cried Steve a trifle heatedly at last, "I tell you that I am going to run the ranch myself. And that I don't like Blenham."

"Damn it," cried the old man violently, "hear the boy! Don't like Blenham, huh? Goin' to run the ranch yourself, huh? Why, I tell you it's as good as mine right now! How are you goin' to pay your men, how are you goin' to buy grub for 'em, where are you goin' to find runnin'-expense money? Go an' tell folks you're mortgaged to me for fifty thousan' dollars an' see how much they'll stake you for on top of that. Or come over my way an' try to borrow some more, if you think I'm an easy guy. Why, Steve Packard, you—you're a tomfool!"

"Thanks," said Steve dryly. "I've heard that before."

"An' you'll hear it again, by the Lord! In ten languages if you'll find men talkin' that many lingos. Here I come chasin' all this way to be decent to you, to see if there ain't some way to help you out—"

"Help me out of my property," amended Steve. "I can't remember anything else you offered to do for me!"

"I said it once," shouted his grandfather, his two big fists suddenly clinched and lifted threateningly; "you're a howlin' young ass! That's what for a man you've turned out to be, Stephen Packard. Come here empty-handed an' try to buck me, would you? Me who has busted better men than you all my life, me who has got my hooks in you deep already, me who ain't no pulin' ol' dodderin' softy to turn over to a lazy, shiftless vagabond all I've piled up year after year. Buck me, would you? Tuck in an' fire my men, butt on my affairs— Why, you impudent young puppy-dog, you: I'll make you stick your tail between your legs an' howl like a kiote before I'm done with you!"

Steve looked at him hopelessly; he might have expected this all along though he had hoped for amity at least. If there were to be a conflict of purpose he could have wished that it be conducted in friendly fashion. But when did Hell-Fire Packard ever clasp hands with the man he opposed in anything, when did he ever see a business rival without cloven hoof, horns, and spiked tail?

"I am sorry you look at it that way, Grandy. It is only natural that I should seek to hold what is mine."

"Then hold your tongue, you young fool!" blazed out the old man. "But don't ask me to hold my hand! I'm goin' after you tooth and big toe-nail! If Ranch Number Ten ain't mine in all partic'lars before you're a year older I want to know why!"

"I think," said the grandson, fighting with himself for calmness and quiet speech, "that any further business I can take up with your lawyer. Past due interest—"

"Lawyer?" thundered Packard senior. "Since when did I ever have call for law an' lawyers in my play? Think I'm a crook, sir? Mean to insinuate I'm a crook?"

"I mean nothing of the kind. A mortgage is a legal matter, the payment of interest and principal—"

"Guy Little!" called the old man. "Guy Little! Goin' to stay under that car all day?"

The mechanician promptly appeared, hands and face greasy and black and took his place on the running-board.

"All ready, sir," he announced imperturbably.

With half-a-dozen strides his master reached the car; in as many seconds the powerful engine was throbbing. The screaming horn gave warning, the quiet herds in the valley heeded, lifted their heads and stood at attention, ready to scamper this way or that as need arose. The wheels turned, the car jolted over the inequalities presented by the field, swerved sharply, turned, gathered speed and whizzed away toward the valley road.

Three times before they shot back into the mouth of Blue Bird Canon the mechanician fancied that his employer had spoken; each time listening, he failed to catch any other sound than that made by the engine and speeding wheels. Once he said, "Sir?" and got only silence for an answer.

He shook his head and wondered; it was not Packard's way to mumble to himself. And again, ready to jump for his life as the big car took a dangerous turn, his eyes glued to the sheer bank a few inches from the singing tires, he caught a sound through the blast of the sparton which surely must have come from the driver's lips.

"What say?" yelled Guy Little.

No answer. He caught a fleeting glimpse of a farmer at the head of his two plunging horses where the man had hurriedly got them out of the way and up the flank of the mountain. They raced on. And again, surely Packard had said something.

"Talkin' to me?" called Little.

Then, for just a wee fraction of a second, Packard drew his eyes from the road and his look met the mechanician's. The old man's eyes were shining strangely.

"Damn it, Guy Little," he boomed out boisterously, "can't a man laugh when he feels that-away?"

And it suddenly dawned upon Guy Little that ever since they had left Ranch Number Ten the old man had been chuckling delightedly.

CHAPTER VIII

IN RED CREEK TOWN

The little town of Red Creek had an individuality all its own. It might have prided itself, had it any civic sense whatever, upon its aloofness. It stood apart from the rest of the world, at a safe distance from any of its rival settlements, even drawn apart as though distrustfully from its own railroad station which baked and blistered in the sun a good half-mile to the west. Grown up here haphazardly long before the "Gap" had been won through by the "iron trail," it ignored the beckoning of the glistening rails and refused to extend itself toward the traffic artery.

More than all this, Red Creek gave the impression, not in the least incorrect, of falling apart into two watchful sections which eyed each other suspiciously, being cynically and unsociably inclined. Its main street was as wide as Van Ness Avenue and down the middle of it, like a border line between two hostile camps, sprawled a stream which shared its name with the town.

The banks here and there were the brick-red of a soil whose chief mineral was iron; here and there were screened by willows. There were two insecure-looking bridges across which men went infrequently.

For the spirit which had brooded over the birth of Red Creek when a sheepman from the north and a cow-man from the south had set their shacks opposite each other, lived on now; long after the old feuds were dead and the whole of the grazing lands had been won over to the cattle raisers, a new basis for quarrels had offered itself at Red Creek's need.

Much of this Steve Packard knew, since it was so in his time, before he had gone wandering; much he had learned from Barbee in a long talk with him before riding the twenty-five miles into the village. Old Man Packard had drawn to himself a host of retainers since his interests were big, his hired-men many, his wages generous. And, throughout the countryside across which he cast his shadow, he had cultivated and grown a goodly crop of enemies, men with whom he had contended, men whom he had branded sweepingly as liars and thieves and cutthroats, men whose mortgages he had taken, men whom, in the big game which he played, he had broken. The northern half of Red Creek was usually and significantly known as Packard's Town; the southern half sold liquor and merchandise, offered food and lodging, to men who harbored few friendly feelings for Packard's "crowd."

Hence, in Red Creek were two saloons, confronting each other across the red scar of the creek; two stores, two lunch-counters, two blacksmith shops, each eying its rival jealously. At this time the post-office had been secured by the Packard faction; the opposition snorted contempt and called attention to the fact that the constable resided with them. Thus honors were even.

Steve Packard rode into town in the late afternoon, his motive clear-cut, his need urgent. If Blenham had stolen his ten thousand dollars for which he had so imperative a call now, then Blenham had been the one who had replaced the large bank-notes with the small; there was the chance that Blenham, just a week ago to-night, had gotten the dollar bills in Red Creek. If such were the case Packard meant to know it.

"There are things, Barbee," he had said bluntly, "which I can't tell you yet; I don't know you well enough. But this I can say: I am out to get Blenham's tag."

"So'm I," said Barbee.

"That's one reason you've got the job you're holding down right now. Here's one point though, which it's up to you to know; I very much suspect that for reasons of his own Blenham hasn't set foot for the last time on Ranch Number Ten. He'll come back; he'll come snooping around at night; he'll perhaps have a way of knowing the first night I'm away and come then. There's something he left there that he wants. At least that is the way I'm stringing my bet. And while I am away you're foreman, Barbee."

A flickering light danced in Barbee's blue eyes.

"Orders from you, if Blenham shows up at night—"

"To throw a gun on him and run him out! The quickest way. To-night I want you to squat out under a tree and keep awake—all night. For which you can have two days off if you want."

"If I thought he'd show," and the boy's voice was little more than an eager whisper, "I couldn't sleep if I tried!"

Then Packard had spoken a little about Red Creek, asking his few questions and had learned that Blenham had his friends in "Packard's Town" where Dan Hodges of the Ace of Diamonds saloon was an old pal, that "Whitey" Wimble of the Old Trusty saloon across the street hated both Hodges and Blenham like poison.

"Us boys," added Barbee, "always hung out at the Ace of Diamonds, bein' Packard's men. After now, when I go on a rampage, I'm goin' to make frien's across the street. Friends sometimes comes in handy in Red Creek," he added smilingly.

The road, as one comes into Red Creek from the east, divides at the first bridge, one fork becoming the northern half of the intersected street, the other the southern half. Steve Packard, filling his eyes with the two rows of similar shacks, hesitated briefly.

Until now he had always gone to the Packard side; when a boy he had regarded the rival section with high contempt, looking upon it as inferior, sneering at it as a thoroughbred might lift lip at an unworthy mongrel. The prejudice was old and deep-rooted; he felt a subtle sense of shame as though the eyes of the world were upon him, watching to see him turn toward the "low-down skunks an' varmints" which his grandfather had named these denizens of the defamed section.

The hesitation was brief; he reined his horse impatiently to the left, riding straight toward the flaunting sign upon the lofty false front of the Old Trusty saloon. But short as was his indecision it had not ended before he had glimpsed at the far end of the street the incongruous lines of an automobile—red racing type.

"Boyd-Merril. Twin Eight," thought Packard. "So we'll meet on the same side after all, Miss Terry Pert!"

There were seeds of content in the thought. If it were to be range war between him and his grandfather, then since obviously the Temples had already been drawn into contention with the old man Packard, it was just as well the fates decreed that he and Terry should be on the same side of the fence, the same side of the fight, the same side of Red Creek.

He tickled his horse with a light spur; despite the manner of their last encounter he could look forward with something akin to eagerness to another meeting. For, he told himself carelessly, she amused him vastly.

But the meeting was not just yet. He saw Terry, jauntily, even saucily dressed, as she came out of the store and jumped into her car, marked how the bright sunlight winked from her high boots, how it flamed upon her gay red scarf, how it glinted from a burnished steel buckle in her hat band. As bright as a sunbeam herself, loving gay colors about her, across the distance she fairly shone and twinkled.

There was a faint shadow of regret in his eyes as she let in the clutch and whizzed away. She was headed down the street, her back to him, driving toward the remote railroad station. Off to the north he saw a growing plume of black smoke.

"Going away?" he wondered. "Or just meeting some one?"

But he had come into Red Creek on a business in no way connected with Terry Temple.

He had figured it out that Blenham, if it had been Blenham who had chanced on Bill Royce's secret and no longer ago than last Saturday night, would have wasted no time in acquiring the one-dollar bills for his trick of substitution; that if he had come for them to Red Creek that same night, after post-office and stores were closed, he would have sought them at one of the two saloons; that, since currency is at all times scarce in cattle towns in the West, he might have had to go to both saloons for them.

Packard began investigations at the Old Trusty saloon whose doors stood invitingly open to the faint afternoon breeze.

In the long room half-a-dozen idle men looked up at him with mild interest, withdrawing their eyes briefly from solitaire or newspaper or cribbage game or whatever had been holding their careless attention as he entered.

A glance at them showed him no familiar face. He turned to the bar.

Behind it a man was polishing glasses with quick, skilful hands. Steve knew him at once for Whitey Wimble. He was a pronounced albino, unhealthy-looking, with overlarge, thin ears, small pale eyes, and teeth that looked like chalk. Steve nodded to him and spun a dollar on the bar.

"Have something," he suggested.

Wimble returned his nod, left off his polishing to shove forward a couple of the glistening glasses, and produced a bottle from behind him.

"Regards," he said apathetically, taking his whiskey with the enthusiasm and expression of a man observing his doctor's orders. "Stranger in Red Creek?"

"I haven't been here," Steve answered, "for several years. I never saw the town any quieter. Used to be a rather gay little place, didn't it?"

"It's early yet," said Whitey, going back to his interrupted task. "Bein' Saturday, the boys from the ranches will be showin' up before long. Then it ain't always so quiet."

Packard made his cigarette, lighted it, and then said casually: "How are you fixed for dollar bills in your strong-box?"

"Nary," returned Whitey Wimble without troubling himself to look into his till. "We don't see overmuch rag money in Red Creek."

"Guess that's so," admitted Steve. "They do come in handy, though, sometimes; when you want to send a dollar in a letter or something of that kind."

"That's a fac', too; never thought of that." Which, since he never wrote or received letters, was no doubt true.

"Men around here don't have much use for paper money, do they?" continued Packard carelessly, his interest seeming to centre in his cigarette smoke. "I'd bet a man the drinks nobody else has asked you for a dollar bill for the last six months."

"You'd lose," said Whitey. "I had three of 'em in the drawer for a coon's age; feller asked me for 'em jus' the other night."

"Yes?" He masked his eagerness as he thrust a quarter forward. "The drink's on me then. Let me have a cigar."

Whitey also took a cigar, indicating friendliwise the better box.

"Who was it asked you for the paper money?" Steve went on. "He might have one he doesn't need."

"It was Stumpy Collins. The bootblack across the street."

"I'll look him up; yesterday he had them, you say?"

Wimble shook his head, gave the matter his thought a moment, and said:

"It was las' Saturday night; I remember 'cause there was a right smart crowd in an' I was busy an' Stumpy kep' pesterin' me until I 'tended to him. He won't have nothin' lef by this, though; it ain't Stumpy's way to save his money long. Firs' time I ever knowed him to have three dollars all at once."

From the Old Trusty Steve went across the street, leaving his horse in front of Wimble's door where there was a big poplar and a grateful shade. Crossing the second of the two bridges he turned his eyes toward the railroad station; the red touring-car stood forth brilliantly in the sunshine, a freight train was just pulling in, Terry was not to be seen.

"She'll eat before she starts back home," he thought, hastening his stride on to Hodges's place, the Ace of Diamonds. "I'll see her at the lunch-counter."

Tucked in beside the Ace of Diamonds was a bootblack stand, a crazy, home-made affair with dusty seat. The wielder of the brush and polish was nowhere in evidence. Steve passed and turned in at the saloon door, wishing to come to Hodges, Blenham's pal. For it required little imagination to suspect that it had been Hodges at Blenham's behest, or Blenham himself, who had sent Stumpy across the street to the Old Trusty.

Here, as in Wimble's place, a few men loitered idly; here as there the proprietor stood behind his own bar. Hodges, a short, squat man with a prize-fighter's throat, chest, and shoulders and a wide, thin-lipped mouth, leaned forward in dirty shirt-sleeves, chewing at a moist cigar-stump.

Jackson Gregory

"Hello, stranger," he offered offhandedly. "What's the word?"

"Know Blenham, don't you?" asked Steve quietly. "Works for old man Packard."

"Sure, I know him. What about him?"

"Seen him lately?"

"Ten minutes ago. Why? Want him?"

Packard had not counted on this, having no idea that Blenham was in town. He hesitated, then said quickly:

"Hasn't left yet, has he? Where is he now?"

"Down to the depot. Trailin' a skirt. An' some skirt, too, take it from me."

He laughed.

Steve wanted suddenly to slap the broad, ugly face. Since, however, he could formulate no logically sufficient reason for the act, he said instead:

"Maybe I'll see him before I pull out. If I don't, ask him if he lost a wad like this?"

Fleetingly he flashed the little roll of banknotes before Hodges's eyes.

"Greenbacks?" asked Hodges. "How much?"

Packard laughed.

"Not so all-fired much," he said lightly. "But enough to buy a hat!"

"If hats are sellin' ten dollars or under?" ventured Hodges.

Packard affected to look surprised.

"What do you know about how much is in this roll?" he demanded innocently.

"One-dollar bills?" said Hodges. "Ten of 'em?"

"You don't look like a mind-reader."

"Well, you're right about the wad bein' Blenham's. Leave it with me, if you want. I'll see he gets it. There ain't enough there for a man to steal," he added reassuringly.

"How do you know it's Blenham's? If he told you that he had lost it he'd have told you where. What's the answer; where did I pick this up?"

"Blenham didn't say he los' nothin'. But I know it's his because he got most of them bills from me."

"Tell me when," and Packard held the roll in a tight-shut hand, "and I'll leave them with you."

"Las' Saturday night," said Hodges, after a brief moment of reflection.

Packard tossed the little roll to the bar.

"There's the money. Tell Blenham I thought it was his!"

He turned to the door, his blood suddenly stirred with certainty: Blenham had stolen the ten thousand dollars, and the theft had been committed no longer ago than last

Saturday night. Just a week—there was the chance—

"Hey, there," called Hodges. "Who'll I say lef this? What name, stranger?"

Steve turned and regarded him coolly.

"Tell him Steve Packard called. Steve Packard, boss of Ranch Number Ten."

And Dan Hodges, dull wit that he was, felt that something was wrong. The look in the stranger's eyes had altered swiftly, the eyes had grown hard. Steve went out. As he reached the sidewalk he glimpsed a red automobile racing townward from the station. Behind it, riding in its dust, came Blenham.

CHAPTER IX

"IT'S MY FIGHT AND HIS. LET HIM GO!"

Steve Packard, walking swiftly, reached the west bridge just before the front tires of Terry's car thudded on the heavy planks. He glimpsed Blenham jogging along behind her and knew that Blenham had seen him.

But his eyes were for Terry now. She, too, had recognized him with but a few yards separating them. She gave him a blast of her horn warningly, and, slowing down no more than was necessary for the sharp turn, came on across the bridge. He read it in her eye that it would be an abiding joy for Miss Terry if she could send him scampering out of her way; the horn as much as said: "You step aside or I'll run you down!"

With no intention of going under the wheels, Steve waited until the last moment and then jumped. But not to the side as Terry had anticipated. Obeying his impulse and taking his chance, he sprang up to her running-board as she whizzed over the bouncing planks of the bridge, grasping the door of her car to steady himself. The feat safely accomplished, he grinned up into Terry's startled eyes.

"We meet again," he laughed sociably. "Howdy!"

Her lips tight-pressed, she gave her attention for a moment to her wheel and the rutty road in front of her. Her cheeks were red and grew redder. Perhaps a dozen men, here and there upon the street, had seen. She had meant them to see; it would have tickled her no little to have had them note Steve Packard flying wildly to the side of the road while she shot by. She had not counted upon him doing anything else.

"Smarty!" she cried hotly.

"Smart enough to climb out from under when an automobile driven by a manslaughter artist comes along," he chuckled, sensing an advantage and drawing a deep enjoyment from it. "Don't you know, young lady, you've got to be careful sometimes? Now, if you had run over me—"

"Serve you right," sniffed Terry.

"Yes, but think! Running over a man who hasn't had time to take his spurs off yet, why you stood all kinds of chances getting a puncture! You don't want to forget things like that."

Terry bit her lip, stepped on the throttle, swung across the street, made a reckless turn, and brought up in front of the lunch-counter.

"Do you know," remarked Packard lightly, ignoring the fact that she had answered him with only the contempt of her silence, "you remind me of my grandfather. Fact! You two have the same little trick of driving. Wonder what would happen if you and he met on a narrow road?"

"At least," said Terry, eying him belligerently, "he is a man, if he is a scoundrel. Not just a hobo!"

"Oh, I didn't mean to call you a scoundrel! Nor yet to say that you struck me as mannish. Of course—"

"Oh, you make me sick!" cried Terry. And she flashed away from him, going into the lunch-room.

He followed her with speculative eyes. Then he glanced across the street. Blenham had dismounted in front of the Ace of Diamonds and was watching. As Packard turned Blenham went into Hodges's saloon.

"Wonder what he'll have to say when Hodges hands him his roll?" mused Packard.

Well, he had accomplished his purpose. He had done all that he had hoped to do in Red Creek this afternoon, had assured himself that his suspicions against Blenham were justified by the fact and that the theft was only a week old. He went back slowly to his horse in front of the Old Trusty. But his eyes were frowning thoughtfully.

What would be Blenham's next move? What would Blenham do, what would he say when Hodges gave him Packard's message? Might he, in an unguarded moment, give a hint toward the answer of that other question which now had become the only consideration: "Were the larger banknotes still hidden at Ranch Number Ten or had Blenham already removed them?"

Instead of mounting to ride away, Packard hung his spurs upon his saddlehorn and turned again into Whitey Wimble's place.

The late afternoon faded into dusk, the first stars came out, Whitey Wimble lighted his lamps. Steve, advised of the fact by the purr of a motor, knew when Terry left the lunch-room and drove to the store for a visit with the storekeeper's wife. Was she going to remain in town overnight? It began to look as though she were.

Across the street Hodges came out and lighted the big lamps at each side of his doorway. A cowboy swung down from his horse and went in, his spurs winking in the lamplight as though there were jewels upon them. A buckboard pulled up and two other men went in after him. A voice in sudden laughter boomed out. Saturday night had come. As Whitey Wimble had predicted, the boys were showing up and Red Creek stood ready to lose something of its brooding afternoon quiet.

Once again Packard crossed the bridge and made his way along the echoing wooden sidewalk to the Ace of Diamonds. A dozen saddle-horses were tied at the hitching-rail. Among them was Blenham's white-footed bay. Up and down the street glowing cigarette ends like fireflies came and went. In front of the saloon a number of men made a good-natured, tongue-free crowd, most of whom had had their first drinks and were beginning to liven up as in duty bound on a Saturday night.

A four-horse wagon came rattling into town from the east to pour out its contents, big, husky men, at Hodges's door. Among them Packard recognized one man. He was the lumber-camp cook from whom he had gotten coffee and hotcakes the other day, that morning after he had refused to accept Terry's cool invitation to breakfast.

"I'll have to look in on those fellows tomorrow," he thought as they shouldered past, boisterous and eager. "Grandy's sure had his nerve cutting my timber with never so much as a by-your-leave."

Their foreman was with them; one glance singled him out. He was of that type chosen always by old man Packard to head any one of the Packard units, a sort of confident mastery in his very stride, the biggest man of them, unkempt and heavy, with a brutal face and hard eyes. Joe Woods, his name. Packard had already heard of him, a rowdy and a rough-neck but a capable timberjack to the calloused fingers of him. He followed the men into the saloon.

At his place behind the long bar was Hodges, busy filling imperative orders, taking in the money which he counted as good as his once it left the paymaster's pocket. But it struck Packard that the bartender did not appear happy; his face was flushed and hot, his eyes looked troubled. Now and then he flashed a quick look at Blenham who stood leaning against the bar at the far end, twisting an empty whiskey-glass slowly in his big hand, staring frowningly at nothing.

"Hodges is a fool and he has just been told so!" was Steve's answer to the situation.

"Hi, Blenham!" called big Joe Woods. "Have a drink."

"No," growled Blenham, deep down in his throat. "I don't want it. I—"

His eyes, lifted to the lumber-camp boss, passed on and rested on Steve Packard. He broke off abruptly, his look changing, probing, seeming full of question.

"Get the money I gave Hodges for you?" asked Packard, coming into the room. "The ten one-dollar bills that you left behind you?"

"They wasn't mine," said Blenham quickly, his hand hard about the whiskey glass, his manner vaguely nervous. "I tol' Dan to give 'em back to you."

Steve smiled.

"Funny," he said carelessly. "Hodges said—"

"I made a mistake," called Hodges sharply. "I got Blenham mixed up with some other guy. I don't know nothin' about this here." He slammed the little roll down on the bar. "Come get it, if you want it." Packard promptly stepped forward, taking the money.

"I figured there was a chance to make ten dollars, easy money, if I just walked across the street for it," he said, looking pleasantly from Hodges to Blenham. "Sure, I want it. It's luck-money; didn't you know? You see, when a man loses anything he loses some of his luck with it; when another man gets it, he gets the luck along with it. Thanks, Blenham."

Blenham made no answer. His eyes were bright with anger and yet troubled with uncertainty. The uncertainty was there to be recognized by him who looked keenly for it. Blenham did not know just which way to jump. From that fact Steve drew a deep satisfaction. For there would have been no reason for indecision if Blenham knew that he had those other, bigger bank-notes, safe.

At the rear of the long room a man was dealing cards for seven-and-a-half. As though to demonstrate the truth of his boast about "luck-money" Steve stepped to the table, the roll of bills in his hand. He was dealt a card. Without turning it up to look at it he shoved it under the ten banknotes.

"Standing?" said the dealer.

Steve nodded.

"Playing my luck," he answered.

The dealer turned lack-lustre eyes upon Steve's card, then upon his own which he turned up. It was the four of clubs.

"I've the hunch that will beat you, pardner," he said listlessly. "But I'll come again."

He turned another card, a deuce.

"That'll about beat you," he suggested. He leaned forward for Steve's card. "Unless you've got a seven in the hole."

And a seven it was; the bright red seven of hearts. The dealer paid, ten dollars to Steve's ten.

"Come again?" he asked.

"Not to-night," returned Packard. "I took just the one flutter to show Blenham."

He turned and saw that Blenham had already slipped quietly out of the room. Dan Hodges, his face a fiery red, was just coming back from the card-room. With him was the big timber boss.

"Tin-horn!" shouted Joe Woods at Packard. "Quitter!"

A quick joy spurted up in Steve Packard's heart; he was right about Blenham. Blenham, filled with anxiety, had gone already, would be rushing back to Ranch Number Ten to make sure if the ten thousand dollars were safe or had been discovered already by the rightful owner. He had slipped away hurriedly but, after the fashion of a careful, practical man, had taken time to confer with Dan Hodges and had commissioned Joe Woods to hold Packard here. And so, though he could not remember of having ever run away from a fight before, Steve Packard was strongly of that mind right now.

"Joe Woods, I believe?" he said coolly, his mind busy with the new problem of a new situation. "Boss of the timber crew on the east side of Number Ten? I was planning on riding out to-morrow for a word with you, Woods."

"So?" cried Woods. "What's the matter with havin' that word to-night?"

"Haven't time," was the simple rejoinder. "I'm about due across the street now; at Whitey Wimble's place."

"Which is where you belong," growled Woods, his under jaw thrust forward, his whole attitude charged with quarrelsome intent. "Over at the White Rat's with the rest of the Willies!"

The ever-ready Packard temper was getting into Steve's head, beating in his temples, pounding along his pulses. He had never had a man bait him like that before. But he strove to remember Blenham only, to take stock of the fact that this was a bit of Blenham's game, and that any trouble with another than Blenham was to be avoided at this juncture. So, though the color was rising into his face and a little flicker of fire came into his eyes, he said briefly:

"Then I'd better go across, hadn't I? See you in the morning, Woods."

But there is always the word to whip the hot blood into the coolest head, to snare a man's caution out of him and inject fury in its stead, and Joe Woods, a downright man and never a subtle, put his tongue to it. On the instant Packard gave over thought of such side issues as a man named Blenham and hidden bank-notes.

He cried out inarticulately and leaped forward and struck. Joe Woods reeled under the first blow full in the face, staggered under the second, and was borne back into the tight-jammed crowd of his followers.

The men about him and Packard withdrew this way and that, leaving empty floor space to accommodate the two pairs of shuffling boots. Joe Woods wiped his lips with the back of a big, hairy hand, saw traces of blood, and charged. The sound of blows given and taken and of little grunts and of scraping feet were for a space the only sounds heard in Hodges's saloon.

Packard's attack had been swift and sure and not without a certain skill; against it Woods opposed all he had, ponderous strength, slow-moving, brutal force, broad-backed, deep-chested endurance. But from the first it was clear to all who watched and was suspected by Woods himself that he had chosen the wrong man.

Steve was taller, had the longer reach, was gifted by the gods with a supple strength no whit less than the bearish power of the timber boss. With ten blows struck, with both men rocking dizzily, it was patently Steve Packard's fight. But a dull, dogged persistence was in Joe Woods's eyes as again he shook his head and charged.

Steve struck for the stomach and landed—hard. Woods doubled up; the sweat came in drops upon his forehead; his face went suddenly a sick white. But the light in his eyes, as again he lifted his head, was unaltered.

"He can lick me—I know it! He can lick me—I know it!" he muttered and kept muttering. "But, by God, he's got to do it!"

And Steve did it and men looked on queerly, appraising him

anew. He took Woods's blows when he must and felt the pain go stabbing through his body; but he stood up and struck back and forced the fight steadily, crowding his adversary relentlessly, seeming always to strike swifter and harder.

It was a bleeding fist driven into Joe Woods's throbbing throat, followed by the other fist, going piston-like, at Joe Woods's stomach, that ended the fight.

The bigger man crumpled and went down slowly like one of his own trees just toppling, and lay staring up into Packard's face with dull eyes. Steve stepped over him, going to the door.

"I'll see you in the morning, Woods," he panted.

But again boots were shuffling on the floor and already several men, Dan Hodges among them, were between him and the door. It dawned upon him that Blenham must have given emphatic orders and that Blenham had the trick of exacting obedience.

"Hold him here," shouted Hodges, and being a man of little spirit he withdrew hastily under Steve's eyes, thrusting another man in front of him. "Keep him for the sheriff. Startin' a fight in my place—it's disturbin' the peace, that's what it is! I won't stand it!"

Packard drew back two or three paces, his eyes narrowing. At that instant he was sure of what he saw in the faces of at least three of the men confronting him; they were going to rush him together.

But now Joe Woods was on his feet again. Packard drew still further back, getting the wall behind him. And then came a diversion. It was Joe Woods speaking heavily:

"I fought him fair an' he licked me. Think I'm the kind of a she-man as stands for you guys buttin' in on my fight? Stand back an' let him go!"

"Blenham said—" screamed Hodges.

"Damn Blenham an' you, too," growled Woods. "It's my fight an' his. Let him go!"

They let him go, drawing apart slowly. With watchful eyes Steve passed down the little lane they made. At the door he turned, saying briefly:

"I'll see you in the morning, Woods!"

Then he went out.

CHAPTER X

A RIDE WITH TERRY

Returning at once to the Old Trusty, on the way passing Terry's car which still stood in front of the store, Steve Packard asked for the use of a telephone. Whitey nodded toward the office, a little room thinly partitioned off from the larger. A moment later Barbee's voice was answering from Ranch Number Ten.

"He's on the way, Barbee," said Steve quickly. "Left Red Creek just a few minutes ago. I'll trail him. Give him the chance to prowl around a little; try and find what he's after. But don't let him get away with it! Understand? Shoot the legs out from under him if you have to. I'll give you a month's pay for the night's work if you nail him with the goods on."

Clicking up the receiver he went out on the street again, giving no heed to the many glances which followed him. They knew who he was; they were speculating on him. "Ol' man Packard's gran'son," he heard one man say.

In the thick darkness lying under the poplar tree it was several minutes before he was certain that his horse was gone. He had tethered the animal himself; there was no dangling bit of rope to indicate a broken tie-rope. Blenham, the practical, had simply taken thought of detail.

"Not missing a single bet, is Blenham," he thought savagely.

He swung about and reentered the saloon. A buzz of talk up and down the long room promptly died away as again the eyes of many men travelled his way. It struck him that they had all been talking of him; he knew that they must have marked those signs which Joe Woods's fists had left on his face; he stood a moment looking in on them, conscious for the first time of his rapidly swelling right eye, seeking to estimate what these men made of him.

It seemed to him that the one emotion he glimpsed on all hands and in varying degrees, was distrust. Little cause for surprise there: he was a Packard and this was not the Packard side of Red Creek.

"Somebody's put me on foot," he announced crisply. "I left my horse outside, tied. It's gone now. Know anything about it, any of you boys?"

They looked their interest. Hereabouts one man did not trifle with another man's horse. But there was no answer to his direct question.

"I've got to be riding," he went on quietly. "Who can lend me a saddle-horse for the night? I'll pay double what it's worth."

Whitey Wimble gave his bar a long swipe with his wet towel.

"If you're askin' favors, seems to me you're on the wrong side the street, ain't you, stranger?"

"Meaning I am a Packard?"

"You got me the firs' time. That's Packard's Town over yonder. Your crowd—"

"Look at my eye!" then said Steve quickly.

A big man with a thin little voice at the far end of the room giggled.

"I seen it already," said Wimble.

"Know Joe Woods? Well, he's got another just like it. Know Blenham? Blenham sicked him on me! Know old man Packard? He's sicking Blenham on me. Want to know what I want a horse for? Blenham's got a head start and I want to overhaul him! To tell him he's a crook and a thief. Now is this side of Red Creek open to me or is it shut? What's the answer, Whitey Wimble?"

Wimble appeared both impressed and yet hesitant. Here was a Packard to deal with and Whitey Wimble when taking over the destiny of the Old Trusty had been set clear in the matter that he had a ripe, old feud to maintain; and still, looking at it the other way, here was a man who carried the sign of Joe Woods's fist upon his bruised face, who announced that he was out to get Blenham, that there was open trouble between him and old man Packard.

Whitey Wimble, beginning by looking puzzled, wound up by turning a distressed face toward Steve.

"It's kind of a fine point," he suggested finally. "Now, come right down to it, it sort of looks to me—"

"Fine point!" cried Steve hotly, a sudden anger growing within him as he thought how Blenham had played the game all along the line, how Blenham might well prove too shrewd for a boy like Barbee, how a set of prejudiced fools here in the Old Trusty by denying him the loan of a horse might seriously be aiding Blenham whom none of them had any love for. "Why, damn it, man, haven't I told you that Blenham has just put a raw deal across on me, that he's coming close to getting away with it, that all I ask is a horse to run him down? Who's going to let me have one? I'm in a hurry!"

Never until now did he realize how strong a factor in the life of the community was the prejudice against his blood. On every hand he saw doubt, clouded eyes, distrust. Plainly many a man there held him for a liar; would even go so far, it was possible, as to suggest later that Steve Packard had meant to steal the horse he asked for. Steve stared about him a moment, his back stiffening. Then, with a little grunt of disgust, he strode across the room.

"At least," he flung over his shoulder at Whitey Wimble, "I am going to use your telephone again!"

Without waiting for an answer and caring not the snap of his fingers what that answer might be, he went to the telephone, jerking down the receiver, saying brusquely to the operator:

"Ranch Number Ten, please. In a hurry."

He waited impatiently and, it seemed to him, an inexcusably long time. Finally the operator said after the aloof manner of telephone girls:

"I am ringing them."

And again—

"I am ringing them."

And then—

"They do not answer."

And at last, and then only when Steve made emphatic that there must be some one at the Number Ten bunk-house at this hour, the girl said:

"Wait a minute."

And after that:

"There seems to be something the matter with the line. I can't raise any of the ranch-houses out that way. We'll send a man out in the morning."

So he couldn't even warn Barbee that Blenham had made good his head-start; that Blenham was plainly of one mind to-night; that it was up to young Barbee to keep his eyes open and his gun cocked. He began to understand why his grandfather had made Blenham one of his right-hand men; he had the cool mind and the way of acting quickly which makes for success.

"I got a horse for you, pardner," said a slow voice as Packard came out of the office. "A cayuse as can't be beat for legs an' lungs. Come ahead."

Steve looked at him eagerly. He was a little fellow, leather-cheeked, keen-eyed, leisurely; a stranger, obviously a cowboy.

"I work for Brocky Lane," offered the stranger as they went out together. "Know him, don't you?"

"I did a dozen years ago," answered Steve absently. "Where's your horse?"

"You're Steve Packard, ain't you? You done Brocky a favor when you was a kid, didn't you? Brocky told me. Brocky's done me a favor. I'm doin' you a favor. That squares us up all 'round. Like a circle, all in a ring, sort of; get me?"

"Yes," agreed Steve, feeling vaguely that the cowman had unknowingly touched upon a problem in higher mathematics. He slipped a hand into his pocket.

But the friend whom an old, long-forgotten kindness raised now for him at his need, shook his head, would have none of Packard's money, and led the way to a shed behind the saloon. Out of the darkness he brought a tall, wall-eyed roan, quickly saddled and bridled and handed over to Steve.

"Heeled?" came solicitously from the little man as Steve swung up into the saddle.

"No."

"Well, Blenham is. He goes that way all the time. An' he's a right good shot, the boys say. If there's some real sour blood stirred up between him an' you there's no use bein' a plumb fool, is there? The store's apt to be open yet; there's a firs'-class double-barrel shot-gun, secon'-hand but as good as new, in the window. Only seven dollars an' a half."

"I'll send the horse over to Brocky's to-morrow," called Steve. "And as for being square—call on me at any time for the next favor. So long."

"So long," responded the slow-voiced man.

Steve swung out toward the east, curbing his mount's eagerness, settling himself in the saddle for a couple of hours of hard riding. Slowly he would warm up the big roan, letting him out gradually, steadily. Already he sensed that in truth here was "a cayuse hard to beat for legs an' lungs." And Blenham's head-start was but a matter of minutes, half an hour at most.

But before he had ridden fifty yards Steve whirled his horse and rode back, going straight to the store. After all, since Blenham was playing a game in which the stakes were no less than ten thousand dollars, since Blenham was without doubt the man who had sought to kill Bill Royce six months ago for the very same money, since Blenham always "went heeled and was a right good shot," why then, as Brocky Lane's cowboy put it, "there was no use bein' a plumb fool." And to ride a hundred yards or so and buy a Colt .45 and a box of cartridges required but a moment.

In the store the long shelves upon one side held dry-goods, while upon the opposite shelves a miscellany of groceries was displayed; toward the rear was the storekeeper's assortment of hardware near a counter piled high with sweaters, boots, chaparejos, all jumbled hopelessly. At the flank of this confusion was a show-case containing a rather fair line of side-arms. Steve, his eye finding what it sought, went straight to the back of the house. And then, looking through an open door which gave entrance to the living-room of the storekeeper's family, his glance met Terry's. She was rising to her feet, drawing on her gauntlets.

"That's your train now," a woman's voice was saying.

Packard heard the whistling of a distant engine. He lifted his hat, she promptly whirled about, giving him her back to look at.

"Here's what I want," said Steve as the storekeeper came to his side. "That .45, and a box of cartridges."

Terry turned again quickly and he surprised a little look of interest in her slightly widened eyes. A man doesn't buy a gun and a box of cartridges at this time of night unless he has a use for them. Packard took up his new purchases, went out, swung again into the saddle, and clattered down the street.

The night was bright with stars, clear and sweet. Presently, with only a handful of miles behind him, the moon rose above the distant ridge, at the full, glorious and generous of light. He loosened his reins a little, gave the big roan his head, and swept on through the ghostly-lighted country.

Now and then, remarking some old remembered landmark, he glanced from it to his watch; more than once, having slipped his watch again into his pocket, he leaned forward and patted the horse's neck.

Then—he had done a little more than half the distance and was riding through the thick shadows of Laurel Canon, which marks the beginning of the long grade—the unforeseen occurred; the unlooked-for which, he knew now, he would have fully expected, had he not counted always upon Blenham playing a lone hand.

In the middle of the inky blotch made by the laurels standing up against the moon there was a spot through which the moon-rays found their way, making a pool of light. As Packard rode into this bright area he heard a rifle-shot, startlingly loud; saw the spit of flame from just yonder, perhaps ten feet, certainly not more than twenty feet away; felt the big roan plunge under him, race on unsteadily, and sink.

He slipped out of the saddle as the horse crashed down in the bushes at the side of the road, and as he did so emptied his revolver into the shadows whence had come the rifle-shot. But he knew that he was a fool to hope to hit; the man had had time to select his spot, to screen his own body with a boulder or fallen log, to leave open behind him a way to safety and darkness.

"Not Blenham himself but one of his crowd did that," muttered Packard as he turned back to the fallen horse. "Just to set me on foot again. He isn't up to murder when he sees another way. And for ten dollars he could hire one of his hangers-on to kill a horse."

Well, it was just another trick for Blenham. On foot now he must make what time he could to the Pinchot farm, some three or four miles further on, demand a horse there, and pray that Barbee was equal to his task. But first he must not leave the big roan to suffer needlessly and hopelessly.

He struck a match and made a flaring torch of a little wisp of dry grass. Loving a good horse as he did, he felt a sudden and utterly new sort of hatred of Blenham go rushing along his blood.

It was with a deep sigh of relief that he straightened up when he saw that either chance or a remarkable skill with a rifle had saved Brocky Lane's roan from any protracted pain.

Packard pushed on, seeking to make what time he could, breaking into a jog-trot time and again upon a down-slope, conserving wind and strength for the up-hill climbs, keeping in the shadows for the most part but taking his chance over and over in the moonlit open.

Yet it was being borne in upon him that it was useless to hurry now; that Blenham had made of his advantage a safe lead; that he might as well slow down, make a cigarette, take his time. And still, being the sort of man he was, he kept doggedly on, telling himself that a race is anybody's race until the tape is broken; that Blenham might be having his own troubles somewhere ahead; that quitting did no good and that it is not good to be a "quitter." But he had little enough hope of coming up again with Blenham that night.

And then, when he had been on foot not more than twenty minutes, a faint, even, drumming sound swelling steadily through the night somewhere behind him put a new, quick stir in his blood. He stopped, stood almost breathless a moment, listening.

The smooth drumming grew louder; suddenly topping a rise the two headlights of an automobile flashed into his eyes. Terry Temple, her errand done in Red Creek, was racing homeward.

"And I'll beat Blenham to it yet!" cried Steve.

Where the moonlight streamed brightest and whitest across the road he sprang out so that she could not fail to see him, tossing up both arms in signal to her to stop. Her headlights blinded him one moment; he heard the warning blast of her horn; he entertained briefly the suspicion that she was going to refuse to stop.

Incredible—and yet he had not thought of her own likely emotions. To have a man leap out into the road in front of her, all unexpectedly, waving his arms and calling on her to stop—Why, she'd think herself fallen into the hands of a highwayman!

She was coming on, straight on, her horn emitting one long, sustained shriek of menace. Packard ground his teeth; either she did not recognize him and was bound upon getting by him, or she did recognize him and was accepting her opportunity to emphasize her attitude toward him.

In any case she was going by, she in whom lay his sole hope

to come to grips with Blenham. If he let her evade he might as well quit, quit in utter disgust with the world.

With the world? Disgust with himself, that he had let Blenham beat him, that he wasn't much of a man, that his old grandfather was right about him. Her car was rushing down upon him; if he let it pass, why, he'd be letting, not only a girl laugh at him, but he'd be letting his chance rush by him. His chance that loomed up bigger than the oncoming machine and more real; his chance not for to-night alone but for ever after.

For if Blenham beat him to-night and his grandfather beat him again later on, he knew that he would pass away from the country about Ranch Number Ten, that he would give over all sustained effort to make something of his life, that he would go back to drifting, rounding out his days after the fashion of the last twelve years. It was while Terry's car was speeding toward him that all of this ran through his mind.

There was the possibility that, knowing who he was, Terry would try to bluff him out of the road, counting confidently upon his leaping to safety at the last moment; there was the other possibility that she mistook his motives and would run him down in a sort of panic of self-defense.

Packard, with his rather clear-cut conception of the girl's character to steer by, saw the one way to master the situation. Whirling about, his back to her now, he broke into a run, speeding along the road in front of her. As he ran the hard lines about his mouth softened into a rare grin: he'd have her guessing for a minute, anyway. And by the time she got through guessing—

He had duplicated his feat of the afternoon at the bridge in Red Creek. Terry, in her first astonishment that the man should turn and run straight on in front of her, slowed down, hesitation in her mind. What was he up to? Then there came sudden shadows in a narrow part of the road, a sharp turn, the absolute necessity of slowing down just a trifle more, and then—

"It's all right; go ahead!" called Packard lightly. He was standing on her running-board.

She had thrown off her hat to the cool of the evening. As they passed out from the shadows he could see her eyes. He pushed back his own hat and Terry saw his eyes. For a moment, while the car sped on, neither spoke.

Looking at her he had glimpsed wonder, an annoyance that was swiftly growing into anger, and a certain assurance that Miss Terry Temple fully intended to remember this day and to square accounts with Stephen Packard.

Returning his look, Terry had seen but one emotion in his eyes: pure triumph. She could not know how the man of him, having but just now succeeded in this first task he had set himself, felt a sudden confidence of the future.

"If I had let you go by," said Packard quietly, "I should have felt that I had let my destiny pass me!"

"Don't you start in getting fresh just because it's moonlight!"

Steve looked puzzled, understood, put back his head and laughed joyously. Then, his face suddenly serious again, he considered her speculatively. Now for the first time he became aware that Terry was already carrying a passenger. A small man, Japanese, immaculate, and frightened so that his teeth were chattering.

He was Iki, who had come into Red Creek this evening by

train and due to cook for the Temple ranch. Just now he was screwed up in his place, ready to jump if Steve moved his way, his purse clutched in his plump hand, half offered already. Steve beamed upon him, then turned his eyes, still speculative, upon Terry.

"Do you care to tell me," said Terry tartly, "why you're always getting in my way? Think you're smart, climbing aboard like a monkey? You've done the trick twice; do I have to look out for you every time I take the car out?"

"I just happen to be in a hurry," said Packard. "And going your way. Somebody shot my horse back there for me."

Her eyes grew actually round; Iki shivered audibly. But in the girl's case the emotion aroused by Packard's words was short-lived. Why should a man shoot the horse under Steve Packard? Disbelief reshaped her eyes; she cried out at him as her foot went down on the accelerator:

"Think I'm the kind to believe all the yarns you can tell? If you want to know what I think, Steve Packard—you're a liar!"

He laughed, well content with the moment and the situation, well content with his unwilling companion just as she was.

"And do you know that what I told you this afternoon was true?" he countered cheerfully. "You're just like my blazing old Grandy! Instead of being my grandfather he ought to be yours. By golly, Miss Terry Pert," teasing the blood higher into her cheeks with his laughter, "that might be arranged, too! Mightn't it? You and I—"

"Oh!" cried Terry, and he had no doubts about her meaning what she said. "Oh, I hate you! Yes, worse than I hate old

Hell-Fire: he keeps out of my trail, anyway. And you, you big bully, you woman-fighter, you—you—"

Just in time he guessed her purpose and threw out his hand across her steering-wheel and grasped her right hand. The car swerved dangerously a moment, then came back to its steady course as Steve's other hand closed over Terry's left. Slowly, putting his greater strength gently against hers, he took her automatic from her.

"Thirty-eight calibre?" he said coolly. "There's nothing little about your way of doing things, is there? And you meant to drill a hole through me, I'm bound!"

Terry's face gleamed white in the pale light; and he knew from the look in her eyes as they seemed fairly to clash with his, that it was the white of sheer rage.

"I'd just as lief blow your head off as shoot a rattlesnake," she announced crisply.

"I believe you," he grunted. "Just the same, if you'd only—"

"Oh, shut up!" she cried, shaking his hand free from hers on the wheel and driving on recklessly.

"I would like to mention," came an uncertain voice from a very pale Japanese, "that I must walk on my feet. I am most regretful—"

"Oh, shut up!" cried Terry. "Shut up!"

And for the rest of the ride both Iki and Steve Packard were silent.

CHAPTER XI

THE TEMPTING OF YELLOW BARBEE

"Here's where I get down," said Steve after a very long silence during which he watched Terry's pretty, puckered face while Terry, gripping her wheel, recklessly assumed the responsibilities of their three lives, hurling the car on through the moonlit night.

Iki, breathing every now and then a long quivering sigh and forgetting to breathe betweenwhiles, held on tightly with both hands.

"Here's where I get down," said Steve again. Here the road followed the line of his north fence; less than a mile to the southward he could see a light like a fallen star, gleaming cheerfully through the trees.

He sensed rather than saw a quick stiffening of Terry's already tense little body; fancied that the car was steadily taking on greater speed, read Terry's purpose in a flash. If he forced her to carry him, why then she would take him as far out of his way as possible.

"Terry Temple!" he cried sharply, leaning in a little toward her. "What's the matter with you anyway? What if we're not friends exactly? I never did you any harm, did I? Why, good

Lord, girl, when a man tells you his horse has been shot under him; when he is trying to overhaul the crook at the bottom of the whole mess whom you hate as well as I do— Oh, I mean Blenham and you know it—"

"Liar!" cried Terry, flashing her eyes at him, and back to the road alternately white with the moon and black with shadows. "Liar on two counts! Didn't I see your horse this afternoon? Tied in front of Wimble's whiskey joint? Oh, it's where I'd expect him! Well—and you needn't think I looked to see or cared, either—when I came by just now, leaving town, I saw your horse standing there yet. So you needn't—"

"That couldn't be," muttered Steve. "And yet—Anyhow, I've got to get off here. Will you stop, please?"

"No, I won't stop please! Nobody asked you to ride that I know of. Get off the same way you got on!"

Packard realized two things very clearly then:

If he jumped with the car going at its present speed he would probably break his neck; if he gave any considerable time to arguing the matter with her he would be carried as far in five minutes as he could walk in an hour.

"I mean business to-night," he told her bluntly. "If you don't slow down before I count ten I am going to lean out a little—like this—and shoot a hole in your tire. Then, if you keep on, I'll shoot a hole in the other tire. Understand?"

Terry laughed mockingly.

"You wouldn't dare!" she told him serenely. "That would be some kind of a crime; they could put you in jail for it. You'd be scared to."

"One, two, three, four, five," he counted briskly.

"I would seek to interrupt to advise, oh, Miss Lady!" chattered Iki. "His voice has the sound of bloodthirstiness."

"Six, seven, eight, nine—ten," counted Packard.

Terry sniffed. He leaned out, she saw the glint of the moon upon his revolver.

She threw out her clutch and jammed down both brakes, hard. Steve swung out and down to the ground. The car, as though it had gained fresh power from the fact of being freed of his weight, shot forward, stopped again.

"Not exactly friends?" cried Terry, and he marked a new trembling in her voice. "I should say not. You—you darned snake, you!"

And she was gone, spinning along into the night, hidden from him by the first hill around whose base the road curved. He stared after her a moment, shrugged, turned his back, and strode rapidly toward the Ranch Number Ten corrals.

He had planned correctly; he had correctly measured Blenham's impulses and desires. Further, he had come in time, just in time.

The light was in the ranch-house. Though but little after eleven o'clock it was dark within the bunk-house, the men long ago asleep. But Barbee was awake, his wits about him; his voice and Blenham's, both quiet, met Steve's ears as he slipped about the corner of the house, coming under the window where the light was.

Blenham was talking now. He sat loosely in a chair, his

hands one upon the other, idle in his lap. Barbee, his eyes narrowed and watchful, stood at the far side of the room. On the floor, near his feet, was a revolver; from its position Steve guessed that Barbee had just kicked it safely out of Blenham's reach. Barbee's own gun was in the boy's hand.

"You're a pretty foxy kid, Barbee," Blenham was saying tonelessly. "You got the drop on me; you're the firs' man as ever did that little trick. Yes; you're a pretty foxy kid!"

Barbee shrugged and spat and answered Blenham with a curse and a grunted:

"Nobody's askin' your opinion, Blenham."

But Steve saw and Blenham must have seen the gleam of triumph in Barbee's eye.

"What are you goin' to do with me?" asked Blenham presently.

"Nothin'," replied Barbee. "Jus' keep you where I got you until Steve Packard comes back. Which ought to be mos' any time now."

"He'll be late," said Blenham. "He won't be here for two or three hours. Suppose while we wait, let's me an' you talk!" he said sharply, sitting forward in his chair.

"Well?" said Barbee. "Talk an' be damned to you, Blenham. Only you don't talk yourself out'n the hole you're in right now. An', I promise you, you make a quick jump for a get-away, an' I'll shoot you dead."

"I know," Blenham nodded. "You'd do it. But I ain't goin' to try any fool thing like that. I'm jus' goin'—Like I said to you, let's talk. What's Packard payin' you for this night's work?"

"He's no tightwad, if that's what you're drivin' at. I'd of done to-night's job an' glad of the chance an' you know it, Blenham, an' never asked pay for it. But I'm drawin' down a whole month's pay extra, if I've got you like you are when he comes in."

Blenham laughed softly. Then he moved the hands resting in his lap. Packard saw that they were folded loosely about an old leather wallet.

"He's sure payin' you generous, Barbee," jeered Blenham. "You know it! Why, look here: This is yours an' more to trail it if you jus' pocket your gun an' let me go! I ain't askin' much an' I'm payin' my way. Look it over, kid!"

Packard saw how he stripped a bank-note from a thin sheaf of its fellows; how he tossed it toward Barbee. It fell to the floor; a little draft set it drifting; Blenham set his foot upon it.

"Look at it!" he snapped, for the first time giving sign of the strain he was laboring under. "It's yours—if you ain't a fool."

Barbee, not to be tricked were this some ruse to snare his attention, said crisply:

"Put you' han's up while I get it!"

Blenham obeyed; Barbee stooped swiftly, all the while with eyes riveted on his prisoner. Then, the muzzle of his gun raised another inch, he looked at what he held. When he looked back at Blenham his eyes were round, his mouth stood a little open.

"My God!" he gasped. "It's a thousan' dollars!"

"Yes," said Blenham quietly. "It's a thousan' dollars. That's quite a little wad, Barbee; it's more, anyhow, than an extra month's wages, ain't it? An' it's yours if you want it! Think of the times you can go on, think of the way you could make Red Creek open its eyes! An' there's more to come if you take that an' let me go an' jus' watch my play an' take a chance with me when I say so. What's the word, Barbee?"

Packard, having held back thus long, remained motionless, glimpsing unexpectedly something of Barbee's soul; watching a little human drama, become spectator to the battle royal of the two contending factions which made up a man's self.

It seemed to him that young Barbee was pale and grew paler; that a shiver ran through him; that he was, for the moment, like one drugged. And, side by side, two emotions, both primal and unmistakable, peered out of his eyes: a savage hatred of Blenham, a leaping greed of gold.

Thus for a little forgetting his own interest in this scene, Packard watched, wondering what the outcome would be. Blenham tempted. Barbee hesitated.

"Right here in my hand," Blenham was saying coldly, "are nine more like that, Barbee. Ten thousan' dollars in all. One thousan' to go to you for jus' keepin' out of my way. I said once you're a foxy kid. Now let's see if you are. Tie to a man like me that's out to make a pile, a damn big pile, Barbee— or hang to a fool like Steve Packard an' take his pay in dribbles an' let him be the one that gathers in all the big kale. Him an' me when I get things goin' right; him an' me with you jus' gettin' the scraps. Which is it? Eh, kid? Which way're you goin'?"

Barbee held the bank-note in his left hand; slowly his calloused fingers closed tightly about it, crumpling it, clutching it as though they would never release it. And then slowly the fingers opened so that the wrinkled bit of paper lay in his palm under his eyes. Barbee ran his tongue back and forth between his dry lips. Steve, staring in at him through the window, saw in his eyes the two lights, that of hate, that of covetousness; they burned side by side as a yellow candle and a red might have done.

Which way would Barbee go? Did Barbee know? Blenham did not; Steve did not. Suddenly, seeing how the two fires flickered in Barbee's eyes, Steve cried out within himself:

"It's unfair! It's asking too much of Barbee!"

And aloud, shoving the nose of a Colt .45 through the window-pane which splintered noisily:

"Hands up there, Blenham! Good boy, Barbee. You've got him, all right! Watch him while I slip in."

Blenham jumped to his feet, threw out his arms, and cursed savagely. Then, grown abruptly quiet, he dropped back into his chair, his two big hands loose about the wallet hidden under them. Steve threw a leg over the window-sill and came in, his gun ready, his eyes taking stock of Barbee while they appeared to be for Blenham only. And Barbee, white now as he had never been until now, shivered, filled his lungs with a long sigh, and fell back a couple of paces, staring at Steve, at Blenham, but most of all at the thing in his hand.

"You put it across, Barbee!" cried Steve heartily.

He reached forward and snatched the wallet from Blenham's knee. Blenham's big hands, clenching slowly, fell to his sides; Blenham's eyes, sullen and evil, clung steadily to Packard's.

"You've saved me my inheritance to-night; you've helped save me my ranch. You've helped me square the game with a dirty dog named Blenham!"

Like a dog Blenham showed his teeth. His drawn face was stamped in the image of fury.

"You're a sweet picture of a dead game sport," he growled, shifting nervously in his chair. "I ain't got a gun; you an' Barbee have; go ahead an' call me all the names you like!"

Steve counted the bank-notes in the wallet. Blenham had spoken truly; there were nine one-thousand-dollar bills. He put out his hand to Barbee for the tenth. Barbee, staring strangely like one rudely awakened from sleep and not yet certain of his surroundings, let the bank-note go. His eyes, leaving it at last to rest steadily on Blenham, looked red and ugly. Packard slipped the wallet into his shirt.

"Barbee," he said quietly, while he busied his eyes with Blenham's slightest movement, "this money was left to me by my father. He gave it to Bill Royce to keep for me. You know all that Bill has stood from Blenham; now you know why. There's quite a load of scoundrelism dumped off at Blenham's door. And, thanks to you, we've got the dead wood on him at last!"

"What are you goin' to do with him?" Barbee, speaking for the first time since Steve's entrance, was husky-voiced. Blenham shifted again in his chair; now there was only cold hatred in the boy's look. "We'd ought to be able to put him in the pen for a good long time."

Blenham laughed jeeringly.

"Try it!" he blustered. "See what you can prove, actually prove to a jury an' a judge! Try it! You go to the law an' see—"

"To hell with the law!" cut in Steve, and though his voice was not lifted for the imprecation Blenham shot a quick, startled look at him.

And both Blenham and Barbee, listening wonderingly, understood that here was a Packard talking; that in the shoes of the grandson, even now, there might be standing the big bulk of the uncompromising grandfather.

"What do I want with the law now? Blenham would wriggle out, I suppose; or he would get a light sentence and trim that down to nothing with good behavior. No, Blenham, if you ever go to jail it will be somebody's else doing; not mine. Is it just jail for the man who shot down my old pardner in cold blood, just for the sake of a handful of money? Is it to be just jail for the man who has made Bill Royce's life a hell for six months? Just jail for the brute who had a horse shot under me to-night? Why, damn you—" and at last his voice broke through the ice of restraint and rang out angrily, full of menace—"do you think I'm going to let you go out of my hands into the hands of judge and jury after all you've done?"

Blenham sprang up, drawing back. The muzzle of Steve's .45 followed him threateningly.

"Barbee," said Packard, his voice once more under control, "go to the bunk-house and send Bill Royce here. Don't wake the other boys. Then you come back here with him. And bring a whip with you."

"A whip?" repeated Barbee.

"Yes; a whip. Any kind you can lay your hands to in a hurry; quirt or buggy-whip or bull-whip!"

Blenham watched Barbee go. Then, drawn back into a corner of the room, sullen and vigilant, he stood biting nervously at a big, clenched, hairy fist.

CHAPTER XII

IN A DARK ROOM

Bill Royce, hastily and but half dressed, came promptly to the house, stumbling along at Barbee's heels. Blenham, his silence and watchfulness unbroken, still chewed at his fist. Barbee brought a heavy blacksnake in his hand.

"Barbee says you want me, Steve?" said Royce from the threshold. "An' that Blenham's here?"

"Yes, Bill," Steve answered. And to Barbee, "Close the door behind you. Lock it. Give me the key. Now fasten the shutters across both windows."

Barbee obeyed silently. Blenham's eyes followed him, seeming fascinated by the whip in Barbee's hand.

"Listen a minute, Bill," said Steve when Barbee had done. "I want to tell you something."

And, as briefly as might be, he told Royce of the ten dollar bills substituted for the real legacy, of the results of his evening in Red Creek, of Barbee's trapping Blenham, of the recovery of the ten thousand dollars, of a horse shot dead on the Red Creek road.

"Then," said Royce at the end of it, his mind catching eagerly one outstanding fact, "I was right, Steve? An' it was Blenham as gave me both barrels of Johnny Mills's shotgun? It was Blenham for sure, wasn't it, Steve?"

"Yes, Bill. It was Blenham."

"An'—an' Blenham's right across there now? It's him I can hear breathin', Steve?"

"Yes, Bill."

"An'—an' what for did you sen' for me, Steve? What are you goin' to do to him?"

Packard beckoned to Barbee. The boy came quickly to his side, giving him the blacksnake. Steve laid it across Bill Royce's hand.

"I'm going to give him a taste of that, Bill," he said. "And I wanted you here. You can't see it; but before I am through with him, you can hear it!"

"Goin' to tie him up an' whip him, Steve? That it?"

"Pack of low-bred mongrel pups!" cried Blenham wrathfully, for the first time breaking his silence. "Sneakin', low-lived curs an' cowards!"

"That it, Steve?" persisted Royce. "Goin' to tie him up an' give him a whippin' with a blacksnake?"

"I am going to whip him—for your sake, Bill," answered Steve sternly.

He threw off his coat, tossing it behind him.

"Get the chairs and table out of the way, Barbee! No, I am not going to tie him up; that isn't necessary, Bill. I can handle him with my hands without tying him; I am going to do it. And then I am going to take the whip and lay it across him until his hide is in strips—or until he begs to be let go. Ready, Blenham?"

"Mean that?" snarled Blenham, a new look in his eye. "Mean you're goin' to give me an even break?"

But Bill Royce, fairly trembling with an eagerness strange to him, had clutched at Steve's arm, had found it, was holding him back, crying out excitedly:

"You're a good pal, Stevie; you're the best pal as ever was an' I know it! Didn't I always know you'd be like this? But can't you see, Stevie, can't you see it ain't enough another man should lick him, even when that man's my pardner, even when it's Stevie himself doin' it! Ain't I been waitin' an' waitin' to get my hands on him!"

Blenham, a little comforted by Steve's words, jeered openly now.

"Come on, Blind Billy," he taunted. "An' when I've throwed you into the junk pile I'll take on your friends! One at the time—you know how the sayin' goes!"

Steve was shaking Royce's hand from his arm.

"Let me do this for you, Bill," he said firmly. "It's only fair. If you could see, it would be different."

But Royce clung on desperately, crying out insistently:

"Blind as I am I can lick him! I know I can lick him! Ain't I done it in my sleep a dozen times, a dozen ways? Ain't I always promised myself sometime I'd get him in my two hands, I'd feel him wriggle an' squirm? This is my fight, Steve, an'—Blenham, where are you?"

"Here!" cried Blenham. "An' gettin' tired of waitin'!"

Royce plunged toward him. But Steve Packard caught his old friend about the body, holding him back a moment.

"Easy, Bill," he said gently. "Easy. I was wrong, you are right. It's your fight. But take your time. Get your coat off. Barbee, stand by that window there; if Blenham tries to get out stop him. I'll stand here. All ready, Bill?"

"Ready!" cried Royce, his voice a roar of eagerness.

"All ready, Blenham?"

"Ain't I said it?" jeered Blenham.

"Then—" and suddenly Steve had snatched up the lamp, blowing down the chimney and plunging the room into thick darkness—"go to it! The light is out, Bill! The room is pitch-black. You're as well off as he is. And now, old pardner. Now!"

It was suddenly very still in the room; the thick, impenetrable darkness seemed almost a palpable curtain screening what went forward; the silence was for a little literally breathless.

Then there came the first faint, tell-tale sound, the slow, tortured creaking of a board as a man put his weight upon it. Through the darkness, across the room, Bill Royce was going slowly, questing the man who, surprised by the action of Steve's which had reduced his advantage over a blind man, held to his corner. And then, stranger sound still through that tense silence, came Bill Royce's low laugh.

"Good boy, Steve," he said softly. "I'd never thought of that! In the dark Blenham's as blind as me! How do you like it, Blenham? How'd you like to have it this way all the time?"

Blenham's only answer lay in his leaping forward, out from his corner, and striking; Royce's answer to that was another quiet laugh. He had slipped aside; Blenham had flailed at the thin air; Royce, grown still again, knew one of the moments of sheer joy which had been his during these last weary months.

Packard and Barbee, frowning unavailingly toward each little noise, could only guess at what went forward so few inches from them. A scraping foot might be either Royce's or Blenham's; a long, deep sigh or quick breathing now here, now there, might emanate from either man. The strange thing, thought both Barbee and Packard, was that even ten seconds could pass without these two men at each other's throats.

But, a supreme moment his at last, Bill Royce found himself grown miserly in its expenditure; he would dribble the golden seconds through his fingers, he would draw out the experience, tasting its joy fully.

For the moment his blindness was no greater than Blenham's; for a little Blenham would grope and wonder and hesitate and grow tense after the fashion the blind man knew so well. And then at the end, when an end could no longer be delayed, Bill Royce would mete out the long-delayed punishment.

But, since the natures of both men were downright, since their hatreds were outright, since there was little of finesse in either and a great impatience stirring both, Royce's playing with Blenham was short.

There came a sudden shuffling of feet—and Royce's laugh; a blow landing heavily—and Royce's laugh; another blow, a grunt, and a panted curse from Blenham—and Royce's laugh.

And then only a scraping of feet up and down, back and forth along the bare floor, the thudding of heavy shoulders into an unexpected wall, the impact of fist against body. In the utter darkness the two men gripped each other, struck, swayed together, staggered apart, only to come together again to strike harder, more merciless blows.

Packard and Barbee now held their breaths while the others panted freely; both Packard and Barbee, stepping quickly now this way and now that as the battling forms swayed up and down, sought to gauge what was happening by the sounds which came to their ears.

Muttered imprecations, scuffling feet in a rude dance of rage, another heavy, thudding blow, a coughing curse. Whose? Blenham's, since after it came Bill Royce's laugh. Another blow, fresh pounding and scraping of boots—blow on top of blow, curse on top of curse—a man falling heavily—

Who was down? Royce of Blenham?

"Bill!" called Packard. "Bill!"

No answer save that of two big bodies rolling together on the floor. Both were down, Royce and Blenham. Both were fighting, wordless and infuriated. Who was on top?

No man on top long, no man under the other more than a

second. The rolling bodies struck against Packard's leg and he drew back, giving them room. The dust puffing up from the floor filled his nostrils. The room was becoming unendurably close, sickeningly close. The sweat must be streaming from both men by now. Packard sniffed, fancying the acrid smell of fresh blood. The big bulks rolled and threshed and whipped here and there—

"Hell!"

It was a cry of mingled rage and pain; it came bursting explosively from Blenham's lips. Royce's laugh followed it; Packard shivered.

"Bill!" he cried. "Bill!"

Royce did not answer; perhaps for the very good reason that he did not hear. There were other matters now engaging his attention solely and exclusively. The fighting fury, the hate frenzy was riding him and he in turn was riding his enemy. Cool sanity and hot blood-lust do not find places side by side in the same brain. A second time came the horrible cry from Blenham. Packard struck a match hastily and lighted the lamp.

Packard and Barbee together dragged Royce away, letting Blenham lie there. Both men were naked to their waists, their shirts and undershirts in rags and strips hanging grotesquely about their hips; Royce looked like some hideously painted burlesque of a ballet-dancer in a comic skirt. Only there was nothing of burlesque or comedy in his face.

Packard, glancing from him down to the tortured body of Blenham that breathed jerkily, noisily, turned with a sudden revulsion of feeling and hurled the heavy blacksnake away from him. He had not fancied the sharp smell of fresh blood.

"I got him!" said Royce shakily. "With my two hands, I got him! Didn't I, Stevie?"

"Better than you know, Bill!" muttered Packard. "Better than you know."

The thing had been an accident, at least in so far as Bill Royce's intent was concerned. Packard knew that; he knew that his old pardner fought hard, fought mercilessly, but fought fair. But in a larger sense was it an accident? Or rather a mere retributive punishment decreed by an eternal justice? There in the pitch dark, for no man to see the how of it, this is perhaps what had happened:

There had been the old, long-rowelled Mexican spur hanging on the wall; Royce's shoulder or Blenham's had knocked it down; their feet had pushed it out to the middle of the floor. They had fallen, together, heavily; they had rolled. Blenham had gone over on his face, Royce's hands worrying him. The spur—

But it mattered little how it had come about. The result was the thing. Blenham would never see with his right eye again.

CHAPTER XIII

AT THE LUMBER CAMP

They did what they could for Blenham—which was but little—and let him go when he was ready. Before daylight he had ridden away, dead white, sick-looking, and wordless save for his parting words in a strangely quiet voice—

"I'll get all three of you for this, s'elp me!"

They had bound his head up in a strip torn from an old sheet; the last they saw of him in the uncertain light was this bandage, rising and falling slowly as his horse bore him away.

Blenham gone, Barbee and Bill Royce went down to the bunk-house again, slipping in quietly. Steve Packard, alone in the ranch-house, sat smoking his pipe for half an hour. Then he went to bed, the bank-notes still in his shirt, his gun under his pillow.

Twice last night he had said to Joe Woods, the lumber-camp boss, "I'll see you in the morning."

Morning come, Steve breakfasted early, saddled his horse, and turned out across the fields to meet the rising sun. And it seemed to his fancies, set a-tingle in the early dawn freshness, that the rising sun, ancient symbol of youth and vigor and hope with triumph's wings, was coming to meet him.

At this period of the day, especially when he rides and is alone and the forests thicken all about him, man is prone to confidence. It had been a simple matter, so he looked upon it now, to have discovered the truth of the substituted bills last night; as simple a matter had been his winning at seven-and-a-half or his whipping big Joe Woods or his recovery of the lost legacy.

Blenham, or rather an agent of Blenham, had killed his horse; what then? His destiny had stepped forward; Terry had come; he had whizzed back to the ranch in her car and on time.

What if the ranch were mortgaged and to the hardest man in seven counties? What though his grandfather had obviously fallen supine before the old man's tempting sin, which is avarice, and was bound to break him? Was fate not playing him for her favorite?

To Steve Packard, riding to meet the sun and to keep his promise to the lumber boss, the world just now was an exceedingly bright and lovely place; in this hour of a leaping optimism he could even picture Terry Temple in a companionably laughing mood.

So early did he take to saddle that the fag end of the dawn was still sweet in the air when he passed under the great limbs of the stragglers of the forests clothing his eastern hill-slopes. He noted how between the widely separated boles the grass was thick and rich and untrampled; reserved against the time of need. There was no stock here yet.

He passed on, swung into the little-used trail which brought him first to the McKittrick cabin where a double-barrelled shot-gun six months ago had brought Bill Royce his blindness; then to the lumber-camp a mile further on. Both were on the bank of Packard's Creek; the flume constructed by Joe Woods's men followed the line of the stream.

The new sun in his eyes, Steve drew his hat low down on his forehead and looked curiously about him. The timberjacks had come only recently; so much was obvious. They had come to stay; that was as plainly to be seen. Rough slabs of green timber, still drying and twisting and splitting as it did so, had been knocked together rudely to make a long, low building where cook and cookstove and a two-plank table indicated both kitchen and dining-room.

A half-dozen other shacks and lean-tos, seen here and there through the trees, completed the camp. Great fallen trees— they were taking only the full-grown timber—looking helpless and hopeless, lay this way and that like broken giants, majestically resigned to the conqueror's axe.

Here in the peace and quiet of the pinking day this inroad of commercialism struck Steve suddenly both as slaughter and sacrilege; among the stalwart standing patriarchs and their bowed brethren he sat his horse staring frowningly at the little ugly clutter of buildings housing the invaders.

"My beloved old granddad had his nerve with him," he grunted as he rode on into the tiny settlement. "As usual!"

The cook, yawning, bleary-eyed, unthinkably tousled, was just bestirring himself. Steve saw his back and a trailing suspender as he went into the cook-shed carrying some kindling-wood in one hand and a bucket of water in the other. It was only when Packard, having ridden to his door and looked in, startled the cook into swinging about, that the dull-eyed signs of a night of dissipation showed in the other's face.

"Up late last night, I'll bet," laughed Steve, easing himself in the saddle. The cook made a face unmistakably eloquent of a bad taste in his mouth and went down on his knees before his stove, settling slowly like a man with stiff, rheumatic joints or else a head which he did not intend to jar.

"Drunk las' night," he growled, settling back on his haunches as his fire caught. "A man that'll get drunk is a damn' fool. I'm t'rough wid it."

"Where's Woods?" asked Steve. "Up yet?"

"Yes, rot him, he's up. He's always up. He's—holy smoke, I got a head!"

"Where is he?" demanded Packard.

The cook rose gently and for a moment clasped his head with both hands. Then he immersed it gradually in his bucket of icy water. After which, drying himself with a dirty towel and setting the bucket of water on his stove, he turned red-rimmed eyes upon Steve.

"You're the guy I fed the other mornin', ain't you?" he asked.

Steve nodded.

"More'n which," continued the cook, "you're the guy as licked Woodsy las' night in Red Crick?"

Again Steve nodded.

"An' again you're claimin' to run the ranch here? An' to own it? An' to be ol' Hell-Fire's gran'son?"

"I asked you where Woods was," Packard reminded him sharply. The cook threw up his hand as though to ward off a blow.

"Whatcha yellin' in my ear for?" he moaned dismally. "Want to split my head off? Woodsy's over yonder; talkin' with a man name of Blenham. Ever hear of him?"

"Over yonder" plainly meant just across the creek where there was a little flat open space among the trees in which stood one of the larger shanties. Steve saw a stove-pipe sticking out crookedly through the shed roof; noted a thin spear of smoke. He spurred across the stream and to the timber boss's quarters.

Woods heard him and came out into the brightening morning, drawing the door closed behind him. His eyes, like the cook's though to a lesser degree, showed indications of a wild night in town. Steve guessed that he hadn't undressed all night; that he was not entirely sober just now though he carried himself steadily and spoke well enough.

"I thought you'd show," said Woods quietly, his big hands down in his pockets, his shoulders against the wall.

"What is Blenham doing here?" Steve asked.

Woods narrowed his eyes in a speculative frown.

"He's damn' near dead. He's waitin' for me to get one of the boys to hitch up an' haul him to a doctor. He says you an' two other guys gouged his eye out for him."

"He's a liar," announced Packard angrily. "The thing was an accident. It was a fair fight between him and Bill Royce. Blenham fell on an old spur. I promised you I'd be here this morning, Woods."

"Yes," said Woods. "I expected you."

"You were square with me last night," went on Packard quietly. "I appreciate the fact. If ever I can do you a favor, just say so. So much for that part of it. Next: Maybe you've heard I'm the owner of Ranch Number Ten? And that I'm running it myself? I've come over to tell you this morning that we're knocking off work here. I don't want any more timber down."

There came a little twitching at the corner of Woods's broad mouth. He made no answer.

"Hear me?" snapped Steve.

"Sure I hear you," said Woods insolently. "So does Blenham; he's right inside where he can hear. I guess it's him you want to talk with. I'm takin' my orders off'n Blenham an' nobody else."

"I've talked already with Blenham. I've told him not to set his hoofs on my ranch again after to-day. Since he's pretty badly hurt I'll let you haul him to the doctor but I don't want him hauled back. Further, I want work stopped here right now. The men will be having breakfast in a few minutes. After breakfast you can explain to them and let them go."

Woods shrugged.

"My orders, hot out'n Blenham's mouth, is to stick on the job here an' saw wood," he said colorlessly. "I'm takin' my pay off'n him an' I'm doin' what he says."

There seemed only a careless indifference in his gesture as he partly turned his back, staring up-stream; but the slight movement served to show Packard that Woods carried a gun on his hip, in plain sight. Well, Woods himself had said—"I expected you!"

Last night and for a definite purpose Steve had armed himself; this morning, setting out on this errand, he had tossed the revolver into a table drawer at the ranch-house. He had never been a gunman; if circumstance dictated that he must go armed, well and good. But his brows contracted angrily at the display of Woods's readiness for gun-play.

"Look here, you Joe Woods!" he cried out. "And listen, too, you Blenham! I'm no trouble-seeker; I know it's a dead easy thing to start a row that will see more than one man dead before it's ended, and what's the use? But I mean to have what is mine in spite of you and Hell-Fire Packard and the devil! The right of the whole deal is as plain as one and one: This is my outfit, if it is mortgaged; nobody excepting me has any business ordering my timber cut. And I say that it's not going to be cut. If there is any trouble it's up to you fellows."

From Blenham in the cabin came no sound; Woods, having glanced swiftly at Packard's angry face, again stared upstream.

For a little Steve Packard gnawed at his lip, caught in an eddy of helpless rage. Never an answer from Blenham, never an answer from Woods; angry already, their silences maddened him. Across the creek he saw the cook standing in his kitchen door, listening and smiling in sickly fashion; two or three of the men, coming out for their breakfasts, were watching him.

They were an ugly, red-eyed bunch, he thought as he swept them with his flashing eyes; they'd fight like dogs for the joy of fighting; soon or late, if Blenham persisted, he'd have the job on his hands of throwing them off his land. Of course he could go "higher up"; he could appeal to his grandfather.

He could, but in his present mood he had no intention of doing any such thing. His grandfather, before now, should have withdrawn these men.

"Don't ask me to hold my hand!" the old man had shouted at him. "I'm goin' after you tooth an' big toe-nail!"

Well, if the old man wanted trouble and range war—

His blood was rushing swift and hot through his veins; his mind working feverishly. One man alone against the crowd of them, he could do nothing. But he could ride back to the ranch, gather up a dozen men, put guns into their hands, be back here in the matter of a couple of hours.

He saw the timberjacks as one by one they came out into the clearing by the cook's shack; counted them as they went in. The thought of a morning cup of coffee was attracting them; among the faces turned briefly his way he recognized several he had seen last night in the Ace of Diamonds saloon. He saw two of them hitching up the big wagon, evidently the only conveyance in the camp. They were getting ready to take Blenham.

Suddenly a new light flashed into Steve's eyes; he turned his head abruptly that Joe Woods should not see.

"How many men have you got here, Woods?" he asked.

Wondering at the question Woods answered it:

"Fourteen; startin' a new camp across the ridge."

Steve had counted nine men go into the cook's shed; with the cook there were ten; the two with the horses made twelve. There should be two more. He waited. Meanwhile, secretly so that Woods might not guess what he was doing or see the busy hand, he loosened his latigo, seeming merely to slouch in his saddle; while he made a half-dozen random remarks which set Woods wondering still further, he got his cinch loose. Another man had gone into the kitchen. Thirteen.

"Fourteen counting you?" he asked Woods.

"Yes."

Then they were all accounted for; two with the horses; eleven in the shed; Joe Woods in front of him.

"My cinch is loose," said Packard and dismounted, throwing the stirrup up across the saddle out of his way, his fingers going to the latigo which he had just loosened.

Woods watched him idly. Then suddenly both men looked toward the kitchen. The door had been slammed shut; there was a fairly hideous racket as of all of the cook's pots and pans falling together; after it a boom of laughter, and finally the cook's voice lifted querulously. Woods grinned. Unruffled by Packard's presence he said casually:

"Cookie mos' usually has the hell of a head after a night like las' night. The boys knows it an' has a little fun with him!"

The two men harnessing the horses had evidently guessed as did Woods what was happening in the cook's domain; at any rate, they hastily tied the horses and hurried to see. Packard, still busied with his latigo, saw them and watched them until the door had shut behind them.

His horse stood between him and Woods. He tickled the animal in the flank; it spun about, pulling back, plunging, drawing Woods's eyes. And the next thing which Woods clearly understood was that Steve Packard was upon him, that one of Packard's hands was at his throat, that the other had gone for the gun on Woods's hip and had gotten it.

"Back into your shack!" commanded Packard, jabbing the muzzle of Woods's big automatic hard into Woods's ribs. "Quick!"

To himself just now Steve had said: "One man against the crowd of them, he could do nothing!" Just exactly what Woods would be thinking; what Blenham inside would be thinking; just exactly what the rest of the men thought since they turned their backs on him and forgot him in their sport of badgering the cook.

What he was doing now was what he would term, did he hear of another man attempting it, "A fool thing to do!" And yet he had told himself many a time that a man stood a fair chance to get away with the unexpected if he hit quick and hard and kept his wits about him.

Woods, taken thoroughly aback, allowed himself to be driven again into his cabin. Packard followed and closed the door. Within was Blenham, lying on Woods's bunk, his head still swathed, a half-empty whiskey bottle on the floor at his side. With one watery eye he looked from one to the other of the two men bursting in on him.

"Blenham," cried Packard, standing over him while he was careful not to lose sight of Joe Woods's working face, "I want work stopped here and this crowd of men off the ranch. You heard what I said outside, didn't you?"

Blenham answered heavily:

"Woods, don't you pay no attention to what this man says.

You keep your men on the job. An' if you got another drop of whiskey—"

"The bottle's where you put it," retorted Woods. "Under your pillow."

Blenham rolled on his side, slipping his hand under his pillow. All the time his one red eye shone evilly on Steve, who, his wits about him, stepped back into the corner whence he might at the same time watch Woods and that hand of Blenham's which was making its stupid little play of seeking a bottle.

"Take it out by the neck, Blenham," said Steve sternly. "Take it out by the neck and pass it to me, butt end first! *Sabe*? I'm guessing the kind of drink you'd like to set up."

Blenham's one eye and Steve's two clashed; Woods watched interestedly. He even laughed as at last, with an exclamation which was as much a groan as a curse, Blenham jerked out his gun and flung it down on his quilt. Steve took it up and shoved it into his pocket.

"There's jus' a han'ful of men over to the cookhouse," said Woods humorously. "Havin' stuck up me an' Blenham you oughtn't to have no trouble over there!"

"How many men?" demanded Steve quietly. "Thirteen, if I counted right, eh, Woods? That's no kind of a number to pin your hopes on! And now listen; I'll cut it short: If there is any trouble this morning, if any man gets hurt, remember that this is my land, that you jaspers are trespassing, that I am simply defending my property. In other words, you're in wrong. You'll be skating on pretty thin ice if you just plead later on that you were obeying orders from Blenham; follow Blenham long enough and you'll get to the pen. Now, I'm going outside. You and Blenham stay in here until I call for you. I'll shut the door; you leave it shut. Take time to roll yourself a smoke and think things over before you start anything, Joe Woods."

Then swiftly he whipped open the door, stepped out, and snapped it shut after him.

"I'm taking a chance," he muttered, his eyes hard, his jaw set and thrust forward. "A good long chance. But that's the way to play the game!"

The door of the cook's shed, facing him from across the creek, was still closed. Steve moved a dozen paces downstream; now he could command Woods's cabin with the tail of his eye, look straight into the kitchen when the door opened, keep an eye upon the one little square window.

"It's all in the cards," he told himself grimly. "A man can win a jack pot on a pair of deuces, if he plays the game right!"

At this point Packard's Creek is narrow; the distance between the spot where he stood and the door of the cookshed was not over forty feet. He shifted Woods's gun to his left hand, taking into his right Blenham's old-style revolver which was more to his fancy. Then, to get matters under way in as emphatic a manner as he knew how, he sent a bullet crashing through the cook's roof.

The murmur of voices died away suddenly; it was intensely still for a moment; then there was a scrambling, a scraping of heavy boots and dragging benches, and the cook's door snapped back against the outside wall, the opening filled with hulking forms, as men crowded to see what was happening. What they saw was the nose of Blenham's gun in Steve's hand.

Jackson Gregory

"Back up there," shouted Packard. "Stand still while you listen to me."

They hesitated, wondering. A man growled something, his voice deep-throated and truculent. Another man laughed. The forms filling the doorway began a slow bulging outward as other forms behind crowded upon them.

Within Woods's cabin there was a little noise.

"You men are leaving to-day," said Steve hastily. "Just as fast as you can pull your freight. Blenham and Woods are going with you. All told there are above a dozen of you and only one of me. But I've got Woods's gun and Blenham's and I happen to mean business. This is my outfit; if you fellows start anything and there is trouble, why you're on the wrong side of the fence. Besides, you're apt to get hurt. Blenham and Woods are quitting cold; so far as I can see you boys would be a pack of fools to make more of a stand than they are doing."

The man who had laughed and who now thrust his face forward through his companions, grinned widely and announced:

"We mightn't worry none about where Blenham an' Joe get off. But we ain't had our breakfasts yet!"

"You don't get any breakfast on my land!" said Steve sharply, more afraid just now of having to do with good nature than with anger.

For if the dozen men there simply laughed and stepped out and dispersed, his hands would be tied; he couldn't shoot down a lot of joking men and he knew it. And they would know it.

"You're on your way right now! You, there!" This to a big, stoop-shouldered young giant in the fore, blue-eyed, straw-haired, northern-looking. "Step out this way, Sandy! And step lively."

The northerner shrugged and looked belligerent. Steve moistened his lips.

"You can't bluff me—" began the northerner.

And Steve knew that, having gone this far, he could not stop at bluffing. And he knew that he must not seem to hesitate.

"I can shoot as straight as most men," he said smoothly. "But sometimes I miss an inch or two at this distance. You men who don't want to take any unnecessary chances had better give Sandy a little more elbow-room!"

The stoop-shouldered man squared himself a little, jerked up his head, took on a fresh air of defiance. Slowly Steve lifted the muzzle of his gun—slowly a man drew back from the northerner, a man fell away to the right, a man drew a hasty pace back at the left. He was left standing in the middle of the open doorway. He shifted a little, doubled his fists at his sides, twisted his head.

Again a noise from Woods's cabin. Steve saw that the door had quietly opened six inches. There was a quick movement within; the door was flung wide open. Woods was standing in the opening, a rifle in his hands, the barrel trained on Steve's chest. Steve saw the look in Woods's eye, whirled and fired first. The rifle bullet cut whistling high through the air; Woods dropped the rifle and reeled and went down under the impact of a leaden missile from a forty-five calibre revolver. The rifle lay just outside now.

The squat young giant with the blue eyes and shock head of

hair had not stirred. His mouth was open; his face was stupidly expressionless.

"Throw up your hands and step outside!" Steve called to him roughly.

The man started, looked swiftly about him, stepped forward, lifting his big hands. They were still clenched but opened slowly and loosely as they went above his head.

"Turn your back this way," commanded Steve, feeling his mastery of the moment and knowing that he must drive his advantage swiftly. "Belly to the wall. That's it. Next!"

A man, the man who had twice laughed, stepped forward eagerly. He needed no invitation to lift his hands, nor yet to go to the other's side, his face to the wall. His eyes were bulging a little; they were fixed not on Steve Packard but on the body of Joe Woods. The timber boss lay across the threshold, half in, half out, twisting a little where he lay.

Now, one after another, speaking in low voices or not at all, the timber crew came out into the stillness of the new day. Steve counted them as they appeared, always keeping the tail of his eye on Woods's door, always realizing that Blenham was still to be dealt with, always watchful of the small square window in the cook's shed. Once he saw a face there; he called out warningly and the face hastily withdrew.

At last they were outside, thirteen men with their backs to him, their hands lifted. Stepping backward Steve went to Woods's cabin.

"Come out, Blenham," he called curtly.

Blenham cursed him but came. Stepping over Woods's body he said threateningly:

"Killed him, have you? You'll swing for that."

"Stand where you are, Blenham." He wondered dully if he had killed Woods. He considered the matter almost impersonally just now; the game wasn't yet played, cards were out, the mind must be cool, the eye quick. "You two boys on the end come over here and help me with Woods."

Again Woods's big body twisted; it even turned half over now, and Woods sat up. His hand went to his shoulder; Steve saw the hand go red. Woods's face was white and drawn with pain. His eyes went to the rifle at his feet. Steve stepped forward, took the thing up, tossed it back into the cabin. Woods swayed, pitched a little forward, caught himself, steadied himself with a hand on the door-jamb, and shakily drew himself to his feet. Steve marvelled at him.

"If you like, Woods," he said quietly, "I'll have you taken over to my place and will send for a doctor for you."

"Aw, hell, I ain't hurt bad," said Woods.

Steve saw how his brows contracted as he spoke. The red hand was laid rather hurriedly on the shoulder of one of the two men whom Steve had summoned across the creek.

Blenham turned away and went down-stream, toward the big wagon. Woods followed, walking slowly and painfully, leaning now and again on his support.

As Steve called to them the men lined up along the wall of the cook's shed, turned, and, their hands still lifted, went down-stream. One after another they climbed up into the wagon. Two or three laughed; for the most part there were only black faces and growing anger. Many of them had drunk much and slept little last night; not a man of them but missed his coffee.

Packard caught up his horse's reins and swung into the saddle calling out:

"I don't know anything you're waiting for. Climb into the seat, somebody. Get started. Blenham and Woods both need a doctor. And you needn't come back for anything you left; I'll have all your junk boxed and hauled into Red Creek this afternoon."

A man gathered up the four reins and climbed to the high seat. The brake was snapped back, the horses danced, set their necks into their collars, and the wheels turned. Behind them Steve Packard, still watchful, rode to escort them to a satisfactory distance beyond the border of his property.

Terry Temple out in front of the dilapidated Temple home was amusing herself with a pair of field-glasses. Her big wolf-hound had just temporarily laid aside his customary dignity and was chasing a rabbit. Terry had her binoculars focussed on a distant field, curious as to the outcome.

Suddenly she lost this interest. Far down the road she glimpsed a big wagon; it was filled with standing men. She altered her focus.

"Dad!" she called quickly. "Oh, dad! Come here!"

Her father came out on the porch.

"What do you want?" he asked irritably.

Terry came running to him, flushed with her excitement, and shoved the glasses up to his eyes. Temple dodged, fussed with the focussing apparatus, lowered the glasses, and blinked down the road.

"It's just a wagon, ain't it?" he demanded. "Looks like—"

Again she snatched the binoculars.

"A lot of men are standing up," she announced. "That's the team from the Packard logging-camp, There's a man sitting on the front seat with the driver and he's got a rag around his head. There's some sort of a bed made in the bottom of the wagon; a man's lying down. I actually believe, Dad Temple—"

She broke off in a strange little gasp. Behind the wagon a man rode on horseback; the sun glinted on a revolver in his hand. They came closer.

"It's Blenham on the front seat with a bandage around his head!" she cried. "He's hurt! And—dad, that man back there is Steve Packard! And he's driving that crowd off his ranch, as sure as you are Jim Temple and I'm Teresa Arriega Temple!"

Temple started.

"What's that?" he demanded with a genuine show of interest.

Together they stared down the road. On came the wagon and the rider behind it. Slowly the look in Terry's eyes altered. In a moment they were fairly dancing. And then, causing her father to stare at her curiously, she broke out into peal after peal of delicious laughter.

"Steve Packard," she cried out, her exclamation meant for her own ears alone and reaching no further than those of her newly imported Japanese cook who was peering out of his kitchen window just behind her, "I believe you're a white man after all! And a gentleman and a sport! Dad, he's nabbed the whole crowd of them and put them on the run. By glory, it looks to me like a man has turned up! Maybe he was telling me the truth last night."

The wagon came on, drew abreast of the Temple gate, passed by. Temple stared in what looked like consternation. Steve, following the wagon, came abreast of the gate, stopped, watched the four horses draw their freight around the next bend in the road, accounted his work done, and turned toward the Temples.

"Good morning," he called cheerily, highly content with life just at this moment. "Fine day, isn't it?"

Terry looked at him coolly. Then she turned her back and went into the house. Iki, the new cook, looked at her wonderingly.

"To me it appears most probable certain," said the astute Oriental within his soul, "that inhabitants of these wilderness places have much madness within their brains."

Steve swung his horse back into the road and set his face toward his own ranch.

"Darn the girl," he muttered.

CHAPTER XIV

THE MAN-BREAKER AT HOME

In a short time the cattle country had come to know a good deal of Steve Packard, son of the late Philip Packard, grandson of Old Man Packard, variously known. Red Creek gossiped within its limits and sent forth word of a quarrel of some sort with Blenham, a winning game of seven-and-a-half, a fight with big Joe Woods. Red Creek was inclined to set the seal of approval on this new Packard, for Red Creek, on both sides of its quarrelsome street, stood ready to say that a man was a man even when it might go gunning for him.

As the days went by Packard's fame grew. There were tales that in a savage melee with Blenham he had eliminated that capable individual's right eye; and though there were those who had had it from some of the Ranch Number Ten boys that Blenham's loss was the result of an accident, still it remained unquestioned that Blenham had suffered injury at Packard's ranch and had been driven forth from it.

Then, Packard had followed Blenham to the logging-camp; he had tackled the crowd headed by Joe Woods; he had come remarkably close to killing Woods; he had broken up the camp and sent the timberjacks on their way. He had had a horse killed under him; he had quarrelled with his grandfather; he was standing on his own feet. In brief—

"He's a sure enough, out an' out Packard!" they said of him.

To be sure, while there were men who spoke well of him there were others, perhaps as many, who spoke ill. There were the barkeeper of the Ace of Diamonds, Joe Woods, Blenham; they had their friends and hangers-on. On the other hand, offsetting these, there were old friends whom Steve had not seen for twelve or more years.

Such was Brocky Lane whose cowboy had loaned Steve a horse which had been killed on the Red Creek road. Young Packard promptly paid for the animal and resumed auld lang syne with the hearty, generous Brocky Lane.

What men had to say of him came last of all to Steve. But some fifty miles to the north of Ranch Number Ten, on the far-flung acres of the biggest stock-ranch in the State, there was another Packard to whom rumors came swiftly. And this was because the old grandfather went far out of his way upon every opportunity to learn of his grandson's activities.

"What for a man is he growed up to be, anyhow?" was what Hell-Fire Packard was interested in ascertaining.

When the old man wanted to get anywhere he ordered out his car and Guy Little. When he wanted information he sent for Guy Little. The undersized mechanician was gifted with eyes which could see, ears which could hear, and a tongue which could set matters clear; he must have been unusually keen to have retained his position in the old man's household for the matter of five or six years.

To his employer he had come once upon a time, half-starved and weary, a look of dread in his eyes which had the way of turning swiftly over his shoulder; the old man had

had from the beginning the more than suspicion that the little fellow was a fugitive from the law and in a hurry at that.

He had immediately taken him in and given him succor and comfort. The poor devil fumbled for a name and was so obviously making himself a new one that Packard dubbed him Guy Little on the spot, simply because, he explained, he was such a little guy. And thereafter the two grew in friendship.

Guy Little's first coming had been opportune. The old man had only recently bought his first touring-car; in haste to be gone somewhere his motor failed to respond to his first coaxing and subsequent bursts of violent rage. While he was cursing it, reviling it, shaking his fist at it, and vowing he'd set a keg of giant powder under the thing and blow it clean to blue blazes, Guy Little ran a loving hand over it, stroked its mane, so to speak, whispered in its ear, and set the engine purring. Old Man Packard nodded; they two, big-bodied millionaire and dwarfed waif, needed each other.

"Climb on the runnin'-board, Guy Little," he said right then. "You go wherever I go." And later he came to say of his mechanician, "Him? Why, man, he can take four ol' wagon wheels an' a can of gasoline an' make the damn' thing go. He's all automobile brains, that's what Guy Little is!"

On the Big Bend ranch, the old man's largest and favorite of several kindred holdings, an outfit which flung its twenty thousand acres this way and that among the Little Hills and on either side of the upper waters of the stream which eventually gave its name to Red Creek, the oldest of the name of Packard had summoned Guy Little.

It was some ten days after the stopping of all activity in the

Ranch Number Ten lumbercamp. He had been sitting alone in his library, smoking a pipe, and staring out of his window and across his fields. Suddenly he sprang to his feet, went to his door, and shouted down the long hall:

"Ho, there! Guy Little!"

The house was big; rooms had been added now and then at intervals during the last thirty or forty years; the master's library was of generous dimensions and could have stabled a herd of fifty horses. This chamber was in the southwest corner of the rambling edifice; Guy Little's quarters were diagonally across the building. But Packard asked no tinkling electric bell; as usual he was content to stick his head out into the hall and yell in that big, booming voice of his:

"Ho, there! Guy Little, come here!"

Having voiced his command he went back to his deep leather chair and refilled his pipe. It was the time of early dusk; not yet were the coal-oil lamps lighted; shadows were lengthening and merging out in the rolling fields. Packard's eyes, withdrawn from the outdoors, wandered along his tall and seldom-used book-shelves, fell to the one worn volume on the table beside him, went hastily to the door. Down the hall came the sound of quick boot-heels. He took up the single volume and thrust it out of sight under the leather cushion of his chair. The mechanician was in the room before he could get his pipe lighted.

"You called, m'lord?"

Guy Little stood drawn up to make the most of his very inconsiderable height, eyes straight ahead, hands at sides, chin elevated and stationary. Nothing was plainer than that he aped the burlesqued English butler—unless it be that it was even more obvious that in his chosen role he was a ridiculous failure. There never was the man less designed by nature for the part than Guy Little.

And yet he insisted; in the beginning of his relationship with his employer, his soul swelling with gratitude, his imagination touched by the splendors into which his fate had led him, awed by the dominant Packard, he had wanted always upon an occasion like this to demand stiffly:

"You rang, your majesty?"

Packard had cursed and threatened and brow-beaten him down to—

"You called, m'lord?"

But not even old Hell-Fire Packard could get him any further.

"Yes, I called," grunted the old man. "I hollered my head off at you. I want to know what you foun' out. Let's have it."

Guy Little made his little butler-bow.

"Your word is law, m'lord," he said, once more rigid and unbending.

Although Packard knew this very well without being told and had known it a good many years before Guy Little had been born, and although Guy Little had repeated the phrase time without number, the old man accepted it peacefully as a necessary though utterly damnable introduction.

"It's like this," continued the mechanician. "Not knowin' what you thought an' not even knowin' what you wanted to think, an' figgerin' to play safe, I've picked up the dope all over. Which is sayin' I bought drinks on both sides the street, whiskey at Whitey Wimble's joint an' more of the same at Dan Hodges's. An' I foun' out several things, m'lord. If it is your wish—"

"Spit 'em out, Guy Little! What for a man is he?"

"Firs'," said Guy Little, shifting his feet the fraction of an inch so that his chin bore directly upon Packard, "he's a scrapper. He beat up Joe Woods, a bigger man than him; later he took part in some sort of a party durin' which, like is beknown to you, somebody gouged Blenham's eye out; after that, single-handed, he cleaned out your lumber-camp, fifteen men countin' Blenham. Tally one, he's a scrapper."

For an instant it seemed that all of the light there was in the swiftly darkening room had centred in the blue eyes under the old man's bushy white brows. He drew deeply upon his pipe.

"Go on, Guy Little," he ordered. "What more? Spit it out, man."

"Nex'," reported the little man, "he's a born gambler. If he wasn't he wouldn't of tied into a game of buckin' you; he wouldn't of played seven-an'-a-half like he did in at the Ace of Diamonds; he wouldn't of took them long chances tacklin' Woodsy's timberjacks before breakfas'. Scrapper an' gambler. That's tally one an' two."

The old man frowned heavily, his teeth remaining tight clamped on his pipestem as he cried sharply:

"That's it! You've said it: gambler! Drat the boy, I knowed he had it in his blood. An' it'll ruin him, ruin him. Guy Little, as it would ruin any man. We got to get that fool gamblin' spirit out'n him. A man that's always takin' chances never gets anywhere; take a chance an' you ain't got a chance! That's the way of it, Guy Little! Go on, though. What else about him?"

"He's a good sport," went on the news-gatherer, "an' he don't ask no help from nobody. He stan's on his two feet like a man, m'lord. When he sees a row ahead he don't go to the law with it; no, m'lord; no indeed, m'lord. He says 'Hell with the law!' Like a man would, like me an' you . . . an' he kills his own rats himself."

"That's the Packard of him! For, by God, Guy Little, he is a Packard even if he has got a wrong start! Rich man's son— silver-spoon stuff—why, it would spoil a better man than you ever saw! Didn't I spoil my son Phil that-a-way? Didn't Phil start out spoilin' his son Stephen that same way? But he's a Packard—an'—an'—"

"An' what, m'lord?"

The old man's fist fell heavily on the arm of his chair.

"An' I'm still hopin' he's goin' to be a damn' good Packard at that! But you go on, Guy Little. What else?"

"Sorta reckless, he is," resumed Guy Little. "But that's purty near the same thing as havin' the gamblin' spirit, ain't it? Nex' an' final, m'lord, he's got what you might call an eye for a good-lookin' girl."

"The devil you say, Guy Little!" The old man, beginning to settle in his chair, sat bolt upright. "Is some female woman tryin' to get her hooks in my gran'son already? Name her to me, sir!"

"Name of Temple," said Little. "Terry Temple as they call her, an' a sure good-lookin' party, if you ask me! Classy from eyes to ankles an' when it comes to—"

"Hold on, Guy Little!" exploded old man Packard, leaping to his feet, towering high above the little man, who looked up at him with an earnest and placid expression. "That wench, that she-devil, that Jezebel! Settin' her traps for my boy Stephen, is she? Why, man alive, she ain't fit to scrape the corral-mud off'n his boots. She's a low-down, deceitful jade, that's what she is, sired by a sheep-stealin', throat-cuttin', ornery, no-'count, worthless cuss! The whole pack of them Temples, he an' she of 'em, big an' little of 'em, ought to be strung up on the firs' tree! The low-down bunch of little prairie dawgs, tryin' to trap a Packard with puttin' a putty-faced fool girl in their snare. I say, Guy Little, I'll make the whole crowd of 'em hunt their holes!"

And he hurled his pipe from him so that on the hearthstone it broke into many pieces.

Now that was a long speech for old man Packard and Guy Little listened interestedly. At the end, when the old man went growling back to his chair, the mechanician took up his tale.

"She's purty, though," he maintained. "Like a picture!"

"Doll-faced," snorted the old man, who had not the least idea what Terry Temple looked like, not having laid his eyes on her for the matter of years. "Dumpy, pudgy, squidge-nosed little fool. I'll run both her and her thief of a father out of the country."

"An'," continued Guy Little, "I didn't exac'ly' say, m'lord, as how this Terry Temple party was after him. I said as how he was after her! That is, as how, roundin' out what I know about him, he's got a eye for a fine-lookin' lady. Which, against argyment, I maintain that Terry Temple girl is."

"Guy Little," cried Packard sharply, "you're a fool! Maybe you know all there is about motor-cars an' gasoline. When it comes to females you're a fool."

"Ah, m'lord, not so!" protested Guy Little, a gleam in his eye like a faint flicker from a dead fire. "There was a time— before I set these hoofs of mine into the wanderin' trail— when—"

The rest might best be left entirely to the imagination and there he left it. But the old man was all untouched by his henchman's utterance and innuendoed boast for the simple reason that he had heard nothing of it.

"Those Temple hounds," he muttered, staring at Guy Little who stared butlerishly back, "are leeches, parasites, cursed bloodsuckers and hangers-on. They think I'm goin' to take this boy in an' give him all I got; they think they see a chance to marry him into their rotten crowd an' slip one over on me this way! That simperin', gigglin' fool of a girl try an' hook my gran'son! I'll show 'em, Guy Little; I'll show the whole cussed pack of 'em! I'll exterminate 'em, root an' branch an' withered leaf! By the Lord, but I'll go get 'em!"

"He'll do it," nodded Guy Little, addressing the invisible third party in order not to directly interrupt his patron's flow of words.

But for a little the old man was silent, running his calloused fingers nervously through his beard, frowning into the dusk thickening over the world outside. When he spoke again it was softly, thoughtfully, almost tenderly. And the words were these:

"Break a fool an' make a man, Guy Little! That's what we're goin' to do for Stephen Packard. He's always had too much money, had life too easy. We'll jus' nacherally bust him all to pieces; we'll learn him the big lesson of life; we'll make a man out'n him yet. An' when that's done, Guy Little, when that time comes—Go send Blenham here," he broke off with sharp abruptness.

Guy Little achieved his stage bow and departed. The door only half closed behind him, he was shouting at the top of his voice:

"Hey, Blenham! Oh, Blenham! On the jump. Packard wants you!"

The door slammed behind him. His back once turned on "m'lord," Guy Little did not wait to get out of earshot to become less butler than human sparrow.

Blenham needed but the one summons and that might almost have been whispered. He was fidgeting in his own room, waiting for this moment, knowing that he was to receive definite instructions concerning Stephen Packard. Over his right eye was a patch; his face was still a sickly pallor; his one good eye burned with a sullen flame which never went out.

Guy Little was the one human being in the world with whom the old man talked freely, to whom he unburdened himself. With his chief lieutenant Blenham he was, as with other men, short, crisp-worded, curt. Now, seeming to take no stock of Blenham's disfigurement, in a dozen snapping sentences he issued his orders.

Their gist was plain. Blenham was to go the limit to accomplish two purposes: the minor one of making the world a dreary place for certain scoundrels, name of Temple; the major one of utterly breaking Steve Packard. When Blenham went out and to his own room again the sullen fire in his good eye burned more brightly, as though with fresh fuel.

A little later Guy Little returned, lighted the lamps, made a small fire in the big fireplace, and ignoring the presence of his master, went to stand in front of the high book-shelves. After a long time he got the step-ladder and placed it, climbed to the top, and squatted there in front of his favorite section. Ultimately he drew down a volume with many colored illustrations; it was a tale of love, its *mise en scene* the mansions of the lords and ladies whose adventures occurred in that atmosphere of romance which had captivated the soul of Guy Little.

When he climbed down and sought the big chair in which he would curl up to read and chew countless sticks of gum, chewing fast when the action hurried, slowly when there was the dramatic pause, stopping often with mouth wide open when tense and breathless interest held him, he discovered that the old man had gone out.

Guy Little pursed his lips. Then he went to the recently vacated leather chair. Not to sit in it; merely to draw out the little volume from under the cushion.

"'Lyrics from Tennyson,'" he read aloud. "What the devil are them things?"

He turned the pages.

"Pomes!" he grunted in disgust.

Whereupon he carried his own book to his own chair. But, beginning to turn the pages, he stopped and looked up wonderingly.

"Funny ol' duck," he mused. "Here I've knowed him all

these years an' I never guessed he read pomes!"

He shook his head, admitted to himself that the "ol' duck" was a keen ol' cuss, returned to his book, began stripping the paper from the first stick of gum, and knew no more of what went on about him.

CHAPTER XV

AT THE FALLEN LOG

Since the hill ranch operated by the Temples and the Packard Ranch Number Ten had over two miles of common border-line, it was unavoidable that Steve and Terry should meet frequently. Truly unavoidable since further they were both young, Terry as pretty as the prover-bial picture, Steve the type to stick somehow in such a girl's mind. She turned up her nose at him; she gave him a fine view of her back; but in riding her father's range she let her eyes travel curiously across the line.

For his part Steve, seeing where some of his calves had invaded Temple property, followed the errant calves himself instead of sending one of his men. And as he rode he was apt to forget his strayed cattle as he watched through the trees for a fluttering, gay-hued scarf.

Certainly of girls and women he had known she was the most refreshing; certainly she was the prettiest after an undeniably saucy style. And life here of late, with Blenham and Woods gone and unheard from, was a quiet, uneventful affair.

Terry, for her part, told herself and any one else who cared to listen, that he was a Packard, hence to be distrusted, avoided, considered as beneath a white person's notice. His breed were all crooked. Sired and grandsired by precious scoundrels, he was but what was to be expected. And yet—

For "yets" and "ifs" and "howevers" had already begun to intrude, befogging many a consideration hitherto clear as cut glass. He had not lied about a horse being shot under him; he had been party to Blenham's departure from the ranch; he had been man enough in Red Creek to whip Joe Woods; and, single-handed, he had driven a crew of rough-and-ready timberjacks off his property.

Further, it was undeniable that he had a good-natured grin, that his eyes though inclined either to be stern or else to laugh at her, were frank and steady, that he made a figure that fitted well in the eye of a girl like Terry Temple.

"Oh, the Packards are men," said Terry begrudgingly, "even if they are pirates!"

This to her father and, it is to be suspected, for her father's sake. For, despite the girl's valiantly repeated hope that Temple "would come back yet" and be again the man he once was, he seemed in fact to grow more shiftless day after day, communing long over his fireplace with his drink, passing from one degree to another of untidiness. He made her "feel just like screaming and running around the house breaking things" at times.

"You are impatient, my dear," said Temple as one speaking to a very young child. "And there are matters which you don't understand; which I cannot even discuss with you. But," and he winked very slyly, less at Terry than just in a general acknowledgment of his own acumen, "you just wait a spell! I've got somethin' up my sleeve—somethin' that— Oh, you just wait, my dear!"

Terry sniffed.

"I ought to be pretty good at waiting by now," she told him, little impressed. "And if you have anything up your sleeve besides the flabby arm of a do-nothing, then it must be another bottle of whiskey! You can't flim-flam me, dad, and you ought to know it."

She whisked out of the house, her face reddened with vexation, a sudden moisture in her eyes. It took all of the fortitude she could summon into her dauntless little bosom to maintain after days like this that there was still a "come-back" left in her father.

In an hour made fragrant by the resinous odors of the upland pines and the freshly liberated perfumes of the little white evening flowers thick in the meadows, Terry on her favorite horse went flashing through the long shadows of the late afternoon, riding as Terry always rode when her breast was tumultuous and her temper rising.

The recently imported Japanese cook and houseboy peered out after her from his kitchen window, his eyes actually losing their Oriental cast and growing round; a trick, this, of Iki's whenever Terry came into his view.

"Part bird," mused Iki, "part flower, big part wild devil-girl! Oof! Nice to look at, but for wife Japonee girl more better. Think so."

Little by little as she rode, letting her horse out until she fairly raced through the fields and into the woods beyond, the pitiful picture of her father faded from her mind. As the vision dimmed of Temple's shoddiness in his worn-out slippers another image formed in Terry's mind; an image which was there more than the girl had as yet come to realize.

Yes, as types the Packards were all right; how many times had she admitted that to herself? But as individuals . . . Oh, how she hated them! And to-day, for some reason not clearly defined in Terry's consciousness, she found it convenient to assure herself with new emphasis that she hated and despised the Packards with a growing detestation, and from this point to go on and inform Miss Teresa Temple exactly why she looked on those of the Packard blood just as she did.

She summoned a host of reasons, set them in ranks like so many soldiers to wage war for her, marshalled and deployed and reviewed and dress-paraded them, and found them all eminently satisfactory mercenaries.

There was one reason which she thrust into the background, seeking to keep it hidden behind the serried ranks of its brothers-in-arms. And yet it insisted in mutinous fashion on pushing to the fore. Seeking to consider the Packards en masse, as a curse rather than as individuals, she found that she was remembering Steve Packard rather vividly.

In the outward seeming Steve Packard was a gentleman; he had that vague something called culture; he bore himself with the assurance and ease of one who knew the world; he had been to college—and Terry knew nothing more of school than was to be learned at a country high school. Steve's father had "broken" her father financially; had such not been the fact Terry herself would have had her own college diploma on her wall; Terry would have known something more of the world than she now knew; she would have been "a lady."

"Oh, pickles!" cried Terry aloud, bringing her runaway thoughts to a sharp halt. "What difference does it make if he knows Latin and I don't? And a hot specimen of a 'lady' I'd make anyhow!"

Over a ridge she flew, the low sun glistening from her spurs and the polished surfaces of her boot-tops, down into the dusk-filled fragrance of a woodsy canon, into the mouth of a silent trail, around a wide curve, and to her own favorite spot of all these woods. A nook of haunting charm with its sprawling stream, its big-boled and widely scattered trees, its grass and flowers. "Mossy Dell," she called it, having borrowed the name from an old romance read in breathless fashion in her room.

Slipping out of her saddle and leaving her horse to browse if such pastime suited him, Terry went through the trees and down along the flashing creek, humming softly, her voice confused with the gurgle of the noisy little stream, her eyes at last growing content.

She was half smiling at some shadowy thought before she had gone twenty paces; she tossed off her hat and let it lie, meaning to come back for it later; she unfastened the scarf about her neck, baring her white throat to the hour's cool invitation, she let her bronze-brown hair down in two loose, curling braids across her shoulders, toying with the ends as she went.

Coming here at troubled moments altered the girl's mood very much as an hour in a quiet cathedral may soothe the soul of the orthodox.

A little further on, lying across the stream and just around another bend, was a great fallen cedar, its giant trunk eight or ten feet through at the base. Approximately it marked the border-line between the Temple Ranch and Ranch Number Ten; it was quite as though the wilderness itself had cast down the big tree across an old trail to indicate a line which must not be crossed.

Upon the top of this supine woodland monarch Terry was

accustomed to sit, her back against one of the big limbs, her heels kicking at the mossy sides, while she glanced back and forth from Temple property to Packard land and told herself how much finer was her side than the other.

Just where the tree had fallen the creek-bed was rocky and uneven; the water eddied and whirled and plunged noisily into its pools. Terry, clambering up from her side of the big log, heard only the shouting of the brook. She grasped the dead branches, pulled herself up, slipped a little, got a new foothold; Terry's head, her face flushed rosily, her eyes never brighter, popped up on one side of the log just in time with the tick of her destiny's clock.

That is to say just as Steve Packard, climbing up from the other side, thrust his head up above the top. An astonished grunt from Steve who in the first start of the encounter came close to falling backward; a little choking ejaculation from Terry whose eyes widened wonderfully—and the two of them settled silently into their places on the cedar and stared at each other. Some three or four feet only lay between the brim of Steve's hat and Terry's upturned nose.

"Well?" demanded Terry stiffly.

"Well?" countered Steve.

He regarded her very gravely. He had never had a girl materialize this way out of space and his own thoughts. This sudden confronting savored of the supernatural; for the moment it set him aback and he was content to stare wonderingly into the sweet gray eyes so near his own and to take note of the curve of her lips, the redness of them, the dimple which, though departed now and, he felt, in hiding, had left a hint of itself behind in its hasty flight.

"If there's one thing I hate worse than a potato-bug," said

Terry, "it's a fresh guy! Think you're funny, don't you?"

"Fresh? Funny?"

He lifted his eyebrows. And then, her suspicion clear to him, his gravity departed the way Terry's dimple had gone and he put back his head and laughed. Laughed while the girl with deepening color and darkening eyes looked at him indignantly.

"Think I did that on purpose?" he cried in vast good nature. "That I was spying on you? That I waited until you started to climb up here and that then I popped my head up just at the same time? All on purpose?"

"That's just exactly what I do think!" Terry told him hotly. "You—you big smarty! Everywhere I go, have you got to keep showing up?"

"I'll tell you something," said Steve. "If I had climbed up here just to give you a little surprise party; if I had known you were there and that I could have poked my head up just as you did yours—know what I would have done?"

"What?" Terry in her curiosity condescended to ask.

"I'd have kissed the prettiest girl I ever saw!" he chuckled. "Honest to grandma! That's just what I'd have done. As it was, you half scared me out of my wits; I came as close as you please to going over backward and breaking my neck."

"Not as close as I please. And as for kissing me, Long Steve Packard, you just try that on sometime when you want your face slapped good and hard and a bullet pumped into you besides!"

"Mean it?" grinned Steve.

"I most certainly do," she retorted emphatically.

"Offered merely as information?" he wanted to know. "Or as a dare? Or an invitation?"

When she did not reply at once but contented herself by putting a deal of eloquence into a look—which, by the way, had no visible effect upon his rising good humor—he went on to remark:

"If you just slapped my face it would be worth it. If you just shot me through the finger-nail or something like that, it would be worth it still." He examined her critically. "Even if you plugged me square through the thumb—"

"If you don't know it," she informed him aloofly, "you are trespassing right now where you are not wanted. The sooner you trail your big feet off Temple land the better I'll like it!"

"Temple land? Since when was a tree considered as land, Miss Teresa Arriega Temple?"

"Think that's funny?" she scoffed.

"And besides," he continued, "the tree is on Packard property. See that old pine stump over yonder? And that big rock there? Those things mark the boundary-line and you'll notice we're on my side!"

Terry's temper flamed higher in her eyes, flashed hotter in her cheeks.

"We are not! And you know we are not! The line runs yonder, just beyond that big white rock on the creek-bank. And you are a good ten feet on my side. Where, if you please, you are not wanted."

"That isn't a pretty enough thought to bear repetition," he offered genially. "Look here, Terry Temple, what's the use—"

"Are you going? Or do you intend just to squat there like a toad and spoil the view for me?"

"Toads are fat animals," he corrected her. "I'm not. More like a bullfrog, if you like. What am I going to do? Why, just squat, I guess."

As he leaned back against the limb which offered its support to his shoulders Terry noted that he wore in full sight at his side the heavy Colt he had bought the other night in Red Creek. A new habit, with Steve Packard.

"Gunman, are you?" she jeered. "I might have known it. Gunmen are all cowards."

He sighed.

"You can be the most irritating young lady I ever met. And why? What have I ever done to you—besides save you from drowning? Since we are neighbors, why not be good friends? By the way, where do you carry your gun?"

"It's different with a girl," she said bluntly. "There's some excuse for her. With the kind that's filling the woods lately she's apt to need it."

"And you wouldn't be afraid to use it?"

"I'm not here to chin with you all day," observed Terry coolly. "And you haven't told me what you're doing on my land."

"Your land?" he demanded.

"On my side of the line, then."

He considered the question.

"I'm here to meet some one," he answered finally.

"I like your nerve! Arranging to meet your friends here! Steve Packard, you are the—the—the—"

"Go on," he prompted. "You'll need a cuss-word now; any other finish will sound flat."

"—the *Packardest* Packard I ever heard of!" she concluded. "You and your friend—"

"No more my friend than he is yours," he said, interrupting her. "An individual named Blenham. And I'm not here so much to meet him as—let's say to head him off."

Terry set it down that, since it was next to impossible at any time for a Packard to speak the truth, he was just lying to her for the sake of the devious exercise. As she was on the point of saying emphatically when Steve said "Sh!" and pointed. She heard a breaking of brush and saw the horns of a steer; the animal was coming into the trail from the Packard side.

"You just watch," whispered Steve. "And sit right still. It won't do you any harm to know what's going on."

The big steer broke through into the trail, stopped and sniffed, and then came on up the stream. Behind came another and another, emerging from the shadows, passing through the swiftly fading light of the open, gone again into the shadows that lay over the wooded Temple acreage. In all nine big fat steers. And behind them, sitting loosely in his saddle, came Blenham.

Only when the last steer had crossed the line did Steve rise suddenly, standing upright on the great log, his hands on his hips. Terry looking up into his face saw that all of the good humor had gone from it and that there was something ominous in the darkening of his eyes.

"Hold on, Blenham!" he called.

Blenham drew a quick rein.

"That you, Packard?" he asked quietly.

"It is," answered Steve briefly. "On the job, too, Blenham. All the time."

Blenham laughed.

"So it seems," he said, his look like his tone eloquent of an innuendo which embraced Terry evilly. "If you're invitin' me to join your little party, I ain't got the time. Thanks jus' the same."

Since one's consciousness may harbor several clear-cut impressions simultaneously, Steve Packard, while he was thinking of other matters, felt that never until this moment had he hated Blenham properly; no, nor respected him as it would be the part of wisdom to do.

The man's glance running over Terry Temple's girlishness was like the crawling of a slug over a wild flower and supplied a new and perhaps the key-note to Blenham's ugliness. It was borne in upon Steve that his grandfather's lieutenant was bad, absolutely bad; that, old adages to the contrary notwithstanding, here was a character with not a hint of redemption in it; after the Packard outright way, this youngest Packard was ready to condemn out of hand.

And further, to all of this Steve marked how Blenham had drawn a quick rein but had shown no tremor of uneasiness; had considered that though the man had been taken completely by surprise he had given no sign of being startled, but had answered a sharp summons with a cool, quiet voice. So, summing it up, here was one to be hated and watched.

"What are you doing on my land, Blenham?" asked Steve sharply. "And where are you driving those steers?"

Blenham eased himself in his saddle, drew his broad hat lower over his eyes; thus he partly hid the patch which he had worn since he came from the doctor's hands.

"I ain't on your land any more," he returned. "An' as for them steers—what's it to you, anyhow?"

Open defiance was one thing Steve had not looked for.

"Looking for more trouble yet, Blenham?" he asked briefly.

Blenham shrugged.

"I'm tendin' to business," he said slowly. "No, I'm not lookin' for trouble—yet. Since you want to know, I'm hazin' them cow-brutes the shortes' way off'n Number Ten an' on to the North Trail. I'm puttin' 'em on the trot to the Big Bend ranch where they happen to belong."

Steve lifted his brows, for the moment wondering. Blenham was not waiting for pitch dark to move these steers; he manifested no alarm at being discovered; now he calmly admitted that he was driving them to old man Packard's ranch where they belonged. It was possible that he was right.

In the few weeks that he had been back Steve had not had the time to know every head on his wide-scattered acreage;

as the steers had trotted through the shadows and into the open his eyes had been less for them than for the coming of Blenham and he was not sure of the brands.

He felt that Terry's eyes, as Terry sat very still on her log, were steadily upon him.

"Blenham," he said curtly, "I don't know whose cattle those are. But I do know this much: If they are mine I am going to have them back; if they are not mine I am going to have them back just the same."

"How do you make that out?" demanded Blenham.

"I make out that neither you nor any other man has any business driving stock off my range without consulting me first."

"They're Big Bend cows," muttered Blenham. "The ol' man's orders—"

"Curse the old man's orders!" Steve's voice rang out angrily. "If he can't be decent to me, can't he at least let me alone? Need he send you here to do business with me? If you want orders, Blenham, you just take these from me: Ride back to the old man on Big Bend ranch and tell him that what stock is on my ranch I keep here until he can prove it is his! Understand? If he can prove that these steers belong to him—and I don't believe he can and you can tell him that, too—why then, let him send me the money to pay for their pasturage and he can have them. And in the meantime, Mr. Blenham, get out and be damned to you!"

For the moment Steve lost all thought of Terry sitting very still so close to him, his mind filled with his grandfather and his grandfather's chosen tool. So when he thought that he heard the suspicion of a stifled giggle, a highly amused and vastly delighted little giggle, he was for the instant of the opinion that Blenham was laughing at him.

But the intruder was all seriousness. He sat motionless, his glance stony, his thought veiled, his one good eye giving no more hint of his purpose than did the patch over the other eye. In the end he shrugged.

"My orders," he said finally, "was simply to haze them steers back to the Big Bend. The ol' man didn't say nothin' about startin' anything if you got unreasonable." Again he shrugged elaborately. "I'll come again if he says so," he concluded and, jabbing his spurs viciously into his horse's flanks, his sole sign of irritation, Blenham rode away through the woods.

"He let go too easy," murmured Terry. "He's got a card in the hole yet."

Her eyes followed the departing rider, she pursed her lips after him.

Steve turned and looked down upon her.

"I hope you don't mind if I trespass to the extent of riding after those steers?" he offered. "I want to drive them back and at the same time I don't mind making sure that Blenham is still on his way."

Terry regarded him long and searchingly.

"Go ahead," she said at last. And, as though an explanation were necessary, she continued: "There's just one animal I hate worse than I do a Packard! For once the fence is down between you and Temple land, Steve Packard."

"Let's keep it down!" he said impulsively. "You and I—"

"No, thanks!" Terry rose swiftly to her feet, balancing on her log, reminding him oddly of a bright bird about to take flight. "You just remember that there's just one animal I hate *almost* as much as I do Blenham; and that that's a Packard."

And so she jumped down from the log and left him.

CHAPTER XVI

TERRY DEFIES BLENHAM

Blenham must have ridden late into the night. For at a very early hour the next morning he was at the Big Bend ranch fifty miles to the north and reporting to his employer. Early as it was, the old man had breakfasted, and now the wide black hat far back on his head, the spurs on his big boots, bespoke his readiness to be riding.

At times he stood stock-still, his hands on his hips, staring down at Blenham's lesser stature; at other times and in a deep, thoughtful silence he strode back and forth in the great barn-like library, his spurs jingling.

"Why, burn it, man," he exploded once during the fore part of the interview, "the boy is a Packard! I'm proud of him. We're going to make a real man out of Stephen yet. Haven't I said the words a dozen times: 'Break a fool an' make a man!' I'm tellin' you, the las' Packard to be spoiled by havin' too much easy money has lived an' died. All we got to do with Stephen is put him on foot; set him down in the good ol'-fashioned dirt where he's got to work for what he gets, an' he'll come through. Same as I did. Yessir!"

Blenham waited for his signal to continue his report, and when he got it, a look and a nod, he resumed, face, voice, and eye alike expressionless of any personal interest in the matter.

"You know them nine big steers as strayed from here some time ago? I tol' you about 'em two or three weeks ago? Well, I found 'em like I said I would, all nine of 'em, an' on Ranch Number Ten."

"It's quite a way for cattle to stray," said the old man sharply. Blenham shrugged carelessly.

"Oh, I dunno," he returned lightly. "I've knowed 'em to go fu'ther than that. Well, I made a pass to haze 'em on back this way an' young Packard blocks my play."

The old man's eye brightened.

"What did he say?" he asked eagerly.

"He said," said Blenham, picking at his hat-band, "as how if the stock was yours which he didn't believe he'd hold 'em until you sent over enough coin to pay for their feed. He said as how, if you couldn't be decent you better anyhow leave him alone. He said hell with both of us."

"He did?" cried old Packard. "He said that, Blenham?"

"He did," answered Blenham with a quick, curious, sidewise glance.

Packard's big hand was lifted and came down mightily upon his thigh as, suddenly released, the old man's voice boomed out in a great peal of laughter.

"Ho!" he cried, shouting out the words to be heard far out across the open meadow. "Say to hell with me, does he? Holds my stock for pasture money, does he? Defies me to do my worst, him a young, penniless whippersnapper, me a millionaire an' a man-breaker! Why, curse it, he's a man already, Blenham! He's a Packard to his backbone, I tell you! By the Lord, I've a notion to jump into my car and go get the boy!"

A troubled shadow came and went swiftly across Blenham's face, not to be seen by the old man who was staring out of his window. All of the craft there was in the ranch foreman rose to the surface.

"Yes," he agreed quietly, "he's got the makin's in him. He ain't scared of the devil himself, which is one right good earmark. He's independent, which is another good sign. Why, when I runs across him an' that Temple girl out in the woods—"

"What's that!" snapped the old man, though he had heard well enough. "Do you mean to tell me—"

"They was sittin' on top a big log," said Blenham tonelessly. "Confidential lookin', you know. I won't say he was holdin' her hands, an' at the same time I won't say he wasn't. An' I won't say he'd jus' kissed her, two seconds before I rode aroun' a bend in the trail." One of his ponderous shrugs and a grimace concluded his meaning. Then he laughed. "Nor I wouldn't say he hadn't. But, like I was tellin' you—"

"You were tellin' me," growled the old man, "that that scoundrel of a Temple's fool of a girl is tryin' her hand at spellbindin' my gran'son Stephen! The dirty little saphead— Look here, Blenham; you've got more gumption than most: tell me how far things have gone an' what Temple's game is. Guy Little has been tellin' me the same sort of thing."

"There ain't much to tell," answered Blenham. "That is, that a man couldn't guess without bein' told. He's your gran'son; even with a scrap on between you an' him, still blood is thicker'n water an' some day, maybe, you'll pass on to him all you got. Leastways, there's a chance, an' also he oughta fit pretty snug in a girl's eye. Fu'ther to all that, it's jus' the same ol' story. A feller an' a girl, an' the girl with a fine figger an' a fine pair of eyes which, bein' a she-girl, she knows how to use. Seein' as you ask the question, I guess I could answer it by jus' sayin' that the Temples are makin' the one move they'd be sure to make."

The senior Packard's scowl had known fame as long as fifty years ago; never was it blacker than right now. For a little he stood still glaring at the floor. Blenham watched him covertly, a look of craft in the one good eye.

"Better go over an' see Temple right away," said Packard presently. "He won't be able to pay up his next instalment. Tell him I'm goin' to foreclose an' drive him out. While you're at it you can show him the plum foolishness of sickin' his idiot girl on Stephen. How it won't bring 'em any good an' will jus' get me out on his trail red-hot. He'll understand." And the stern old mouth set into lines of which Blenham read the full and emphatic meaning. "Go on: anything else to report?"

After his fashion in business matters he had pondered deeply but briefly upon this interference of Terry, had planned, had instructed his agent, and now turned to whatever might next demand his attention in connection with his campaign against and for Steve Packard. And Blenham, deeming that he had scored a certain point, moved straight on to another.

"He said—an' she watched an' listened an' giggled—as how he was in right an' you was in wrong; as how the law was on his side an' he'd stick it out; how he could take the whole ruction into court an' beat you; how—"

Jackson Gregory

Old Hell-Fire Packard stared at him, mumbling heavily:

"He said that? Stephen, my gran'son said that?"

"Yes," lied Blenham glibly. "Them was his words. An', not knowin' a whole lot about law an' such—"

He ended there, knowing that his words went unheeded. The look upon the old man's face changed slowly from one of pure amazement to one of pain, grief, disappointment. Stephen, his gran'son, threatened to go to law! It was unthinkable that any one save a thief and an out-right scoundrel, such by the way as were all of his business rivals and the men who refused to tote and carry at his bidding, should make a threat like that; worse than unthinkable, utterly, depravedly disgraceful that one of the house of Packard should resort to such devious and damnable practices. For an instant Blenham thought that tears were actually gathering in the weary old eyes.

But the emotion which came first was gone in a scurry before a sudden windy rage. The face which had been graven with humiliation and chagrin went fiery red; the big hands clenched and were uplifted; the great booming voice trembled to the shouted words:

"Let him; burn him, let him! I can break the fool quicker that way than any other; don't he know it takes money, money without end, for the perjurin', trickery, slippery law sharks that'll bleed a man, aye, suck out his life-blood an' then spit him out like the pulp of an orange? Infernal young puppy-dawg! See what it's done for him already, this rich-man's-son business. To think that one of my blood, my own gran'son, should go to law! Why, by high heaven, Blenham, the thing's downright disgraceful!"

Swiftly, deftly, employing a remark like a surgeon's lancet,

Blenham offered:

"I have the hunch that Temple girl put it in his head."

"You're right!" This new suggestion required no weighing and fine balancing. You could attribute no villainy whatever to one of the old man's enemies that he would not admit the extreme likelihood of your being right. "Stephen ain't that sort; she's got him by the nose, hell take her! She's drivin' him to it, an' it's Temple drivin' her. An' it's up to you an' me to drive him clean out'n this corner of the universe. Which we can do without goin' to the law!" he interjected scornfully. "I reckon you understan', don't you, Blenham?"

Blenham nodded and put on his hat.

"I'm to hound him from the start to finish; until we drive him an' her out the country. An' I'm to pound at your gran'son too an' at the same time until we bust him wide open. That right?"

"Right an' go to it!" cried Packard.

Blenham saluted as he might have done were he still a sergeant down on the border, wheeled and went out. Five minutes later he was riding again toward the south. And now the look on his face was one of near triumph. For at last the time had come when the old man had given outright the instructions which could make many things possible.

That same day, about noon, Terry Temple, flashing across country in her car, met Blenham on the country road. She was going toward Red Creek, her errand urgent as were always the errands of Terry. Half a mile away she knew him, first by the white stocking of his favorite mare, second by his big bulk and the way it sat the saddle.

So, quite like the old Packard whom she so heartily detested, she gave him the horn and never an inch of the road which was none too wide. Blenham, his mouth working, jerked his horse out of the way, down over the edge of the slope, and cursed after her as she passed him.

Terry, in Red Creek, went straight to the store and to a shelf in a far and dusty corner where were all of the purchasable books of the village. A thumb in her mouth, a frown in her eyes, she regarded them long and soberly.

In the end she severed the Gordian knot by taking an even dozen volumes. There were a grammar, an ancient history, some composition books, and, most important of all, a treatise upon social usages.

How to write letters, what R. S. V. P. meant, "Mr. and Mrs. So-and-so request and so forth," how a lady should greet a gentleman friend—in short, an answer to all possible questions of right and wrong ways of appearing in polite society. With her purchases stowed away in a cracker-box Terry turned again toward the ranch.

In the ordinary course of events Terry should have returned to her home well ahead of Blenham. But this afternoon she made a wide, circling detour to chat briefly with Rod Norton's young wife at the Rancho de las Flores, and so came under the Temple oaks after dusk.

As she turned in at the gate she saw Blenham's horse standing tied down by the stable. Terry's eyes opened wonderingly and a little flush came into her cheeks. Plainly Blenham was closeted with her father. Terry bit her lip, gathered her books in her arms, and hastened toward the house.

The bawling of a mother cow and a baby calf, separated by a corral fence, had quite drowned out the purr of her motor; her step as usual was light upon the porch. The first that Temple and Blenham knew of her coming was her form in the doorway, her face turned curiously upon them.

And in that instant, while all three stood motionless, Terry saw and wondered at a look of understanding which had flashed between her own father and the despised representative of a hated race. Further she noted how the glass in Temple's hand was still lifted, as was the glass in Blenham's, the whiskey still undrunk, winking at her in the pale lamplight.

"Isn't your eternal drinking bad enough without your asking such as that to drink with you?" she asked quietly. Very, very quietly for Miss Terry Temple.

Her father shifted a trifle uneasily. Blenham watched her intently, admiringly after a gross fashion and yet a bit contemptuously. Blenham could put a look like that into his eye; to him a girl was a thing that might be both sneered at and coveted.

"My dear," said Temple, striving for clear enunciation and in the end achieving it heavily, "I am glad you came. I want you to listen. We must act wisely. We must not misjudge Mr. Blenham."

While Terry remained silent, looking from one to the other of the two men. Temple drank his whiskey hastily, furtively, snatching the second when her gaze had gone to Blenham.

"What's the game?" asked Terry in a moment.

She set her books down upon the table at her side, put out

her hand to the back of a chair, and like the men remained standing.

Temple looked to Blenham, who merely shrugged his thick shoulders and sipped at his whiskey, as though it had been a light wine and very soft to an appreciative palate. In some vague way the act was vastly insolent. Temple appeared uncertain, no uncommon thing with him; then, going to set his emptied glass down he put an elbow on the mantel, dropped his head, and spoke in a low, mumbling voice:

"The game? It's what it always was, Terry girl; what it always will be. The game of the ear of corn and the mill-stones; the game of the unfortunate under the iron heel."

"Unfortunate!" cried Terry in disgust. "Pooh!"

"Listen to me," commanded her father. "You ask: What's the game? and I'm telling you." His head was up now; Terry noted a new look in his eyes, as he hurried on. "It's just the game of life, after all. The war of those who have everything against those who have nothing; of men like Old Hell-Fire Packard against men like me. A game to be won more often than not through the sheer force of massed money that squeezes the life out of the under dog—but to be lost when the moneyed fool, curse him, runs up against a team like Blenham and me!"

"Blenham and you?" she repeated. "You and Blenham? You mean to tell me that you are chipping in with him?"

Blenham turned his whiskey-glass slowly in his great thick fingers. His eye shone with its crafty light; his lips were parted a little as though they held themselves in readiness for a swift interruption if Temple said the wrong thing or went too far.

"You are prejudiced," said Temple. "You always have been. Just because Blenham here has represented Packard, and Packard—"

"Is an old thief!" she cried passionately. "And worse! As Packard's *Man Friday* Blenham doesn't exactly make a hit with me!"

"Come, come," exclaimed Temple. "Curb your tongue, Teresa, my dear. If you will only listen—"

"Shoot then and get it over."

Terry sank into her chair, clasped her gauntleted hands about a pair of plump knees which drew Blenham's gaze approvingly, and set her white teeth to nibbling impatiently at her under lip as though setting a command upon it for silence.

"Let's have it, Dad."

"That's sensible," mumbled Temple. "You always were a smart girl, Teresa, when you cared to be. Let's see; where had I got? Oh, yes; speaking of Blenham chipping in with us, as you put it."

"With *you*!" corrected Terry briefly.

"We're mortgaged to old man Packard," continued Temple, somewhat hasty about it now that he had fairly plunged into the current of what he had to say, as though the water were cold and he was anxious to clamber out upon the far side. "Not much in a way; a good deal when you figure on how tight money is and how little we've seen of it these last few years. Now, Packard sends Blenham across with a message; he's going to foreclose; he is going to drive us out; to ruin us. That is Packard's word."

Terry stiffened in her chair; her chin rose a little in the air; her eyes brightened; the color in her cheeks deepened. That was her only answer to Packard's ultimatum as quoted to her father by Blenham and by Temple to her. Knowing that there was still more to come, she sat still, her clasped hands tightening about her knees. Blenham, as still as she, was sipping at his whiskey.

"But Blenham is a white man."

Temple attempted to say it with the force of conviction, but Terry merely sniffed, and Temple himself failed somewhat to put his heart into his words. He hurried on, repeating:

"Yes, a white man. And he's got a little money of his own that he's been tucking away all these years of working for Packard. He comes over this evening, Teresa, my dear, and makes us a—curse it, a generous offer. You see, as things are, we are bound to lose the whole place, lock, stock, and barrel, to Packard; you don't want to do that, do you?"

"Go on," said Terry. Her face was suddenly as white as the hands from which she was swiftly, nervously stripping her gauntlets. "Just what is Blenham's generous offer, Dad?"

"It's one of two things."

He hesitated and licked his lips. Terry's heart sank lower yet; it took him so long to set the thing into words! "You see, as Old Man Packard's foreman and agent he comes to tell us that he is ordered to foreclose; to break us utterly. As a friend to us he says—"

"For God's sake!" cried Terry sharply. "What does he say?"

"He will pay us a thousand dollars to let him take over everything! He will assume the mortgage; he will scrap it out with old Packard; he will clear the title; and, if we get where we want the ranch back some time, he will let us buy him out for just what he has put in it."

Terry looked at him gravely.

"In words of one syllable," she said quietly, "Blenham plans to give you one thousand dollars; then to pay to old Packard the seven thousand you owe him; and for this amount of eight thousand to grab an outfit that is worth twenty thousand if it's worth a nickel! That's his generous offer, is it?"

"My dear—"

"Don't my dear me!" she snapped impatiently. "Just go on and get the whole idiotic thing out of your system. What else?"

"That's all. As I have said already, as things are we are bound to lose everything to Packard. Blenham steps up and offers us a thousand—"

"I should think he would step up! Lively! Well, I can't stop you, can I? You don't have to have my consent to make a laughing-stock out of yourself? Have you signed up with Blenham already?"

Temple sought to assume an air of dignity which went poorly with his ragged slippers and bleary eye.

"Blenham has his money in a safe in Red Creek. There will be papers to be signed. We are going there now. I—I am sorry you take it this way, Teresa."

Then she sprang to her feet, her two hands clenched, her eyes blazing.

Jackson Gregory

"And I," she cried hotly, "am sorry. Oh, I am ashamed! that one of the name of Temple should sink so low as to hobnob with a cur and a scoundrel, a cheat, a liar, and all that Blenham is, and that you and I and the whole country know he is! I'd rather see Old Hell-Fire Packard break you and grind you under foot than see you stand there and drink with that thing!"

And that there should be no mistake her finger shot out, pointing at Blenham.

"Terry!" commanded her father, "be silent. You don't know what you are saying!"

"Don't I, though! I—I—"

Blenham laughed as she broke off, laughed again as he stood watching how she was breathing rapidly.

"Pretty puss," he said impudently, "you need them pink-an'-white nails of your'n trimmed."

"Don't you dare say a word to me," she flung at him. "Not a word."

"Not a single little word, eh?" He tossed off his whiskey, dropped the empty glass to the floor behind him, and came a quick stride toward her, an ugly leer twisting at the corner of his mouth, his one eye burning. "I've got your ol' man where I want him; he knows it an' I an' you know it. An' when I like I can have you where I want you, too. Understan'?"

He had taken another step toward her. The sudden thought leaped up in her mind that he and her father had had many drinks together before her arrival. She drew back slowly. Temple, seeing that for the moment all attention had been drawn from him, reached out for a bottle on the far end of the mantel.

Then suddenly and without another word being spoken Terry was galvanized into action. Blenham was coming on toward her and she saw the look in his eye. She whipped back; her breath caught in her throat; the color ran out of her cheeks. She glanced wildly toward her father; his fingers were closing about the neck of a bottle when they should have been at the neck of a man.

Terry whipped up a book from the table—it was a volume answering many a question about how to act in society but without any mention of such a situation as now had arisen—and flung it straight into Blenham's hectic face. Then she slipped through the door behind her, slammed it, and ran out, down the porch and into the night. Behind her she heard Blenham's heavy, spurred boots and Blenham's curse.

"If he comes on I will kill him!"

She was at her car; her revolver was in her hand. She saw Blenham come outside. A moment he seemed to hesitate, his big bulk outlined against the door's rectangle of light. Then she heard him laugh and saw him return to the room. She came back slowly, tiptoe, to stand under the window.

"You can drive the girl's car, can't you?" Blenham was asking. And when Temple admitted that he could: "Let's pile in an' be on our way. Like I said, you close with me tonight or I won't touch the thing."

Then again Terry ran back to her car. She sprang in, started her engine, opened the throttle as she let in the clutch, and making a wide circle shot up the road, out the gate, and away into the darkness.

"I'll take this pot yet, Mr. Cutthroat Blenham!" she was crying within herself.

CHAPTER XVII

AND CALLS ON STEVE

Though a tempest brewed in her soul and her blood grew turbulent with it, Terry did not hesitate from the first second. Just the other day upon a certain historic log had she not said:

"I hate Blenham worse than a Packard!"

True, she had gone on to intimate that the youngest of the house of Packard was scarcely more to her liking than was the detested foreman. But—Well, if Steve didn't know, at least Terry did, that that remark was uttered purely for its rhetorical effect.

"He's been a pretty decent scout from the jump," Terry admitted serenely to herself as she threw her car into high and went streaking through the pale moonlight. Then she smiled, the first quick smile to come and go since she had hurled a book in Blenham's face. "A pretty decent scout from the jump!"

He had literally jumped into her life, going after her quite as though—

"Oh, shucks!" laughed Terry. "It's the moonlight!"

There came a certain sharp turn in the road where even she must slow down. Here Terry came to a dead stop, not so much in hesitation as because she was conscious of a departure from the old trails and felt deeply that the act might be filled with significance. For when she had made the turn she would have crossed the old dead line, she would have passed the boundary and invaded Packard property.

"Well," thought Terry, "when you are between the devil and the deep sea what are you going to do?"

So she let in her clutch, opened her throttle, sounded her horn purely by way of defiance, and when next she stopped it was at the very door of the old ranch-house where Steve Packard should be found at this early hour of the evening.

The men in the bunk-house had heard her coming, and to the last man of them pushed to the door to see who it might be. Their first thought, of course, would be that the old mountain-lion, Steve's grandfather, had come roaring down from his place in the north. Terry tossed up her head so that they might see and know and marvel and speculate and do and say anything which pleased them. Having crossed her Rubicon, she didn't care the snap of her pretty fingers who knew.

"I want Steve Packard," she called to them. "Where is he?"

It was young Barbee who answered, Barbee of the innocent blue eyes.

"In the ranch-house, Miss Terry," he said. And he came forward, patting his hair into place, hitching at his belt, smiling at her after his most successful lady-killing fashion. "Sure I won't do?"

"You?" Terry laughed. "When I'm looking for a man I'm not going to stop for a boy, Barbee dear!"

And she jumped down and knocked loudly at Steve's door, while the men at the bunk-house laughed joyously and Barbee cursed under his breath.

Steve, supposing that it was one of his own men grown suddenly formal, did not take his stockinged feet down from his table or his pipe from his lips as he called shortly—

"Come in!"

And Terry asked no second invitation. In she went, slamming the door after her so that those who gawked at the bunk-house entrance might gawk in vain.

And now Steve Packard achieved in one flashing second the removal of his feet from the table, the shifting of his pipe from his teeth, the swift buttoning of his shirt across his chest. And as he stared at her he gasped:

"I'll be—"

"Say it!" laughed Terry. "Well, I'm here. Came on business. There's a hole in the toe of your sock," she ended with a flash of malice, as she noted how, embarrassed for the first time since she had known him, he was trying to hide a pair of man-sized feet behind his table.

Steve grew violently red. Terry laughed deliciously.

"I—I didn't know—"

"Of course you didn't," she agreed. "Now, I'm in something of a rush of the red streak variety, but in a little book of mine I have read that a young gentleman receiving a young lady caller after dark should have his hair combed, his shirt buttoned, and at least a pair of slippers on. I'll give you three minutes."

Packard looked at her wonderingly. Then, without an answer, he strode by her and to the window. The shade he flipped up so that anyone who cared to might look into the room. Next he went to the door and called:

"Bill, oh, Bill Royce. Come up here. Here's some one who wants a word with you!"

Terry Temple's face went a burning, burning red. There came the impulse to put both arms about this big shirt-sleeved, tousled Packard man and squeeze him hard—and at the end of it pinch him harder. For in Terry's soul was understanding, and he both delighted her and shamed her.

But when Steve came back and slipped his feet into his boots and sat down across the table from her, Terry's face told him nothing.

"You're a funny guy, Steve Packard," she admitted thoughtfully.

"That's nothing," grinned Steve, by now quite himself again. "So are you!"

She had come from the Temple ranch without any hat; her hair had tumbled down long ago and now framed her vivacious face most adorably. Adorably, that is, to a man's mind; other women are not always agreed upon such matters. At any rate, Steve watched with both admiration and regret in his eyes as Terry shook out the loose bronze tresses and began to bring neat order out of bewilderingly becoming chaos. Her mouth was full of pins when Bill Royce came in. But still she could whisper tantalizingly—

"If you picked on Bill for a chaperon because he's blind—"

Royce stopped in the doorway.

"That you, Terry Temple?" he asked. "An' you wanted me? What's up?"

"I came to have a talk with Steve Packard," answered Terry promptly.

She got up and took Royce's hands between hers and led him to a chair before she relinquished them. And before she went back to her own place she had said swiftly:

"I haven't seen you since you licked Blenham. I—I am glad you got your chance, Bill."

"Thank you, Miss Terry," said Royce quietly. "I sorta evened up things with him. Not quite. But sorta. Then you didn't want me?"

"Not this trip, Bill. It's just a play of Mr. Packard's here. He didn't like to have it known that I had him all alone here; afraid it might compromise him, you know."

She giggled.

"Or queer him with his girl, mos' likely!" chuckled Royce.

Whereat Steve glowered and Terry looked startled.

"You're both talking nonsense," said Packard. He reached out for his pipe but dropped it again to the table without lighting it. "If there is anything I can do for you, Miss Temple—"

He saw how the look in her eyes altered. Nothing less than

an errand of transcendent importance could have brought her here and he knew it. And now, in quick, eager words she told him:

"Blenham has almost put one across on us. Our outfit is mortgaged to your old thief of a grandfather for a miserable seven thousand dollars. Old Packard sent Blenham over to tell dad he is going to shove us out. Blenham plays foxy and offers dad a thousand dollars for the mortgage. Oh, I don't understand just how to say it, but Blenham has a few thousand dollars he has saved and stolen here and there, and he means to grab the Temple ranch for a total of eight thousand dollars; seven thousand to old Packard, one thousand to dad—"

"But surely—"

"Surely nothing! Dad's half full of whiskey as usual, and a thousand dollars looks as big to him as a full moon. Besides, he's sure of losing to old Hell-Fire sooner or later."

"And you want me—"

"If you've got any money or can raise any," said Terry crisply, "I'm offering you a good proposition. The same Blenham is after. The ranch is worth a whole lot better than twenty thousand dollars. My proposition is—But can you raise eight thousand?"

Steve regarded her a moment speculatively. Then, quite after the way of Steve Packard, he slipped his hand into his shirt and brought out a sheaf of banknotes and tossed them to her across the table.

"I'm not a bloodsucker," he said quietly. "Take what you like; I'll stake you to the wad."

Terry looked, counted—and gasped.

"Ten thousand!" she cried. "Good Lord, Steve Packard! Ten thousand—and you'd lend me—"

"To pay off a mortgage to my grandfather, yes," he answered soberly, quite conscious of what he was doing and of its recklessness and, perhaps, idiocy. "And to beat Blenham."

She jumped up and ran around the table to put her two hands on his shoulders and shake him.

"You're a God-blessed brick, Steve Packard!" she cried ringingly. "But I'm not a bloodsucker, either. If you're a dead game sport—Well, that's what I'd rather be than anything else you can put a name to. Lace your boots, get into a hat, shove that in your pocket." And she slipped the roll of bills into his hand. "By now dad and Blenham will be on the road to Red Creek; we'll beat them to it, have a lawyer and some papers all ready, and when they show up we'll just take dad out of Blenham's hands."

"I don't quite get you," said Steve. "If you won't borrow the money—"

"I'll make dad sell out to you for eight thousand; he pockets one thousand and with the other seven your money-grabbing, pestiferous old granddad is paid off. Then you and I frame a deal between us—"

"Partners!" ejaculated Bill Royce. "Glory to be! Steve Packard an' Terry Temple pardners—"

"Don't you see?" Terry was excitedly tugging at Steve's arm. "Come on; come alive. We're going to play freeze-out with Hell-Fire Packard and his right-hand bower, both. And we're going to keep dad from doing a fool thing. And we're going to—Oh, come on, can't you?"

Steve got up and stood looking down at her curiously. Then he laughed and turned away for his coat and hat.

"Lead on; I'm trailing you," he said briefly.

Bill Royce rubbed his hands and chuckled.

"Even if I ain't got eyes," he mused, "there's some things I can see real clear."

CHAPTER XVIII

"IF HE KNOWS—DOES SHE?"

There seemed no particular need for haste. And yet Terry ran eagerly to her car, and Steve hurried after her with long strides while the men down at the bunkhouse surmised and looked to Bill Royce for a measure of explanation. Steve was not beyond the age of enthusiasm; Terry was all atingle. Life was shaping itself to an adventure.

And so, though it appeared that all of the time in the world was theirs for loitering—for it should be a simple matter to come to Red Creek well in advance of Blenham and his dupe—Terry yielded to her excitement, Steve yielded out of hand to the lure of Terry, and, quite gay about it, they sped away through the moonlight. While Terry, driver, perforce kept her eyes busied with the road, Steve Packard leaned back in his seat and contented himself with the vision of his fellow adventurer.

"Terry Temple," he told her emphatically and utterly sincerely, "you are absolutely the prettiest thing I ever saw."

"I'm not a thing," said Terry. "And besides, I know it already. And—"

Then it was that they got their first puncture; a worn tire

cut through by a sharp fragment of rock so that they heard the air gush out windily. Terry jammed on her brakes. Steve jumped out and made hasty examination.

"Looks like a man had gone after it with a hand-ax," he announced cheerfully. "Good thing you've got a spare."

Terry flung down from her seat impatiently.

"I need some new tires," she said, as she from one side and he from the other began seeking in the tool-box under the seat for jack and wrench. "That spare is soft, too, and half worn through; I'll bet we get more than one puncture before the job's done. But it's mounted, anyway."

Steve went down on his knee and began jacking the car up; Terry standing over him was busy with her wrench loosening the lugs at the rim. Then, while he made the exchange and tightened the nuts, she strapped the punctured tire in its carrier and slipped back into her seat. As Steve got in beside her he marked how speculatively her eyes were busied with the road.

"We've got them behind us, haven't we?" he asked.

Terry nodded quickly.

"Yes. We've got the head start and they're on horseback. It's no trick to beat them to it. But—Oh, I saw a look on Blenham's face to-night! He's bad, Steve Packard; all bad; the kind that stops at nothing! And somehow, somehow he's got a strangle-hold on poor old dad and is making him do this. We've got the head start, we can beat them to Red Creek, but—"

"But you don't like the idea of leaving your father alone in Blenham's company to-night?" he finished for her. "Is that it?"

Again she nodded. He could see her teeth set to nibbling at her lips.

"Then," he suggested, "why go to Red Creek at all? Why not turn back here and stop them? You can take Mr. Temple back home with you. I imagine that between the two of us we can make Blenham understand he is not wanted this time."

"I was thinking of that," said Terry.

And where the Ranch Number Ten road runs into the country road, Terry turned to the right, headed again toward her own home.

When, with Steve at her heels, she ran up on the porch it was to be met by Iki, the Japanese cook, his eyes shining wildly.

"Where's my father?" she asked, and Iki waving his hands excitedly answered:

"Departed with rapid haste and many curse-words from his gentleman friend. The master could not make a stop for one little more drink of whiskey. The other strike and vomit threats and say: 'Most surely will I cause that you tarry long time in jail-side.' Saying likewise: 'I got you by the long hair like I want you and yes-by-God, like some day soon I get your lovely daughter!' Only he say the latter with unpleasant words of—"

Terry was shaking him by both shoulders.

"Where did they go?" she demanded. "How long ago?"

"On horses, running swiftly," gibbered Iki. "Ten minutes, maybe—perhaps twenty or thirty. Who can tell the time when—"

"Why didn't we meet them?" asked Steve of Terry. "If they are really headed for Red Creek?"

"They are taking all of the short-cuts there are," she answered promptly. "They'll take a cow-trail through the ranch, cut across the lower end of your place, and come into the old road just beyond. Blenham's all fox; he has guessed that I am out to put a spoke in his wheel somehow. He won't be wasting any perfectly good moonlight. Come on!" And again she was running to the car. "We'll overhaul them just the same.

"I believe you," grunted Steve, once more seated beside her, the engine drumming, the wheels spinning. "You don't know what a speed law is, do you?"

"Speed law?" she repeated absently, her eyes on the next dark turn in the road. "What's that?"

He chuckled and settled back in his seat. His eyes, like the girl's, were watchfully bent upon the gloom-filled angle which Terry must negotiate before the way straightened out again before her. Her headlights cut through the shadows; Terry's little body stiffened a bit and her hands tensed on her wheel; her flying speed was lessened an almost negligible trifle; she made the turn and opened the throttle. Steve nodded approvingly.

For the greater part they were silent. He had never seen her in a mood like to-night's. He read in her face, in her eyes, in the carriage of her body, one and the same thing; and that was a complex something made of the several emotions of determination, sorrow, and fiery anger.

He read her thought readily; it was clear that she made no attempt to conceal it: She was going to consummate a certain deal, she was grieved and ashamed for her father, she remembered the "look on Blenham's face to-night," and again and again her fury shot its red tide into her cheeks.

"Blenham put his dirty hands on her," was Steve's thought; "or tried to."

And he found that his own pulses drummed the hotter as he let his imagination conjure up a picture for him, Blenham's big, knotted hands upon the daintiness that was Terry. In that moment it seemed to him that he had been drawn home across the seas to help mete out punishment to a man: a man who had stricken old Bill Royce, and who now dared look evilly upon Terry Temple.

Then came their second puncture, an ugly gash like the first caused by a flinty fragment of rock driven against the worn outer casing.

"I ordered new tires a month ago," said Terry by way of explanation, as she and Steve in the road together set about remedying the trouble.

While he was getting the inner-tube out, squatting in front of her car so as to work in the glow from her headlights, she was rummaging through her repair kit.

"These rocky roads, you know, and the way I drive."

He laughed. "The way she drove!" That meant, "Like the devil!" as he would put it. Over rocky roads, racing right up to a turn, jamming on her brakes when she must slow down a little; swinging about a sharp bend so that her car slid and her tires dragged; in short getting all of the speed out of her motor that she could possibly extract from it, regardless and coolly contemptuous of skuffed tires and other trifles.

Finding the cut in the inner-tube was simple enough; the moonlight alone would have shown it. He held it up for her to look at and she shook her head and sighed. But making the patch so that it would hold was another matter; and pumping up the tire when the job was done was still another, and required time and ate up all of Terry's rather inconsiderable amount of patience.

"A little more luck like this," she cried as once more they took to the road, "and Blenham will put one over on us yet!"

It was borne in upon Steve that Terry's fears might prove to be only too well founded. The time she had taken to drive to him at his ranch, the time lost in returning to her home and in changing tires and mending a puncture, had been put to better use by Blenham. True, he was on horseback while they motored. And yet, for a score or so of miles, a determined, brutally merciless man upon a horse may render an account of himself.

But while they both speculated they sped on. They came to the spot where the "old road" turned into the new; Blenham and Temple were to be seen nowhere though here the country was flat and but sparsely timbered, and the moon pricked out all objects distinctly.

And so on and on, beginning to wonder at last, asking themselves if Blenham and Temple had drawn out of the road somewhere, hiding in the shadows, to let them go by? But finally only when they were climbing the last winding grade with Red Creek but a couple of miles away, they saw the two horsemen.

Terry's car swung about a curve in the road her headlights

for a brief instant aiding the moon in garishly illuminating a scene to be remembered. Blenham had turned in his saddle, startled perhaps by the sound of the oncoming car or by the gleam of the headlights; his uplifted quirt fell heavily upon the sides of his running horse; rose and fell again upon the rump of Temple's mount, and the two men, their horses leaping under them, were gone over the ridge and down upon the far side.

In a few moments, from the crest of the ridge, they made out the two running forms on the road below. Blenham was still frantically beating his horse and Temple's. Terry's horn blared; her car leaped; and Blenham, cursing loudly, jerked his horse back on its haunches and well out of the road. With wheels locked, Terry slid to a standstill.

"Pile in, dad," she said coolly, ignoring Blenham. "Steve Packard and I will take you into Red Creek. Packard is ready to make you a better proposition than Blenham's. Turn your horse loose; he'll go home, and pile in with us."

"He'll do nothing of the kind!" shouted Blenham, his voice husky with his fury. "Just you try that on Temple, an'— He'll do nothing of the kind," he concluded heavily, his mien eloquent of threat.

"We know you think you've got some kind of a stranglehold on him, Blenham," cut in Terry crisply. "But even if you have, dad is a white man and—dad! What is the matter?"

Temple slipped from his saddle and stood shaking visibly, his face dead white, his eyes staring. Even in the moonlight they could all see the big drops of sweat on his forehead, glistening as they trickled down. He put out his hand to support himself by gripping at his saddle, missed blindly, staggered, and began slowly collapsing where he stood as though his bones were little by little melting within him. Blenham laughed harshly.

"Drunker'n a boiled owl," he grunted. "But jus' the same sober enough to know—"

"Dad!" cried Terry a second time, out in the road beside him now, her arms belting his slacking body. "It isn't just that. You—"

"Sick," moaned Temple weakly. "God knows—he's been hounding me to death—I don't know—I wanted to stop, to rest back there but—I'm afraid that—"

He broke off panting. Steve jumped out and slipped his own arms about the wilting form.

"Let me get him into the car," he said gently. And when he had lifted Temple and placed him in the seat he added quietly: "You'd better hurry on I think. Get a doctor for him. I'll follow on his horse."

Terry flashed him a look of gratitude, took her place at the wheel and started down grade. Her father at her side continued to settle in his place as long as Steve kept him in sight.

"Well?" growled Blenham, his voice ugly and baffled and throaty with his rage. "You butt in again, do you?"

Steve swung up into the saddle just now vacated by Temple.

"Yes," he retorted coolly. "And I'm in to stay, too, if you want to know, Blenham. To the finish."

With only the width of a narrow road between them they stared at each other. Then Blenham jeered:

"Oho! It's the skirt, huh? Stuck on her yourself, are you?"

Steve frowned, but met his piercing look with level contempt.

"Your language is inelegant, friend Blenham," he said slowly. "Like yourself it is better withdrawn from public notice. As to your meaning—why, by thunder, I half believe you are right! And I hadn't thought of it!"

Blenham caught In one of his rare bursts of heady rage shook his fist high above his head and cried out savagely:

"I'll beat you yet, the both of you! See if I don't. Yes you an' your crowd an' him an' her an'—"

"Don't take on too many all at once," suggested Steve.

Only the tail of his eye was on Blenham; he was looking wonderingly and a bit wistfully down the moonlit, empty road.

"I got him where I want him right now," snarled Blenham. "An' her—I'll have her, too, where I want her! An', inside less time than you'd think I'll have—"

But he clamped his big mouth tight shut, glared at Steve a moment and then, striking with spur and quirt together, so that his frightened horse leaped out frantically, he was gone down the road after Temple and Terry.

As Steve followed a smile was in his eyes, a smile slowly parting his lips.

"The scoundrel was right!" he mused. "And I hadn't even thought of it. Now how the devil do you suppose he knew?"

And then, before he had gone a dozen yards a curious, puzzled, uncertain look come into his face.

"If he knows," was his perplexity, "Does she?"

CHAPTER XIX

TERRY CONFRONTS HELL-FIRE PACKARD

"Father's got it in his head he is going to die!" cried Terry. "He sha'n't. I won't let him!"

Steve Packard, riding into Red Creek, met Terry coming out. She was just starting, her car gathering speed; seeing him she drew down abruptly.

"I left him at the store," she added breathlessly. "He is sick. They are friends there; they'll take care of him. He knows you are coming; he has promised to do business with you and shut Blenham out of the running. You are to hurry before Blenham gets there—he's across the street at the saloon already. After his money, I guess; next thing, unless you block his play, he'll be standing over poor old dad's bed, bullyragging him. Come alive, Steve Packard, and beat him to it."

And with the last words she had started her car, after Terry's way of starting anything, with a leap. Steve reined in after her, urging his horse to a gallop for the first time, calling out sharply:

"But you—where are you going? Why—"

"After Doctor Bridges," Terry called back. "The fool is over at your old thief of a grandfather's, playing chess! The telephone won't—"

He could merely speculate as to just what the telephone would not do. Terry was gone, was already at the fork of the roads, turning northward, hasting alone on a forty-mile drive over lonely roads and into the very lair of the old mountain-lion himself. Steve whistled softly.

"I wish she had invited me to go along," he grunted.

But, instead she had commissioned him otherwise. So, though his eyes were regretful he rode on to the store. A backward glance showed him a diminishing red tail-light disporting itself like some new species of firefly gone quite mad; it was twisting this way and that as the road invited; it fairly emulated the gyrations of a corkscrew what with the added motion necessitated by the deep ruts and chuck-holes over and into which the spinning tires were thudding.

Then the shoulder of a hill, a clump of brush, and Terry and her car were gone from him, swallowed up in the night and silence. He looked at his watch. It was twenty minutes after eight. She had forty miles ahead of her, a return of forty miles.

"It will take her two hours each way," he muttered, "unless she means to pile her car up in a ditch somewhere. Four hours for the trip. That means I won't see her until well after midnight."

And then he grinned a shade sheepishly; Blenham was right. He had thought of those four hours as though they had been four years.

But for her part Terry had no intention of being four hours

driving a round trip of any eighty miles that she knew of; she had never done such a thing before and could see no cause for beginning to-night. True, the roads were none too good at best, downright bad often enough.

Well, that was just the sort of thing she was used to. And to-night there was need for haste. Great haste, thought the girl anxiously, as she remembered the look on her father's face when she and the storekeeper's wife had gotten him into bed.

"I'll have the roads all to myself; that's one good thing."

She settled herself in her seat, preparing for a tense hour. She, too, had marked the time; it had been on the verge of twenty minutes after eight as she left the store. "What right has the only doctor in the country to play chess, anyway? And with old Hell-Fire Packard at that? Two precious old rascals they are, I'll be bound. But a rascal of a doctor is better than no doctor at all, and—Ah, a good, open bit of road!"

The car leaped to fresh speed under her. She glanced at her speedometer; the needle was wavering between twenty-seven and thirty miles. She narrowed her eyes upon the road; it invited; she shoved the throttle on her wheel a little further open; thirty miles, thirty-three, thirty-five—forty, forty-five—there she kept it for a moment—only a moment it seemed to her breathless impatience. For next came a series of curves where her road, rising, went over the first ridge of hills and where on either hand danger lurked.

Beyond the ridge the road straightened out suddenly. Better time now: twenty-five miles, thirty, thirty-five—and then, down in the valley, forty-five miles, fifty, fifty-five—her horn blaring, sending far and wide its defiant, warning echoes, her headlights flashing across trees, fences, patches of brush, and rolling hills—sixty miles.

"If my tires only stick it out—they ought to—this road hasn't a sharp rock on it."

But from sixty miles she must pull down sharply. Far ahead something was across the road; perhaps only a shadow, perhaps a tangible barrier; she didn't know these roads any too well.

She cut off her power, jammed on foot and emergency brakes, and so came to a stop just in time. Here a fence stretched across the road; the tall gate throwing its black shadows on the white moonlit soil was not five feet from her hood when she stopped.

She jumped down, threw the gate wide open, propped it back with a stone knowing full well how the farmers and cattlemen hereabouts builded their gates to shut automatically, drove through in such haste that she grazed the gate itself and so jarred it into closing behind her, and was again glancing from road to speedometer—twenty-five, thirty-five, a turn to negotiate, seen far ahead, dropping back to twenty-five, to twenty. A straight, alluring stretch—twenty-five, thirty-five, forty-five, fifty, fifty-five, sixty, sixty-two, sixty-three—the far rim of the valley, another line of hills black under the stars—fifty again and down to twenty-five, to twenty and horn blowing as she sped into the mouth of the first canon.

And again, when at last she was down in Old Man Packard's valley and within hailing distance of his misshapen monster of a house, she set her horn to blaring like the martial trumpet of an invading army. Cattle and horses along her road awoke from their dozing in the moonlight, perhaps leaped to the conclusion that it was old Hell-Fire himself in their midst, flung their tails aloft and scampered to right and left, and Terry's car stood in front of Packard's door.

Right square in front of the door so that Terry herself could jump from her running-board and so that her front wheels were planted firmly in the old man's choice bed of roses. There were two flat tires, punctured on the way; two ruined, battered rims; her tank still held perhaps a gallon of gasoline. But she had arrived.

Before she leaped out Terry had glanced at her clock; she had made the trip of forty miles in exactly fifty-three minutes. Considering the state of the roads—

"Not bad," admitted Terry.

Then with a final clarion call of her horn she had presented herself at Packard's door. She had got a few of the wildest blown wisps of brown hair back where they belonged before the door opened. She heard hurrying feet and prepared herself by a visible stiffening for the coming of the arch villain himself. There was a sense of disappointment when she saw that it was only the dwarfed henchman come in the master's stead. Guy Little stared at her in pure surprise.

"Terry Temple, ain't it?" gasped the mechanician. "For the love of Pete!"

"I want Doctor Bridges," said Terry quickly. "He's here, isn't he?"

Guy Little instead of making a prompt and direct answer presented as puzzled a countenance as the girl ever saw. He was in slippers and shirtsleeves; he had a large volume which in his hands appeared little less than huge; his hair was as badly tousled as Terry's own; his eyes were frankly bewildered. Terry spoke again impatiently:

"Answer me and don't gawk at me! Is the doctor here?"

"For the love of Pete!" was quite all that Guy Little offered in response.

She sniffed and pushed by him, standing in the hallway and for the first time in her life fairly in the lion's den. She looked about her with lively interest.

"Say," said Little then. "Hold on a minute."

He came quietly close to her, his slipper-feet falling soundlessly.

"Doc Bridges is in there with the ol' man." He jerked his head toward the big library and living-room whose door stood closed in their faces. "They're playin' chess. Unless your sick man's dyin' I guess you better wait until they get through. Even if he is dyin'—"

"I'll do nothing of the kind!" retorted Terry emphatically. "When I've raced all the way from Red Creek, banging my car all up, risking my precious life every jump of the way, doing the trip in fifty-three minutes do you think that—"

"Hey?" cried Guy Little. "How's that? How many minutes? Fifty-three, you said, didn't you? Fifty-three minutes from Red Crick to here? Hey?"

"Is the man crazy?" demanded Terry. "Didn't I say I did? I could have done it in less, too, only with a flat tire and—"

"Hey?" repeated Guy Little, over and over. "You done that? Hey? You say—"

"I say," cut in Terry starting toward the closed door, "that there is a man sick and a doctor wanted."

"Oh, can that part of it!" cried Little, coming after her again in his excitement. "Chuck it! Forget it! The thing is that you made the run from there to here—an' in the night time—an' with tire trouble an'—"

"Doctor Bridges—"

"Is in there. Like I said. Playin' chess with the ol' man. You don't know what that means. I do. Mos' usually, askin' a lady's pardon for the way of sayin' it, it means Hell. Capital H. An' to-night the ol' man has got the door locked an' he's two games behind an' he's sore as a hoot-owl an' he says that anybody as breaks in on his play is— No, I can't say it; not in the presence of a lady. There's times when the ol' man is so awful vi'lent he's purty near vile about it. Get me?"

"Guy Little, you just stand aside!" Terry's eyes blazed into his as she threw out a hand to thrust his back. "I came for the doctor and I'm going to get him."

Guy Little merely shook his head.

"You don't know the ol' man," he said quietly. "An' I do. I'm the only man, woman or child livin' as does know him. You stan' aside."

He stepped quickly by her and rapped at the door. When only silence greeted him he rapped again. Now suddenly, explosively, came Old Man Packard's voice, fairly quivering with rage as the old man shouted:

"If that's you, Guy Little, I'll beat your head off'n your fool body! Get out an' go away an' go fast!"

"It's important, your majesty," returned Guy Little's voice imperturbably.

He rubbed one slippered toe against his calf and winked at Terry, looking vastly innocent and boyish.

"I'm pullin' for you," he whispered. "There's jus' one way to do it." Aloud he repeated. "It's important, your majesty. An' there's a lady here."

"Lady?" shouted the old man, his voice fairly breaking with the emotion that went into it. "Lady? In my house? What do you mean?" Then, without waiting for an answer, "I don't care who she is or what she is or what the two of you want. Get out! This fool pill-roller in here thinks he can beat me playin' chess; you're in league with him to distract me, you traitor!"

Guy Little smiled broadly and winked again.

"Ain't he got the manner of a dook?" he whispered admiringly. And to his employer, "Say, Packard, it's the little Temple girl. Terry Temple, you know. An'—"

Even Terry started and drew back a quick step from the closed door. She did not know that a man's voice could pierce to one's soul like that.

"An'," went on Guy Little hurriedly, knowing that he must rush his words now if he got them out at all, "she's jus' drove all the way from Red Crick—in a Boyd-Merrill, Twin Eight car—had tire trouble on the road—an' done the trip in fifty-three minutes!"

He got it all out. A deep silence shut down after his words. A silence during which a man's eyes might have opened and stared, during which a man's mouth too might have opened and closed wordlessly, during which a man's brain might estimate what this meant, to drive forty miles in fifty-three minutes over such roads as lay between the Packard ranch and Red Creek.

"It's a lie!" shouted Packard. "She couldn't do it."

"I want Doctor Bridges—"

"Sh!" Guy Little cut her short. "I got the ol' boy on the run. Leave it to me." And aloud once more: "She done it. She can prove it. An'—"

There came a snort of fury from the locked room followed by the noise of a chess-board and set of men hurled across the room and by an old man's voice shouting fiercely:

"It's a cursed frame-up. Bridges, you're a scoundrel and I can beat you any three games out of five and I'll bet you ten thousan' dollars on it, any time! An' as for that thief of a Temple's squidge-faced girl—Come in. Damn it all, come in and be done with it!"

And as he unlocked the door with a hand that shook and flung it wide open he and Terry Temple confronted each other for the first time.

CHAPTER XX

A GATE AND A RECORD SMASHED

The man never yet lived and knew old man Packard who would have suggested that he was not a good and thorough-going hater. His enemy and all of his enemy's household, wife and child, maid-servant and man-servant were all as the spawn of Satan.

Now he stood back, his face flushed, his two hands on his hips, his beard thrust forward belligerently and fairly seeming to bristle. Terry Temple, her heart beating like mad all of a sudden and for no reason which she would admit to herself, lifted her head and stepped across the threshold defiantly. For a very tense moment the two of them, old man and young girl, stared at each other.

Doctor Bridges still sat at the chess-table, his mouth dropping open, his expression one of pure consternation; Guy Little stood in the doorway just behind Terry, rubbing a slippered toe against his leg and watching interestedly.

"So you're Temple's girl, are you?" snorted the old man. "Well, I might have guessed it!"

And the manner of the statement, rather than the words themselves, was very uncomplimentary to Miss Teresa

Arriega Temple.

And, as a mere matter of fact—and old man Packard knew it well enough down in his soul—he would have guessed nothing of the sort. So long had he held her in withering contempt, just because of her relationship to her father, so long had he invested her with all thinkably distasteful attributes, so long had he in his out-of-hand way named her squidge-nosed, putty-faced, pig-eyed, and so on, that in due course he had really formed his own image of her.

And now, suddenly confronted by the most amazingly pretty girl he had ever seen, he managed to snort that she was just what he knew she was—and in the snorting no one knew better than old man Packard that, as he could have put it himself, "He lied like a horse-thief!"

Terry had seen him once when she was a very little girl. He had been pointed out to her by one of her father's cowboys who, for reasons of his own, heartily hated and a little feared the old man. Since then the girl's lively imagination had created a most unseemly brute out of the enemy of her house, a beetle-browed, ugly-mouthed, facially-hideous being little short of a monstrosity.

And now Terry's fine feminine perception begrudgingly was forced to set about constructing a new picture. The old man, black-hearted villain that he was, was the most upstanding, heroic figure of a man that she had ever seen.

Beside him Doctor Bridges was a spectacle of physical degeneracy while Guy Little became a grotesque dwarf. The grandfather was much like the grandson, and—though she vowed to like him the less for it—was in his statuesque, leonine way quite the handsomest man she had ever looked on.

Perhaps it was at just the same instant that each realized that rather too great an interest had been permitted to go into a long, searching look. For Terry suddenly affected a look of supreme contempt while the old man jerked his eyes away, transferring his regard to the serene Guy Little.

"You said, Guy Little—"

"Yes, sir, I said it!" Guy Little nodded vigorously. "Them forty miles in fifty-three minutes. In the dark. An' with tire trouble. It's a record. The best you ever done it in was fifty-seven minutes. She beat you four minutes. Her!"

He indicated Terry.

"Doctor Bridges—" began Terry.

"It's a lie!" cried the old man, smashing the table top with a clenched fist. "I don't care who says it; she couldn't do it! No girl could; no Temple could. It ain't so!"

"Call me a liar?" cried Terry, a sudden flaming, surging, hot current in her cheeks, her eyes blazing. "You are a horrid old man. I always knew you were a horrid old man and you are a lot horrider than I thought you were. And—you just call me a liar again, Hell-Fire Packard, and I'll slap your face for you!"

For a moment, gripped by his ever-ready rage, the old man stood towering over her, looking down with blazing eyes into eyes which blazed back, a little tremor visibly shaking him as though he were tempted almost beyond resistance to lay his hands on her and punish her impudence. A bright, almost eager, fearlessness shone in her eyes.

"I dare you," said Terry. "Old man that you are, I'll slap you so that you'd know who it is you're insulting. Pirate!" she flung at him. "And land-hog—Oh!

"Doctor Bridges, you are to come with me right now." She had flung about giving her shoulder to Packard's inspection. "We must hurry back to Red Creek."

"Say, Packard," chimed in Guy Little. "Her car's all shot to pieces. An' her gas is all gone. An' her ol' man is awful sick in Red Creek an' needin' a doc in a hurry—or not any. You understan'—"

"What's it got to do with me?" boomed Hell-Fire Packard. "What do I care whether her old thief of a father dies to-night or next week? What do I—"

"Aw, rats," grunted Guy Little. "What's eatin' you, Packard? Listen to me: She says how she done it in fifty-three minutes an' you can't do it any better'n fifty-seven; how you ain't no dead-game sport noways; how she's short of change but would bet a man fifty dollars you couldn't an' wouldn't."

"She said them things?" roared the old man.

"I—" began Terry.

"She did!" answered Guy Little hastily and loudly. "She did!"

"Bridges," snapped old Packard, "grab your hat an' black poison bag an' be ready in two minutes." Packard was on his way to the door. "Guy Little, you get my car at the front door—quick! An' as for you—" He was at the door and half turned to stare angrily into Terry's eyes—"You can do what you please. I'm goin' to take the only pill-slinger in the country to the worst ol' thief I ever heard a man tell about."

"I'm going back with you," said Terry briefly.

Old man Packard shrugged. Then he laughed.

"If you ain't scared," he grunted, "to ride alongside a man as swears, so help him God, in spite of smash-bang-an'-be-damn', is goin' to make that little run back to Red Creek—in less'n fifty minutes!"

"Mind you," said old man Packard at the front door, his eye stony as it marked how Terry's car stood among his choice roses, "I ain't doin' this because I got any use for a Temple, he or she. Especially she. You jus' get that in your head, young lady. An' before we start let me tell you one more thing: You keep your two han's off'n my gran'son!"

"What!" gasped Terry.

"I said it," he fairly snorted. "Come on there, Guy Little, with that car. Ready there, Bridges, you ol' fool? Pile in."

He took his seat at the wheel, his old black hat pushed far back on his head, his eye already on the clock in the dash. Terry slipped ahead of Doctor Bridges and took her seat at the old man's side.

"You said—just what?" she demanded icily.

"I said," he cried savagely, "as I know how you been chasin' my fool of a gran'son Stephen, an' as how you got to stop it. I won't have you makin' a bigger fool out'n him than he already is."

Terry sat rigid, speechless, grown suddenly cold. For once in her life no ready answer sprang to her lips.

Then Hell-Fire Packard had started his engine, sounded his horn, and they were on their way. And Terry, because no words would come, put her head back and laughed in a way that, as she knew perfectly well, would madden him.

The drive from Hell-Fire Packard's front door to the store in Red Creek was made in some few negligible seconds over forty-eight minutes. The three occupants of the car reached town alive. Never in her life after that night would Terry Temple doubt that there was a Providence which at critical times took into its hands the destinies of men.

There had been never a word spoken until they had come to the gate which had closed behind Terry on the way out. Old man Packard had looked at speedometer, clock and obstruction. Terry had seen his hands tighten on his wheel.

"Set tight an' hang on," he had commanded sharply.

The big front tires and bumper struck the gate; there was a wild flying of splinters and at sixty miles an hour they went through and on to Red Creek.

"The old devil!" whispered Terry within herself. "The old devil!"

CHAPTER XXI

PACKARD WRATH AND TEMPLE RAGE

No far-sighted, inspired prophet's services were needed to predict a rather stormy scene upon the arrival of old Hell-Fire Packard and Miss Terry Temple at the place of the storekeeper of Red Creek. It was to be expected that Steve Packard would be on hand; that he would be impatiently awaiting the drum of a racing motor; that he would be on the sidewalk to greet Temple's daughter.

"Terry!" he called. "So soon?"

He couldn't have made a worse beginning had he pondered the matter long and diabolically. Blenham had been right and Steve had had ample time to admit the fact utterly and completely; now there was a ringing note in his voice, the effect of which, falling upon his grandfather's ears, might be likened with no great stretch of imagination to that of a spark in a keg of gunpowder.

The old man's brakes, applied emphatically, brought his car to a standstill.

"Look at that clock!" was his first remark, at once apprising Steve of his relative's presence and hinting, by means of its no uncertain tone, at an unpleasant situation on hand or about to burst upon them. "Made it in fifty-three minutes, did you? Well, I done it in less'n forty-nine! What have you got to say about that?"

But Terry ignored him and jumped down, her hand impulsively laid on Steve's arm. Thus she, in her turn, may be said to have added another spark to young Packard's in the powder keg.

"How's dad?" she asked quickly.

Steve patted the hand on his arm and either Terry did not notice the act or did not mind. Old man Packard both noted and minded. His grunt was to be heard above Doctor Bridges's devout "Thank God, we're here!" as the physician stepped stiffly to the sidewalk.

"Better," said Steve. "I think he's going to be all right after all. I hope so. He—"

"Blenham?" she asked insistently. "He didn't put one over on you? The mortgage—"

Steve tapped his breast pocket.

"The papers have been signed; we got a notary; everything is shipshape. Go in; I'll tell you all about it later."

He turned toward the car and the stiffened figure of the man gripping the wheel with tense, hard hands.

"Grandy—"

"Grandy, your foot!" boomed old Packard suddenly, one hand jerked away to be clenched into a lifted fist. "An' *Terry*! My God!"

"What do you mean?" asked Steve. "I don't understand."

"I mean," shouted Packard senior, his voice shaking with emotion, "that no mouth in the world is big enough to hold them two words the same night! If you want to chum with any Temple livin', he-Temple or she-Temple, if, sir, you intend to go 'round slobberin' over the low-down enemies of your own father an' father's father, why, sir, then I'm Mr. Packard to you and the likes of you!"

Still was Steve mystified.

"I thought," he muttered, "that since you two came together, since you yourself have driven her in—"

"If I, sir," thundered his grandfather, "have chosen to bring that petticoated wildcat there an' that ol' pill-slinger from my place to Red Creek in a shake less'n forty-nine minutes—jus' to show her that anything on God's earth done by a Temple can be better done by a Packard—you got to go to thinkin' things, have you? Why, sir, so help me, sir, I've a notion to jump down right now an' give you the horsewhippin' of your life!"

Steve, in spite of himself, chuckled. Terry, reassured about her father, giggled. Both sounds were audible; the two, mingled, were entirely too much to be borne.

"You—you disgrace to an honorable name," the old man called bitterly and wrathfully. "You—"

He broke off, hesitated, glared from Steve at the car's side to Terry already on the steps of the store, and concluded something more quietly though not a whit less furiously for all that: "You speak of papers signed. You don't mean you're actually havin' any kind of business dealin's, frien'ly dealin's, with the Temples?"

"Blenham brought word you were foreclosing on Temple; he had some sort of a crooked scheme to cheat Temple out of his land. I have just framed a deal whereby I put up the money to pay you your mortgage and—"

"You? *You*, Stephen Packard?"

"Yes," said Steve, wondering whether the old man were the more moved because of the shock of finding his nephew able to pay off so large a sum or because of the "frien'ly dealin's with the Temples."

There was a brief silence. Doctor Bridges mounted the steps; he and Terry were going in. Then again Hell-Fire Packard's voice burst out violently and Terry stopped short, her hands going suddenly to her breast. Her face, could they have noted in the pale light, was flaming scarlet.

"That hussy, that jade, that Jezebel!" came the ringing denunciation. "The tricky, shameless, penurious, graspin' unprincipled little she-devil! She's after you, my boy, after you hard. An', you poor miserable blind worm of a fool, you ain't got the sense to see it! Everybody knows it; the whole country's talkin' about it; how Temple's baitin' his trap with her an' she's baitin' her trap with herself an'—"

"Grandfather!" cried Steve, his own face flushing under the scathing torrent. "You don't know what you are saying!"

"I know what he's saying."

Terry, her hands still tight pressed to her breast, came slowly down the steps. Though but a moment had passed her face was now dead white in the moonlight.

"You are saying," and her eyes shone straight up into the old man's, "that I am setting a trap for your grandson? That I,

Teresa Arriega Temple, would for an instant consider a Packard, the son and the grandson of a Packard, as worthy of shining my boots for me? Why, I spit upon the two of you!"

She whirled and was gone into the house. Steve instead of watching her going kept his eyes hard upon his grandfather's face. Now that the door closed he said quietly:

"Grandfather, we have seen rather little, of each other. I think we had better see even less from now on. You have insulted that girl in a way that makes me want to climb into your car and drag you down—and beat you half to death!"

His restraint was melting under the fire of his passion; his voice grew less quiet and began to tremble.

"I am going to make that girl the next Mrs. Packard or know the reason why!"

"Defy me, do you? Defy me an' go an' run with a pack of thieves an'—"

"That's enough!" shouted Steve. "I am going right straight and ask her—"

"Ask her an' hell swallow you!" came the vociferous permission from the infuriated old man. "But remember one thing: Blenham has slipped up to-night, maybe, an' let you an' her an' her lyin', thievin', scoundrelly father steal a march on me. But it's the last one; mark that! Blenham gets his orders straight from me to-night; he goes after you to break you, smash you, literally pull you to pieces root an' branch—an' with me an' Blenham workin' on the job night an' day, stoppin' at nothin'. Hear me? I mean it!" His two fists were now lifted high above his head. "Stoppin' at nothin' I'll step on you an' your Temple frien's like you was a nest of caterpillars. You hear me, Stephen!"

But Stephen, his lips tight pressed as he fought with himself to keep his hands off his own father's father, turned and went the way Terry had gone.

"You hear me, Stephen. There's nothin' I'll stop at to smash you!"

So his grandfather's voice followed him mightily. But young Packard had already set his thought upon another matter. Before him in the tiny living-room of the ramshackle store building a kerosene lamp was burning palely and lying upon an old sofa, face down, shaken with sobs was Terry.

"Terry!" he called softly. "Your father isn't—"

He thought that she had not heard. He came closer and laid his hand gently—there was a deep tenderness even in the action—upon her shoulder. But Terry had heard and now flung his hand violently aside and sprang to her feet, her eyes blazing angrily into his.

"My father is asleep. Doctor Bridges rather thinks there is nothing very much the matter with him," she remarked crisply. "I am sorry I troubled you in any way, Mr. Packard. You say you arranged matters with dad? Well, I want you to tear up the papers; I'll see that your money is returned to you."

"Terry!" he muttered.

Then she flared out hotly, her two small hands clenched at her sides, her chin lifted, her voice a new voice in his ears, bitter and hostile.

"Don't you Terry me, Steve Packard! Now or ever again. I

am sorry that I ever saw you; I am ashamed that I ever spoke to you. I had rather be dead or—yes, I'd rather be in Blenham's arms than have you look at me!"

"Good Lord!" ejaculated Steve, utterly at sea. "I don't understand."

"You don't have to," snapped Terry. "All you've got to know is that I won't have anything further in any way whatever to do with you. I won't have you helping us with our mortgage; I won't have you advancing money to us; I won't stand one little minute for any of your—your wretched interference with our affairs! If you think you can—can butt in on our side of any fight in the world—"

She ended abruptly, beginning to flounder, panting so that the swift rise and fall of her breast was an outward token of inward emotion. Steve Packard stared and flushed hotly and began to feel his own anger mount quickly.

"Butt in on your affairs!" he snorted after a fashion more than vaguely reminiscent of his grandfather. "I like that! As if I'd have come a step without your invitation."

And so he blurted out the one thing he should have left unsaid, the thing which already rankled in Terry's proud heart. She had asked him to come; she had in a way suggested a—a sort of partnership.

"Oh! how I hate you!" cried Terry. "You—you Packard!"

"If there's some crime, some string of crimes that I have committed—"

"Will you tear up those papers? I'll get you back your money. Will you tear up those papers?"

"Will you explain what's gone wrong?"

"I will not."

He shrugged exasperatingly.

"I'll keep the papers," he returned stonily. "I put over rather a good deal to-night, come to think of it."

He put on his hat, jamming it down tight, and half turned to go.

"When you want to talk ranch matters over with me—come to my ranch-house, little pardner!"

"Oh!" cried Terry. "Oh!"

CHAPTER XXII

THE HAND OF BLENHAM

"Each man's life is what he shapes it for himself."

"A stupid, bare-faced, platitudinous lie!"

Steve Packard, grown irritable here of late, flung the offending book through an open window and got to his feet.

"A man's life is what the evil little gods of chance make it, curse them. Or what a fool of a girl tangles and twists it into."

He shook himself viciously and went to his door, staring out across the hills vaguely moulded under the stars.

Life was just a very unsatisfactory sort of a proposition. It was a game that wasn't worth the players' serious attention, a game all of chance and not in the least of skill, and not even interesting! So, in the sombre depths of his soul Steve Packard admitted freely. And, until a certain night only some six months ago, he had never divined this great truth.

That night Blenham had sneered, "Stuck on her yourself, are you?" and Steve had recognized a vital fact inelegantly expressed; that night Terry Temple had appeared to him more than just a "good little sport"; that night he had somewhat brusquely considered the sweet femininity of her under her assumed surface of *diablerie* and had found her infinitely desirable; that same night Terry, for no reason in the world that Steve Packard could discover, had suddenly congealed into a thing of ice that had never since thawed save only briefly before burning fits of wrath.

Two hours after he had admitted to himself that he loved her she informed him with all of the emphasis she could summon for the occasion that she hated him. And life hadn't been what he had made it at all.

The papers which Temple had signed were still in existence, safely deposited in a bank in San Juan. Steve had paid off the Temple mortgage to his grandfather; he had paid Temple a thousand dollars in cash; thereby he had acquired a half interest in the Temple ranch. That had all been quite in accordance with Terry's suggestions and entirely satisfactory.

Not being a thief, Steve counted upon relinquishing his right to his half at any time that Temple paid back just what had been advanced. But it became evident very soon that Temple would never pay back anything. Though Doctor Bridges found nothing very much the matter with him, nevertheless Temple died less than two weeks later.

During those two weeks Steve had not seen Terry. With word of the girl's bereavement, however, he had gone immediately to her. She looked at him curiously, saying quietly that the boys were doing all that was necessary and had asked him to go.

Then, after another two weeks, he had ridden again to the Temple ranch. He found it deserted, doors and windows shut, dead leaves thick in the path. His heart sank and thereafter knocked hard at his ribs; Terry was gone and had said nothing to him. He turned and went home, bitter and angry and hurt.

Where had she gone? He didn't know; he told himself he didn't care; certainly he would bite his tongue out before he would ask any of her friends. But he knew within himself that he did care as he had cared about nothing else in the world; and he asked himself a thousand times:

"Where has Terry gone?"

For the world was not right without her; the sunlight was thin; the season of bursting buds was but a pale, lack-lustre imitation of spring. And as the long, hot days dragged by and the verdure died on hill and plain and dusty moun-tainside, he asked himself "When will she come back to us?"

Long after every one else had heard and forgotten the story, or at least had given over all thinking upon it, Steve heard how Terry had drawn against the last of the inconsiderable legacy left her long ago by her Spanish mother, and had gone to San Juan.

She had friends there; the banker's wife, Mrs. Engle and her fluffy-haired daughter, Florrie, had opened their arms to her and made her tarry with them until the family made their annual trip East. Then Terry had gone with them.

And never a word to Steve Packard. He cursed himself, tried to curse her, and found that he couldn't quite make a go of it, and settled down to good, hard work and the job of forgetting what a pair of gray eyes looked like and how two certain red lips smiled and the tinkly notes of a laughing voice.

In the good, hard work of stock ranching he succeeded more than well; in the other task he set himself he failed utterly. Never, when alone out on the range a shadow fell across, did he fail to look up quickly with his lips half forming to the word, "Terry!" And, after all this time, still no word from her, no word of her.

Eight thousand dollars he had paid to Temple. The remaining two thousand of his father's heritage he had turned over promptly to his grandfather to apply on his own indebtedness. He had consulted with Bill Royce and Barbee and had cut down his crew of men, thereby curtailing expenses.

He had sold a few head of beef cattle and banked the money for the men's wages and current expenses. By the same means he had managed to keep abreast of his interest payments to old man Packard and had even paid off a little more of the principal. Then, catching the market right "going and coming," he had bought a lot of young cattle from an overstocked ranch adjoining, and had made a second profitable sale a month later.

Finally, to indicate that he was still in the game and playing it to win, consequently overlooking never a bet, he had cashed in pretty fortunately on a section of his timber-land.

The Rollston mills were just opening upon the other side of the mountains; he showed the firm's buyer a stretch of his big timber and closed the deal to their common satisfaction. And with every deal of this sort old man Packard felt his grip being pried loose from Ranch Number Ten.

From the beginning Steve had been puzzled to know what to do with the Temple outfit. Terry had paid off the men and had let them go; the stock on the place she had left, and without a word, to Steve's care. Since the place was well stocked, chiefly with young cattle, there was enough here to demand the attention which so busy a man as Steve Packard could not give.

He talked matters over with Bill Royce and in the end sent both Bill and Barbee to the Temple place, riding over once or twice a week himself to see how matters went.

And so the months dragged by. Twice, swearing to himself that he was doing so only because the management of the business made it absolutely necessary, Steve wrote to Terry. He got no answer. He did not even know if she had received his notes. The first he had signed, by the way, "Yours very truly, Steve." The second ended "Respectfully, S. Packard."

"Terry's havin' the time of her life," Bill Royce startled him by announcing one day out of a clear sky.

"How do you know?" asked Steve sharply.

"Oh, she writes letters to her frien's," said Royce. "One of the boys brought word from the Norton place. Terry wrote her an' wrote some folks in Red Creek an' wrote the Lanes an'—"

"Appears to be quite a letter-writer," remarked Steve stiffly. "And she's having the time of her life, is she?"

"Sure," said Royce innocently. "Why not? The boys are bettin' she's dead gone on some young down-East jasper an' that maybe she'll be married in no time. What do you think, huh, Steve?"

"Where is she?" demanded Steve, very brusque about it.

"Blessed if I know," admitted Royce. "Chicago, I think. Or New York. Or Pennsylvany. One of them towns. Shucks.

She'd ought to come on home where she belongs."

"Oh, I don't know," said Steve.

But in Royce's ears the voice didn't ring quite true. It was meant to be careless in the extreme and—no, it didn't ring quite true.

Hot, cloudless skies as the season dragged on, dry, burning fields under a blazing sun, the cattle seeking shade wherever it was to be had, crowding at the water-holes, browsing early and late and frequenting the cooler canons during the heat of the days. And nights of stars and a vast silence and emptiness.

A girl had come, had for a little posed laughing outlined against the window of a man's soul, had flashed her unforgettable gray eyes at him and had gone. And so, and just because of her, the blistering hills seemed but ugly, lonely miles, the nights under a full moon were just the more silent and empty.

But Steve Packard held on, grown grim and determined. He had entered the game, lightly enough he had demanded his stack of chips, now he would stay for the show-down. Either he would clear his ranch of its mortgage and thus make clear to his meddlesome old grandparent that he was a man grown and no mere boy to be disciplined and badgered willy-nilly, or else his meddlesome old grandparent would in truth "smash" him.

In either case there would be the end soon. For, win or lose, Steve, tired of the game, would draw out and set his back to Ranch Number Ten and the country about it and go back to the old rudderless life of vagabondage. Just because a girl had come, had tarried, and then had gone.

So, though the game had long ago lost its zest, Steve Packard like any other thoroughbred played on for a finish. Now and then, but seldom, he saw Blenham. Often, in little, annoying, mean ways Blenham made himself felt. Early in the season Steve's riders had found three of his steers dead on the outskirts of the range; a rifle bullet had done for each one of them.

Since old man Packard had promised to stop at nothing, since Blenham was full of venom, Steve never for a moment doubted whose hand had fired the three shots. But he merely called his cowboys together, told them what had happened, ordered them to keep their eyes open and their guns oiled, and hoped and longed for the time when he himself could come upon Blenham busied with some act like this.

There were other episodes which he attributed to Blenham though he must admit in each case that anything in the vaguest way approaching a proof was lacking. Just before he closed the deal with the lumber company that had taken over his timber tract a forest fire had broken out. Luck and a fortuitous shifting of the wind had saved him from a heavy loss.

Incidents, these and others of their kind, to fill Steve Packard with rage; but Blenham's supreme blows— Blenham's and old man Packard's—were reserved for late in the dry season when they fell hardest.

A growing shortage of feed and the necessity for cash for the forthcoming substantial sum to be paid on the mortgage held by his grandfather, combined with the fact that his lean acres were overstocked, drove Steve in search of a market late in the summer. Bill Royce shook his head and raised his objections.

"Everybody else is doin' the same thing an' at the same time," he said lugubriously. "Which'll mean the market all glutted up so's you won't get no kind of figger. If you could only hold on till next spring."

But Steve merely said—

"Oh, well, Bill, it's all in a lifetime," and shaped his plans for a sale.

And within ten days there came an offer which startled him. It was from the big buyers, Doan, Rockwell, and Haight, who, their communication said, knew his line of stock thoroughly and were prepared to pay the top prices for all he had. He estimated swiftly and sent a man hurrying into town with a message to go by wire; he would round up between a hundred and fifty and two hundred head and would have them in San Juan when desired.

"Old Doan's a sport and a wise boy, both," announced Steve triumphantly when he made the news known to Bill Royce. "He knows high-grade stuff and he's willing to pay the price." He narrowed his eyes speculatively. "We'll scare up close to two hundred head, William. And they'll bring us just about twenty thousand. Maybe a thousand or so above that. And, Bill, did you ever know the time when twenty thousand dollars would look more like twenty thousand full moons just showing up over the skyline?"

Bill's grin reflected Steve's lively satisfaction. Now there would be the money for old Hell-Fire Packard's next payment, there would be a long respite from him, there would be ample feed for the rest of the cattle. Steve might even spend a part of the money for a herd of calves to be had dirt-cheap just now from the Biddle Morris dairy outfit, down near San Juan.

The prospect was exceedingly bright; just as though in truth a string of full moons were shining down upon them. And still there was the shadow, even at this time, the shadow cast by Terry's absence and silence. If she were only here to rejoice with them.

Steve snorted his disgust with himself, got on a horse and went streaking across the fields, riding hard as was a habit here of late, yelling an order to Barbee as he went. Barbee's innocent blue eyes followed him thoughtfully: then Barbee shrugged and spat and thereafter called to his men to "get busy." The round-up began immediately.

Then came a handful of long, hot, feverishly busy days. Strayed steers carrying the Number Ten brand were hazed back to the big fenced-in meadows from the mountain slopes, were counted and held, in an ever-swelling herd. There was little rest for the men, who, shifted from one sweating horse to another, rode late and early.

Word came from Doan setting the date for the delivery in San Juan. Steve wired his satisfaction with the arrangement, undertaking to have the cattle in the stock pens just out of the town two or three days before Doan's coming. And no one knew better than did Steve Packard the true size of the job he had on his hands at this time of year and with a herd of close to two hundred wild steers.

The drive began one morning in the dark long before the dawn. Steve estimated that he could make the Rio Frio the first night and had arranged beforehand with the Talbot boys for the night's pasturage. The second day would find them on the edge of the bad lands; his wagons hauling baled hay were to push on ahead and be waiting at the only sufficient water-holes to be found within a number of miles. San Juan in four days was the schedule.

"We'll lose weight all along the road," he conceded. "But it can't be helped. And a couple of day's rest and lots of feed and water in San Juan before Doan shows up will put back a part of the lost weight."

He had made allowances for a hard drive. Nevertheless the actuality was a sterner matter than he had foreseen. All along the way the feed was scant. Water was low in the holes, Rio Frio for the first time in years was a mere series of shallow pools. The blazing heat was such that men and horses and steers all suffered terribly.

At the end of the second day he ordered a full dozen of the less hardy of his beasts cut out from the herd and turned into a neighboring range; it was questionable if they would have been able to drag on the two remaining days and even had they done so they would have brought no top price from the buyer.

The drive was made on schedule time. Circumstances not only permitted but insisted. There were no places for loitering, there were only the major water-holes upon which Steve had counted, the distances between them regulating each day's progress. And so the stock was in San Juan a full two days before the time for Doan's coming.

For Steve the two days dragged heavily. He camped with his herd on the edge of the settlement, allowing the boys to disport themselves as they saw fit a large part of the time, himself having little desire for the bad whiskey and crooked gaming of La Casa Blanca.

Tuesday morning Doan was to arrive. Steve met the stage and one glance showed him that Doan was not on it. He asked the driver if he knew anything of Doan and the man shook his head. Steve supposed that he was coming up from the railroad by auto and so idled about the town all forenoon, waiting.

By midday, when Doan still failed to put in an appearance, Steve had grown impatient. By the middle of the afternoon his impatience gave place to anger. He had kept his appointment bringing his herds over a hard trail, and Doan with nothing to do but travel luxuriously, had failed him.

But it was not until the stage came in Wednesday morning and again brought no Doan and no word of Doan that Steve telephoned a message to the nearest Western Union office at Bidwell demanding to know what the trouble was. Not only was he on heavy expenses; his mood never had been one to take kindly to the long waiting game. And yet he was forced to wait all that day and all the next day with no word from Doan.

He telegraphed again Wednesday night, a third time Thursday morning. No answers came. But a little before noon, Thursday, Doan came. Came by automobile from the railroad, a man with him. Steve saw them as they drove into town; he noted Doan's thin face and his tall form in the gray linen duster; then he marked the man with him. The man was Blenham.

Steve, raw-nerved through these long hours of inaction and uncertainty, pushed straightway to Doan bent upon demanding an explanation. He got an inkling of one from an unexpected quarter, Blenham's lips.

"We sure appreciate this, Mr. Doan," Blenham said, getting down and offering his hand to the cattle-buyer. "Count on me an' ol' man Packard doin' you a favor any time. So long."

And casting to Steve a look of blended triumph and venom he hurried down to the stable and his horse.

"Mr. Doan," said Steve bluntly, "what in hell's name do you mean by treating me this way?"

Doan turned his thin impassive face with the hawk-eyes toward young Packard.

"Who do you happen to be?" he asked coolly.

"I'm Steve Packard from Ranch Number Ten. And I've got a herd of steers out here that's been waiting for you some time now."

"Oh, yes," said Doan, still very cool. "Got my wire, didn't you, saying that I was unavoidably detained?"

"I did not!" snapped Steve. "Detained by what? Blenham?"

"Strange," murmured Doan.

He got down from his car and stretched his long legs.

"I've had a new secretary, Mr. Packard. I found out that he drank. He has been discharged. Hem. Let me see: you've got about fifty steers, haven't you?"

"I've got a hundred and eighty-six," Steve said sharply, staring at Doan's inscrutable face and wondering just what was up.

"A hundred and eighty-six!" Doan shook his head. "I couldn't take that many on just now; I've made other plans. Unless, of course, you are in a position to tempt me to buy by making me a very attractive figure!"

Steve came a sudden step nearer, his eyes blazing, his two fists clenched.

"What's this game of yours?" he demanded. "Out with it. What are you up to? You wired me an offer of ten to twelve cents, twelve and a half for the fancy."

"What!" cried Doan. "Why, my dear fellow, you must have lost your senses! With the market the way it is now I don't have to pay more than seven and eight cents."

Steve waited for no more. His days of waiting were past. He drew back, swung from the shoulder and struck with all of his might. His fist against Doan's chin hurled the lean body of the cattle-buyer half across the street.

"Barbee," said Steve quietly, "round up the boys. We start our herd back in ten minutes."

And Barbee, taking stock of Steve's white face, went hastily on his errand.

CHAPTER XXIII

STEVE RIDES BY THE TEMPLE PLACE

"Dear me, Mr. Man! How savage you do look!"

Steve started and whirled. No; this time he was not dreaming. It was Terry.

Terry laughed lightly, deliciously. She had grown prettier. She had learned a new way to smile. No, it was just the old way, after all. But she had discovered a new way to do her hair, an amazingly charming way. Her lips were redder than ever before; her eyes were gayer and grayer and softer and sweeter. Her voice tinkled with new, thrilling music. She was just exactly perfect in Steve Packard's eyes.

"You're super," said Steve. "You're superlative. You haven't done a thing all these long, weary months except grow more devilishly attractive."

"Are you as savage as you looked?" she asked swiftly.

For a brief instant he turned his eyes away from her and gazed after a herd that was moving slowly toward the north, Barbee and the other boys heading again toward the home range. But, no matter what rage and sullen chagrin lay in his heart, his eyes, returning to Terry, showed that already her coming had worked its change. He appeared almost content.

"Are you going to shake hands?" he asked.

"Shall I?" she asked. "We are to be good friends after all?"

"Or, are you going to kiss me?"

Terry arched her brows at him. But there was a live fire in her eyes and a crimsoning tide under her lovely skin.

"Smarty!" cried the old Terry. "Just try getting fresh with me and you'll get your face slapped!"

Whereupon Steve's laughter boomed out joyously.

"It's Terry come home again!" he announced to the open meadow about them. "Terry herself."

Was it Terry herself? She seemed strangely embarrassed all of a sudden. Just why? Terry didn't know.

"We are going out in my car," she said hurriedly. It seemed that she must hasten to make some safe remark each time that his eyes, busied with her, rested upon her eyes. "We'll be at the ranch long before you get your cows home. You may come to see me—if you please to."

"Who is we?" he asked.

"Oh," said Terry, "that means Mrs. Randall who is going to be cook and chaperon."

San Juan dozed in the late afternoon heat. The corrals were between them and the quiet street. He threw out his arms, caught Terry in them and kissed her. And Terry, whipping back, slapped his face.

"You—you—" she panted, her face scarlet.

He touched tenderly with his finger-tips the place where her hand had struck him.

"I'll be over to call on you and Mrs. Randall," he said. "Real soon."

Now as Steve Packard rode slowly after his cowboys and a diminishing herd, the dust-filled air, dry and hot as it was, seemed sweet and caressing to his temples, his eyes mused happily. Blenham had just worsted him, Blenham had tricked him, had put him to the heavy expense of the long drive, had knocked his steers up for him, had laughed at him.

Very well; tally for Blenham. A matter to be considered in due time. A body blow, perhaps, but then what in God's good world is a strong body for if not to buffet and be buffeted? He and Blenham would come to grips again, soon or late, and in some way still hidden by the future matters would finally adjust themselves.

All considerations with which only some dim future was concerned. Just now, in the living, breathing, quivering present there was room for but the one thought: Terry had come back to him.

Yes. Terry had come back to him. And he had kissed her. And she had slapped him. He smiled and again his finger-tips went their way tenderly to his cheek. He had kissed her because he loved her, meaning her no harm, offering her no insult. She had slapped him because she was Terry, and because she couldn't very well help it. Not because she did not love him!

Somewhere in the world, off in some misty distance, there was a man named Blenham, a trickery, treacherous, cruel hound of a man. He would require attention presently. Just now—

"You've come back to me!" whispered Steve Packard.

And he sighed and shook himself and wished longingly that the return drive were over and that he had a bath and a shave and were just calling at the Temple ranch.

Though presently he overhauled his men Steve rode all that day pretty well apart, maintaining a thoughtful silence which Barbee and the others supposed had to do solely with the failure of his plans for a good market. His men knew that he had banked pretty heavily on this deal; and that now again he would be confronted by the old problem of finding sufficient feed to pull his herds through.

Hay was scarce and high and would need to be hauled far, making its final cost virtually prohibitive. The herders, grumbling among themselves, were for the most part of the opinion that he should have accepted his defeat at Blenham's hands and sold to Doan at a sacrifice figure.

That night they camped at the Bitter Springs, making but a brief stop to water and feed and rest the road-weary cattle. Then in the night and moving slowly they pushed on planning to get to the next water-holes before the heat of another day. And now Steve, giving his orders to Barbee, left them and struck out ahead.

There was small need of accommodating his impatience to the sluggish progress of the leg-dragging brutes and there were matters to be arranged. Further, it was his intention to have a talk with Terry Temple just as soon as might be.

That day Terry's automobile with shrieking horn swept on by him. He caught a glimpse of two veils, a brown and a black; the car's top was up. Terry appeared not to see him.

"She hasn't lost a speck of her impudence!"

He frowned after her departing car, praying in his heart for a puncture or a stalled engine. She deserved as much for the way in which she tooted her infernal horn. But his prayer went unanswered and his displeasure vanished presently as he pushed on steadily in her wake, eager to come to the end of his ride.

But he must never entirely forget the panting herd straggling on far behind him, choking and coughing in its own dust. He must arrange somewhere, somehow for pasturage. So he made a detour and looked in on Brocky Lane first, then on Rod Norton. Both old friends were glad to see him and gave him hard brown hands in grips that were good to feel.

But they merely shook their heads when he mentioned his errand. Lane had sold a few head last week; Norton was afraid that he would have to make a sacrifice sale himself. They would do anything that they could but it was only too clear that they could not give him that which they themselves did not have and could not get.

"Old man Packard," offered Norton bluntly, "is the only man I can think of who has pasture to rent. Drop Off Valley, just up in the mountains back of your place."

Steve laughed shortly and swung up into his saddle.

"So long, Nort," he said colorlessly "The old man would burn his grass off before he'd let me have it."

And he rode on, two problems in his mind, both growing more difficult as he drew nearer the home ranch. Problem One: Just what was Terry going to say? Problem Two: How was he going to pull his stock through?

As though he did not already have enough on his hands, Bill Royce greeted him at the home ranch-house with the significant word—

"Trouble!"

"I know it," grunted Packard, swinging down stiffly from his saddle. "What kind this time, Bill?"

"Blenham-brand, I'd reckon," said Bill angrily. Steve noted that both of the old hand's cheeks were flushed hotly. "Barbee telephoned in about four hours ago. Seven steers dead, some more sick. An'," the explanation coming quickly, "Barbee's got the hunch Blenham had rode on ahead an' had poisoned the water-holes an'—"

"Damn him!" cried Steve, a sudden fury seeming to leap out upon him and take him by the throat. "Am I to stand everything from that man and from my old fiend of a grandfather? It's this and that and any other thing they want to turn loose and here I stick like a cursed toad-stool, doing nothing for want of proof! Proof," he snorted disgustedly. "Bill Royce, let's quit waiting for anything but just go get the trouble-seeking outfit!"

"Which sounds good to me," retorted Royce eagerly.

And yet when his rage cooled a bit Steve ground his teeth in his impotence. He must wait until Barbee came with what God chose to leave him of his steers, he must hear the foreman's account and decide whether Blenham were really at the bottom of this or if it were just his way and his men's to blame all things upon Blenham.

"The first thing, Bill," he said when he had turned his tired horse loose in the pasture, "is to decide what we are going to do with what cattle Blenham hasn't poisoned for us. We are fed off pretty short down at this end. I'll ride over to the Temple place and see if we can't arrange with Miss Terry to run a few head there."

"Yes," said Royce dryly. "I'd hurry if I was you, Steve. But, say!" He slapped his leg and jerked up his head. "How about the old Indian Valley, Drop Off Valley, as they call it now?"

"Gone crazy, Bill? When did my grandfather ever show any inclination to help out?"

Then Royce, thoroughly excited, explained. Andy Sprague from beyond the ridge had ridden by only yesterday afternoon. If Royce had only known at that time that Steve was bringing back the cattle from San Juan he would have arranged with Andy. For the man had said that he had just bought Drop Off Valley from old Packard; that he wouldn't want the range this year as he had only recently sold close. He would rent and reasonably.

"There's close on a couple of thousan' acres in there; there's plenty water an' enough good grass to run two or three hundred head easy until your feed comes in again down this way. Nail him, Steve; for the love of Mike, nail Andy Sprague quick before the crooked little cuss finds out jus' how bad you need the pasture an' sticks you accordin'. Go nail him, Steve."

And Steve, seeing hope like a brightening flush of a new day, hurried to the corrals and a fresh horse. He was going straight after Andy Sprague. But—

"Guess I'll ride by the Temple place," he said carelessly.

CHAPTER XXIV

DOWN FROM THE SKY!

Drop Off Valley, its name won to it by its salient feature, was but a long, narrow, and very high plateau in the mountains lying to the east of Ranch Number Ten. It was well watered from springs at the upper end which wandered the entire length of the tract and spilled down the cliffs which cut in abrupt fashion across the lower end, making a natural and fearsome boundary.

From this portion of the "valley" one might kick a stone a sheer and dizzy distance down into the head-waters of Indian Creek, which indicated the beginning of the narrow pass which led through the mountains and to the misty blue hills of Old Mexico.

Here in the abundant, rich, dry feed wandered upward of two hundred head of Ranch Number Ten and Temple Ranch cattle, mingling freely, the herds of one outfit carrying their brands in and out of the herds of the other. A sign and a token that at last a certain dead-line had ceased to exist.

Steve had found Andy Sprague, as crooked a little man as he looked to be according to Bill Royce and others who should know, and had arranged with him for the leasing of the mountain pasturage. Less than a week later Sprague was back saying that he had seen Hell-Fire Packard and that that old mountain-lion had roared at him terribly, had threatened him with utter ruin if ever again he helped out Steve Packard and had bade him carry a message.

"Tell that smart young fool of a gran'son of mine," was the word Sprague gave Steve, "that right now I'm gettin' ready to polish him off final. Tell him what I done to him, blockin' his sale in San Juan, wasn't a patch on what I can do; tell him he'll lose more steers than he ever los' before. Tell him if he don't want to get hisself all mussed up in this deal he'd better come over to my place an' throw up his han's. I'm gettin' mad!"

Before having these words from Andy Sprague's twisted mouth Steve Packard had been puzzled to explain two matters: According to count, on one hand there were too few cattle by perhaps a score while on another hand there were too many by at least a half dozen. And, though Terry Temple was directly concerned, he had said nothing to her.

The first mystifying suggestion that some strange juggling of stock had been going on came to him just before he had driven the hundred and eighty-six steers to San Juan. Rounding up his own stock and cutting it out from Temple stock, he had had the opportunity to check up carefully in Terry's interests.

Calves, cows, steers, and horses, he knew to the head just what Terry numbered them. And in the round-up, going over his figures carefully, he had found that wearing the Temple brand there were six steers more than there should be. A matter of some five or six hundred dollars.

Were it only the financial end of it Steve would have thought little of the matter. But, going over the herd animal by animal, he made a discovery which shocked him. He found six big steers in the lot which wore fairly recently burned Temple brands—crudely scrawled over the brands of the Big Bend ranch, old man Packard's favorite outfit in the north.

It was impossible to know just how long ago a searing-hot iron had altered the range indication of ownership; Steve could merely stare and wonder and finally hazard a guess. Temple had been hard-driven; he had succumbed to temptation and opportunity as he had to whiskey and many other things. Seeing life obliquely he had no doubt told himself that he was squaring accounts. So, in the end, Steve was inclined to believe.

Just what to do he did not know. It seemed best to him to bide his time, to keep his eyes open, to hope for the way out of an embarrassing situation. He would willingly have made restitution himself, to save Terry from knowing and to save her name from the smudge which old man Packard would eagerly put upon it were he offered the opportunity. And right here was the trouble; he did not care to let his grandfather know what had happened.

While striving with this matter the other was brought to his attention. Also at the time of the round-up Barbee reported a black-and-white steer missing, the prize of the beef herd, said Barbee. Strayed into some far out-of-the-way canon, perhaps. But as the days went by other cattle, finally totalling a score, were reported missing. And Steve remembered how one evening he and Terry from a log had watched Blenham driving off a string of steers.

"My beloved grandfather has no love for the courts of law," mused Steve many a time. "And he knows that in that I am like him. So to his way of thinking it's just Packard eat Packard and the rest of the world 'Hands Off.' And so he is going the limit. Well, I guess that's as good a way as any other."

The day came when Steve put his cattle into Drop Off Valley. The herds, his and Terry's, were counted twice, once as they filed through the gate of the round-up corrals, again as they were turned into the upland range. Two hundred and thirty-four head.

"Two hundred and thirty-four head where I defy Blenham or the devil himself to steal a single one of them," said Steve positively.

For though there were no fences here nature had raised sufficient barriers in the way of the sheer Drop Off Chasm cutting across the southern end of the plateau and in rocky, uninviting and all but impassable mountain peaks on north and east and a section of the western boundary.

It seemed the simplest matter in the world here with but ordinary diligence and vigilance on the part of his cowboys to make good Steve's vow. Therefore, with Barbee in charge of the men here and under instructions to keep the eyes of trusted night riders always open, Steve thought to have heard the last of cattle losses.

The steers were to be counted every day if Barbee thought necessary; so much Steve had said coolly, merely for the emphasis of the words. Barbee had looked at him curiously, making no rejoinder and going about his business with a puzzled look on his face.

A week later Barbee reported to Steve down at Ranch Number Ten.

"Five steers gone," he said succinctly, his eyes hard and expectant, challenging his employer's.

"Gone?" repeated Steve. "Where? And when?"

"I don't know," replied Barbee. "I missed 'em four days ago. I wouldn't believe they'd gone for good. I didn't see how they could of gone. I've looked for 'em ever since; I've rode into an' out of every canon an' pass; I've been everywhere they could go. But—they're gone. Five big steers."

For a moment their eyes, Steve's as hard as Barbee's, held steady and unwinking in a deeply probing gaze.

"Barbee," said Steve after a little, "remember the night Blenham tried to bribe you with a thousand-dollar bill?"

Barbee flushed and nodded.

"I get you," he said quietly. "Think he's bought me up, maybe?"

"I don't know what to think. But this much is clear; If you are on the level it's up to you to see that I don't lose any more stock. And it's also up to you to find where those five steers went. And get them back. Every single hoof of them."

That night Steve himself spent in Drop Off Valley, a rifle over his arm. He had ordered his men to carry guns, and if Blenham or another man were detected driving off his cattle, to shoot and to shoot to kill.

But the next day he returned to the home ranch. He trusted his cowboys—all but Barbee, and in Barbee's case he was not sure what to think—and it was only too clear to him that there were enough men there to cope with the situation without his interference. Two days later Barbee reported to him again.

The boy's face was haggard and drawn, his eyes

burned sullenly.

"Six head more gone!" he announced defiantly. His look said plainly: "What are you going to say about it? They're gone."

"So you've turned cattle-thief, have you, Barbee?" was what Steve said.

A sickly flush stained Barbee's hollow cheeks.

"No!" he snapped hotly. "I ain't. But—"

He swung on his heel and started to the door. Steve called him back.

"What are you going to do, Barbee?"

"I'm goin' an' get Blenham," said Barbee between his teeth. "I been wantin' him a long time. Now this is his work an' he makes it look like it's mine. I'm goin' an' get him."

"If it is Blenham," Steve offered coldly, "and if you are playing square with me, how does it happen that he can get away with a thing like this? Right under your nose—and you not know? It sounds—You know how it sounds, Barbee."

"I don't know how he does it," growled Barbee. "I don't know how a man could run off a string of cows like that in them mountains an' not leave no tracks. Why, there ain't half-a-dozen places where they could be drove out'n the valley an' through the cliffs, an' I been watchin' every one of them places myself all night an' keepin' the other boys ridin' until they're saddle-weary. An'—an' six head more gone—"

"You're either a clever little actor, Mr. Barbee," muttered

Steve sharply, "or you are straight, and I'm hanged if I know which. Just leave Blenham alone for a while; go back to your job."

Barbee, his spurs dragging disconsolately, went out. Steve saw how the boy's shoulders slumped and again asked himself if Barbee were acting or if Blenham were simply too sharp for him? In the end he decided that he had better move his headquarters to Drop Off Valley.

That same day there came a cowboy riding from the Big Bend ranch bringing a brief note from Steve's grandfather. It ran:

DEAR STEPHEN: Better not go too far, my boy. Eye for an eye is first-class gospel. And there ain't no game yet I ever been bluffed out on. Guess you understand.

PACKARD.

Steve didn't altogether understand but the messenger could add nothing save that the old man was chuckling with Blenham when he gave the message. Steve, in no mood to hear of his grandfather's high good humor, tore the letter to bits, distributed them upon the afternoon wind and told the lean cowboy that he could tell Grandfather Packard and Blenham to go straight to everlasting blazes. The cowboy laughed and rode away.

Steve, riding slowly through the lengthening shadows falling through the pines of the mountain slopes before one comes to Drop Off Valley, was overtaken by Terry Temple riding furiously. Terry's horse was dripping with sweat; Terry's face was troubled; there was a look almost of terror in her eyes.

"Steve Packard," she cried out as she came abreast of him

and they stared into each other's eyes in the dusk under the big trees. "Tell me everything you know about those stolen steers! Everything."

So she knew, too? Yet he had cautioned Barbee not to talk and to instruct the other boys to keep their mouths shut until such time as they could understand this hand being played in the dark.

"Who told you?" he asked quickly.

"I saw them!" she told him, her spirit shining like fire in her eyes. "The whole six of them. I knew they were not our cattle. I saw how the brands had been worked, clumsily worked. Oh, my God, Steve Packard, what does it mean?"

Now it flashed upon him. Terry was not speaking of the cattle lost from the upland valley; she referred to those half-dozen big steers roaming on the Temple ranch whose brands had been crudely altered from the sign of the Big Bend outfit to the sign of her father's. Slowly the red blood of shame, shame for her, crept up into his cheeks, dusky under his tan.

"Terry," he began lamely.

But she halted him with the word, her ear catching the subtle note of sympathy, her hand upflung, her temper flaring out that he, of all men, should think shame of her blood.

"My father was never a thief!" she cried hotly, her voice ringing clear and certain. "Not that, Steve Packard. Don't you dare say that! And yet—You saw them, you knew, and you didn't say a word to me, to anybody?"

"I didn't know what to say or what to do,", he explained

gently. "I thought it best just to wait, to hope for the sense of all this infernal jumble. I hoped—"

"You big fool!" she called him with all due emphasis. "Just like all of the rest of your blundering sex. If the good Lord had stopped with the job of making Adam, his whole creation wouldn't have been worth the snap of my thumb and finger."

"It isn't, anyway," said Steve. "I wouldn't swap your little finger for a king's gold crown—"

"Moonshine," cut in Terry. "Listen to me, Steve Packard: You saw those swapped brands and you kept your mouth shut."

"It is generally considered—"

"I said to listen to me! You didn't say a word to me because you believed my dad was a cattle-thief!"

Steve, despite himself, shifted uneasily in his saddle and finally dropped his eyes. Terry sat there staring at him fixedly, her own eyes wide open and again harboring that look that was almost fear.

"You—you—Oh, Steve Packard! This is contemptible of you!"

Then he lifted his eyes and looked at her solely enough.

"Terry Temple," he said very gently, "I pray God that you are right and that I am wrong. I did not know, I only saw what I saw, and wondered and kept my mouth shut. But— listen to me now, Terry Temple. You are not the one to dodge an issue, no matter how hard it is to face it. Tell me: If your father did not shift those brands, then who did? And why? Don't you see that is what it amounts to, that is what we've got to answer?"

"Blenham!" she told him swiftly, hardly waiting for him to finish. "Blenham, under orders. Orders from your precious old thief of a grandfather!"

He smiled back at her, hoping to coax an answering smile to her lips and into her troubled eyes. But she only shook her head and went on steadily.

"Recrimination of a sort—"

"Recrimination is quite some word, no matter what it means," sniffed Terry. "But we can leave it out. In words of one syllable, your old thief of a grandfather ordered his pet dog and sub-thief to go tie something on poor old dad. And you fell for it! You ought to go to a school for the simple-minded."

"Just what," demanded Steve equably, "do you suppose a play like that would win for anybody? Any time my old thief of a grandfather, as you call him, hands an enemy of his several hundred dollars in beef cattle, why, just please wake me up."

"A play like that is just what old Hell-Fire would be up to right about now," she told him positively. "You have been proving something too much for him to swallow whole and boots on; your chipping in with us that time you took the mortgage over made him hungrier than ever to gobble up the crowd of us. So he plays the dirty trick of making it appear my father is a cattle-thief."

"Blenham might do a trick like that. My grandfather wouldn't. That is, I don't think he would."

"Better hedge! Wouldn't he, though! He's always been as mean as gar-broth; the older he gets the meaner and nastier he is. He'd do anything to double-cross a Temple and you know it. It's one crooked play; there'll be more like it. Just you see, Steve Packard. And the next one—at least if it concerns me—you see that you let me know about it instead of going around like a dumb man."

Then he blurted out word of the recent losses from Drop Off Valley. For her herds mingled there with his and a part of the losses were to be borne by her.

"I'm on my way there now," he concluded. "I've an idea—"

"You haven't!" she interrupted. "Steve Packard, I don't believe you ever had an idea in your life. Don't you know— don't you know what's going with those steers up there?"

"Do you?"

"You just bet your life I do! It's that crook of a Yellow Barbee, in cahoots with that crook of a Blenham who's taking orders from that crook of an old Hell-Fire Packard! Can't you see their play?"

"I rather think I can. But I don't happen to be as positive about the unknown as you do."

"You're just a man," said Terry. "That's why. And now you are on your way to the feeding-grounds up there, to come in and say, 'Here I am, Barbee, come to watch you and see that you don't steal any more stock for me to-night.' That the idea?"

Steve laughed.

"Not exactly. I had intended leaving my horse before I got

to the rim of the valley and going on on foot, not telling everybody what I was about."

"And you'd come to the rim of the valley either by Hell Gate pass or through the old Indian Trail, wouldn't you? And Barbee or Blenham would see that both ways were watched."

"You seem to know the trails rather well," he began, but she merely broke in:

"That's not all I know about this neck of the woods, either, Steve Packard. Maybe it's lucky for you and for me too that you told me all this. I'll take you into Drop Off Valley to-night, and Blenham and Yellow Barbee can watch all they please and never guess we're there. For there's a way up that not even Blenham knows and where they will never look for us. Come on, Steve Packard; use a spur."

She shot by him, leading the way.

So Steve and Terry rode through the forests, passing from the dull fringe of the day into the calm glory of the night, feeling the air grow cooler and sweeter against their faces, sensing the shutting-in about them of the gentle serenity of the wilderness. They followed little-travelled trails where she rode ahead and he, following close at her horse's heels, was glad each time that an open space beyond or a ridge crested showed him her form pricked clearly against the sky.

They spoke less and less as they went on. Deeper grew the silences into which they made their way, with only the gush of a mountain brook or the fluttering of a startled bird or the rustle of dead leaves under some alert little wild thing, just these sounds occasionally and ever the soft thud of shod hoofs on leaf mould and loose soil.

The stars multiplied swiftly, grew in brilliancy. But down here close to the face of the earth where the shadows were, the dark was impenetrable.

For many a mile Terry led the way through the forests. Steve was on the verge of suggesting that she had lost her way, when she turned off to the right and down a long slope in so decided a fashion that he closed his lips to his suspicion.

She knew where she was going; as he once again saw her body against a patch of sky—she had gone down the slope and climbed a ridge ahead—and as he noted her carriage and the poise of a chin for the instant clearly outlined, he knew that she was sure of herself. Well, she was that sort of a girl; she might have confidence in herself and a man might place his confidence with hers.

So at last Terry brought him down into a creek-bed and the bottom on a steep-sided canon. He merely said, "I'll take your word for it!" when she told him that this was the deep-cleft ravine which lay like a gash at the base of the sheer Drop Off Cliffs.

Yonder, perhaps a mile ahead and yet prominently asserting itself to their view because of a certain widening and straightening of the canon here, a bold head of cliffs stood out like a monster carving in ebony. Up there, at the top of these cliffs, was the southern end of Drop Off Valley.

"And it is up those cliffs that we are going," Terry announced when, having drawn nearer, they stopped again to gaze upward. "There's a trail climbing straight up from the bed of the pass; a trail to go hand-and-foot style. Once on top we'll be among Barbee's herds, Barbee guessing nothing of our coming since he'll be busy watching the other ways in. And—Look!"

They were close together and she gripped his arm in her sudden amazement while she threw out one hand pointing. He heard her little gasp; he looked upward; an astonished ejaculation broke from his own lips. A breathless moment and already the thing, appearing from the black nothingness, silhouetted but a moment against the sky, was gone and he vaguely saw Terry's face turned toward him while they sought to find each other's eyes and know if each had seen what the other had glimpsed.

"It's impossible!" he muttered. "We are imagining things."

"Wait!" said Terry. "Maybe after all—"

They waited impatiently, their blood atingle. And in a very few moments there was, seeming absurd and impossible, a repetition of the vision which had so startled them: a black form at the head of the cliffs, the field of star-strewn sky back of it limning it into vivid distinctness—the ebon bulk of a steer moving straight out from the top of the precipice, straight out a half-dozen feet into nothingness of empty space, then slowly descending through the air, gone silently in the deeper shadows of the canon below!

"Block and tackle!" muttered Steve abruptly. "A small steel cable. Two or three men up there; a man on horseback down below. And while Barbee and the boys guard the other end—"

"Blenham puts one across on us down here!" Terry finished it for him.

"Only here's where we put one over on Blenham," rejoined Steve hotly. He threw a cartridge into his rifle-barrel and spurred ahead of her. "You stay here, Terry. I—"

"Will I?" Terry retorted with animation. "Not on your life,

Steve Packard! If this is the beginning of Blenham's finish—
Well, I'm in on it."

CHAPTER XXV

THE STAMPEDE

Terry had sensed something of the truth. In its way here was the beginning of the end of many things. Before she and Steve Packard, making what haste was possible in the thick dark and with what silence was allowed them, had gone a score of paces deeper into the canon, the crack of a rifle shouted its reverberating message of menace back and forth in the rocky ravine, a spurt of flame showed where the rifleman stood upon a pinnacle of rock almost directly above their heads and there came the further sounds of men's startled voices and the scampering of horses' hoofs, fleeing southward through the pass.

"They had lookouts all along!" cried Steve over his shoulder, discarding caution and secrecy and throwing his rifle to his shoulder. "Better hold back, Terry!"

He fired, accepted the precarious chances offered him by an uneven and unknown trail in the dark and raced on deeper and deeper into the long chasm. It seemed to him that he had glimpsed something moving at the top of the cliffs just about the place whence Blenham's men had lowered the steers. He asked no question but threw up his gun-barrel and fired again.

From straight in front of him there came back to his ears the clang and thud of iron horseshoes upon granite, the rattle of rocks along the trail; now and again he saw a spark struck out underfoot. Then, far ahead as the canon widened suddenly and a little thinning of the darkness resulted, he made out dim, running forms, and again he fired from his own leaping horse.

A flying bullet might find a target and it might not; at any rate the sound of the shots volleyed and boomed echoingly between the stone wails imprisoning them, and Barbee or one of Barbee's men should hear. Steve was estimating hopefully as he dashed on after the fugitives and as Terry dashed on after him, that the men at the top of the cliffs would not try to come down now, not knowing who or how many the attackers were, but would seek escape above.

Then, if his cowboys heard and rode toward the cliffs, it was all in the cards that they might intercept at least a couple of Blenham's tools.

A running form almost at his side drew his attention briefly, and all but drew hot, questing lead after it. Then he made out that it was but one of the stolen steers, abandoned now; he pressed by, firing time after time into the canon ahead of him. And behind him he heard Terry's voice, eager and fearless, crying out:

"Good boy, Steve Packard! We'll get 'em yet!"

A spurt of flame from far ahead and close to the wall of the canon, the crack of another rifle, long drawn out, and the whine of a bullet singing its vicious way overhead, and again Steve fired, answering shot with shot. He heard a man shout and fired in the direction of the voice. And then the only sounds rising from the narrow gorge were those of running horses and the accompanying noises of rattling stones.

Jackson Gregory

Now the way was again tortuous, pitch-black, boulder-strewn. Steve slowed down rather than break his horse's legs or his own neck, not knowing whether to turn to right or left. In a moment of uncertainty he felt and heard Terry push ahead of him. He heard her hurrying on and followed, shouting to her to come back. Ten minutes later, out of the pass now and upon a low-lying ridge whence he could look across the hills billowing away darkly toward the southland, he came up with her again.

"They got off that way." She pointed south. "Saw one figure and maybe two going down the slope. There's no use following. The way is too open and it's too dark. They've got away after all."

"For to-night," said Steve. "But maybe the fellows at the top of the cliffs—"

"I'll show you the way up," said Terry.

So without delaying they turned back and came presently under Drop Off Cliffs again. Here they left their horses and, Terry showing the way, found the old path up the precipice. Along many a narrow shelf of rock they went, over many a gigantic granite splinter where foothold was precarious enough, up many a steep climb. But in their present mood they would have achieved even a more difficult and more hazardous task with eagerness and assurance. Twenty minutes brought them to the top.

"Who's that?" shouted a sudden voice as Steve's hat came up out of the void. "Hands up!"

"That you, Barbee?" grunted Steve. "Hands up? I'd drop a clean hundred feet if I did a fool trick like that. Did they get away? The men up here?"

He wriggled up to the top, lay on his stomach and gave a hand to Terry, drew her to lie a moment breathless at his side and then again turned to Barbee. There was another man with him and both were looking wonderingly at Steve and Terry.

"I never heard a man say," muttered the astounded Barbee, "that there was stair-steps up here! For a man an' girl to come up—"

"And for our cows to go down!" cried Steve, on his feet now and coming to Barbee's side. "You heard everything, Barbee? You know what has happened?"

"Yes," said Barbee. "A hundred yards over that way—" he pointed along the cliff's edge—"where a twisted cedar-tree stands in a little washout, not hardly to be noticed unless you're on the lookout for it, they had their pulleys hitched an' a long steel cable. It was easy shootin', come to think of it. Jus' rope a cow, cinch her up tight with two big straps they had all ready, slip a hook through the belly-band, an' lower away! Pretty smooth, huh?"

"And they all got away?"

"No, they didn't," said Barbee queerly. "I got one of 'em!"

"You did?" Steve swung back toward him eagerly. "Who is he, Barbee? And where is he? I want a talk with him."

Barbee shook his head and reached for his tobacco and papers. He was young after all, was Barbee, and this was his first man.

"Andy Sprague, it was," said Barbee. "He's dead now."

There fell a heavy, breathless silence upon the three standing there under the stars. Terry shivered as though with cold and drew a step closer to Steve; he felt her hand on his arm. Barbee lighted his cigarette, his hands steady, but his face looking terribly serious in the brief-lived light shed upon it.

"I heard you shootin'," said Barbee. "I rode this way, on the jump. I was only about a mile up the valley; maybe a shade less. He had his horse close an' was on him an' poundin' leather lively to get out. We come pretty close to runnin' into each other. I hollered at him to hold on an' he jus' rode on his spurs an' I shot. Emptied my gun. Got him twice, bein' that lucky, an' him that unlucky. He slid off his cayuse an' clawed aroun' an'—an' he's dead now," ended Barbee briefly.

"Did he tell you anything? Did he say anything that would implicate anybody?"

"Meanin'," said Barbee steadily, "did he squeal on his pals?"

"Just that. Did he mention any names?"

"No," replied Barbee thoughtfully. "He jus' cusses me an' dies game. But this here was in his pocket."

He passed it to his employer. It was a bit of note-paper. Steve and Terry read it together as Steve struck one match after another. Then they looked into each other's faces, grown very tense, while Barbee smoked in silence. The few words were:

BLENHAM: This here Mex don't seem to know what I mean. Next time send a man as can talk English. Anyway I am coming to-night. I don't want no killing if it ain't necessary, but there ain't going to be a hide or hoof left in Drop Off by morning.

And the signature, cramped and stiff, was that of Steve's grandfather.

"So," muttered Steve heavily. "The old man has gone the limit, has he? He meant it when he said he'd stop at nothing to smash me. And yet I can't believe—"

"Let me see it again," Terry commanded.

She took the paper from his fingers and with it his block of sulphur matches. For even Terry, to whom old man Packard was as relentless and unscrupulous as Satan himself, hesitated to believe that he was hand in glove with Blenham in this.

There might be a way to read between the lines, to come to some other understanding of the baffling situation. Evidently the old man had given the note to the "Mex" who did not know enough of the English language to carry word of mouth; the Mex had passed it to Sprague.

Steve and Barbee and the man with Barbee—an old Ranch Number Ten hand named Bandy Oliver—had stepped aside quietly. Terry stood with the note in her hand, forgetting it for the moment. So, at the last, matters had come to this: There lay a man over yonder, dead, with Barbee's lead in him.

And old man Packard was coming to-night, now of all times when Steve's heart was hard, when his brain was hot with his fury, when he had just come upon men stealing his stock and had learned that his own grandfather, the old mountain-lion from the north, was one of them.

"If they meet to-night," said Terry, "those two Packards, there are going to be other men killed. Good men and bad men. And, as likely as not, Blenham won't be one of them."

"There was another jasper with Sprague. He got away. That way, I think. Couldn't say, but there might have been more; what with the dark an' the cattle scared an' churnin' aroun'."

Steve with Barbee and Bandy Oliver had moved slowly away and toward the upper end of the plateau. Detached words, fragments of their speech, floated back to her more and more indistinctly on the night wind that never sleeps upon these uplands.

Terry turned from them and stood for a little looking down into the black void of the canon into which the stolen cattle had been lowered, from which she and Steve had just climbed. She fancied that the darkness down there was thinning. The dawn was coming up almost imperceptibly over the mountain-tops, filtering wanly into the depths of the canons. The night had rushed by; it would soon be day.

And old man Packard had not come. Thank God for that. Down in her heart Terry was conscious of a leaping gladness. She knew, admitted now, that she had been afraid. A man lay dead over yonder; if Packard met Packard to-night there would be other men dead. Terry shivered and drew back from the edge of the precipice.

"It's always colder just before day," she told herself.

"Sunrise already?"

Steve's voice, borne to her ears with startling distinctness. He had not come nearer; maybe the dawn wind was stiffening, thus bearing his words to her more clearly. Or it might be that Steve had lifted his voice suddenly.

Why should a man be startled by a new sunrise? True, the night had gone quickly, but—

"The sun never rose there!" Steve's voice again, thrilling through her with its portent. "It's fire—range fire—in a dozen places!"

A bright glow lay across the far, upper end of Drop Off Valley. At first one might have done as Steve Packard did and wondered what had happened to the sun. The sky had merely brightened warmly, slowly, gradually, showing a hint of pink. And then, as the bone-dry grass here and there had caught, vivid streaks of flame and a veritable devil's dance of a myriad sparks shot high skyward. And, as Steve had cried out, not in one place only, but in a dozen spots had the fires been lighted.

"To herald the wrathful coming of Hell-Fire Packard!"

Such was the thought springing full-fledged into Terry's brain, into Steve's, into Yellow Barbee's. A chain of fires had been started across the whole width of the feeding grounds. Now the rising wind made of it a sudden burning barrier that extended from side to side of Drop Off Valley, came rushing toward the lower end, threatening to leave but a black charred devastation of the precious pasturage.

Barbee had run and thrown himself upon his horse. Steve had grasped the dragging reins of Andy Sprague's mount. Terry saw him and his two cowboys swing about toward the upper end.

"Terry!" he shouted over his shoulder. "Down the cliffs again; quick! The fire is coming this way; the herds will stampede!"

There was only the sound of thudding hoofs as the three men rode furiously to meet the menace the dawn had brought and seek to grapple with it. Then that sound had gone and its place, for a little taken by heavy silence, gradually gave way to new sounds. The crack of rifles, faintly heard—thin voices of men shouting a long way off—a sound like that of a distant sea, moving restlessly—grown to suggest the coming of a storm that ever swelled in violence—and then a deep and deepening rumble, like thunder.

The herd had stampeded.

To Terry there came then, for the first time in her life, the sense of utter helplessness and hopelessness. At least the others were doing something, no matter how fruitless it might prove, while she was doing nothing. Steve was riding full-tilt to meet the herd. She saw him and his men, strange figures in the uncertain light, looming big against the dawn sky and the fires' glow. They were shouting, waving their arms. Then, going down over a swell of earth they were lost to her.

Again and again there came to her the sound of shots and men's voices shouting, cursing, yelling wild commands, a rising clamor meant to divert the blind rush of frightened beasts, to turn them to right and left so that they might scramble out of the valley before they came to the lower end where Terry stood—where was the yawning chasm down into which many a great, terror-filled body was doomed to plunge to annihilation unless the way were found to swing the flood of fear aside in time.

Barbee and Bandy Oliver and the other boys were obeying Steve's commands, doing all that they could, seeking frantically to split the herd and divert it and so save it. But all of the time the wind strengthened, the fires rose higher and higher against the sky, the sparks soared to rarer altitudes, were flung further out, new fires were catching everywhere.

The tall, dry grass was burning in a hundred places. The herd, sweeping on, was snorting its terror, yielding absolutely to the blind instinct of flight. And steadily the thunderous murmuring sound from the hoof-smitten earth rose and swelled. Closer and closer they came. Terry could distinguish Steve's voice.

In her hand were the matches he had given her in order that she might read again his grandfather's letter. A little gasp broke from her lips. The letter fluttered from her hand, no longer of the slightest importance and on the wings of the wind went outward and then down into the chasm. She ran forward swiftly, a hundred yards from the precipice's edge. She struck a match, stopped briefly, set it to the grass.

The flame caught, leaping up avidly, licking hungrily for more fuel, a demon for desire, newly born, yearning to rage a giant of destruction. The girl snatched a handful of the burning grass and ran with it; a little further forward, then to the side, scattering burning wisps as she went.

Everywhere that a spark fell it made of itself a blaze. Already, in twenty seconds, she had created a broad belt of flame that rose swiftly and spread to right and left.

About her everywhere the air grew stifling, hot, filled with smoke and ash and cinder so that as she ran her lungs began to hurt her. But she kept on. Nearer were the herds coming; Steve and his men had not been able to stem the mad torrent; not yet had they succeeded in turning it.

And in another handful of minutes the black, tight-jammed mass of big panting bodies would be hurtling out into space. Unless she made her fire extend from side to side in a wall of leaping, roaring, swirling menace that would do what no men and horses could accomplish.

Terry was racing as never had Terry run before, her breath coming in choking sobs, her eyes shining wildly, her body shaken with the effort she put upon it. She had her burning barrier across the more dangerous end of the valley, where the cliffs dropped sheerest, she had but another few yards to go and there would be hope that she would succeed. But she must not stop yet, not yet.

She ran on toward the nearer rim of the valley, scattering burning wisps of grass as she went, her heart beating wildly, seeming ready to burst through her side. She fell, rose, ran on. She stood still a moment, turning her back to the fires of her own building, looking toward the upper end whence came the steady roar.

For an instant she stood fascinated. It looked as though the ground itself, in many a low-lying swell, were racing on to meet her. Then she saw the hundreds of horns glistening dully in the new light. That black mass, surging forward, was the herd and she was still in its path.

She cried out and threw down her last torch and ran just as the frightened steers were running, fear in her heart, racing away from death, just running for her life. She saw a form ahead of the others, breaking away from them, sweeping down upon her. She cried out in terror; then she knew and cried out again and threw up her arms and turned toward the rider who had remembered her and feared for her and come for her. And Steve, bending from his saddle, equal to the need of the moment, swept her up and caught her tight in his arm and rode out of the way of herd and fire.

From a little crag-crested knoll, standing hand in hand, their forms blended in silhouette against the dawn, they watched breathlessly the end of the stampede. The maddened brutes rushed on, straight toward Terry's barrier of flame. Then those in the van sought suddenly to alter their headlong courses.

Steve's face was white with anger as he saw the result. A full half-dozen, perhaps ten, big bodies at the fore passed through the far end of the flaming line, swept on, sought to swerve only at the last frantic moment with their fellows crowding them to the brink, and, struggling wildly, went over and down and out of sight. Terry shuddered.

The herd, however, broke, divided, swung to right and left and passed about the burning danger-signal and to the outer rims of the valley, achieving safety somewhere in the night, scattering, tossing their gleaming fronts, snorting, and beginning to bellow their rage.

"If it hadn't been for you, Terry Temple—" Steve began, his voice a little hoarse.

"If it hadn't been for you, Steve Packard,"' laughed Terry a trifle unsteadily but quite happily, "where would I have been?"

And then, quite as though their destiny wished it made plain that not yet had the time come for them to devote exclusively to themselves, Barbee rode down toward them, spurring through the last of the fleeing herd, shouting:

"There's a dozen men ridin' this way an' ridin' like—! An' the firelight's shinin' on their guns; every man's totin' one. An' it's ol' Hell-Fire Packard ridin' at their head."

"I'm glad he has come," muttered Steve heavily.

And then, as though he were uncertain of his return to her, he kissed Terry's lips that were lifted toward his. In a dull stupor, so much had she experienced these last few minutes, she watched him swing again to the back of a horse and ride to meet those who came. The very way he carried his rifle in front of him bespoke with rare eloquence his readiness for anything.

CHAPTER XXVI

YELLOW BARBEE KEEPS A PROMISE

Terry started, shook off her apathy with a sudden effort and called out:

"Steve! Steve! Come back!"

He had gone but a half-dozen paces. He swung about and returned to her. It was not light enough yet for her to see his eyes; they seemed just unfathomable, sombre pools in the shadow of his hat-brim. As he turned his head a little, harking to the distant sounds of men's voices earning on, the rigid profile was harsh and implacable.

"Terry," he said sternly, "you mustn't ask me to come back again. I am just standing on my own rights this time, as a man must now and then. Old man Packard is over there. He is coming on. He wants trouble. He doesn't want the law courts. He always preferred to play the game man to man. He has cost me a number of cattle; when I can figure just how many I am going over and collect from him—if we are both left alive, which is to be doubted. And now, if he wants fight—"

Again he glanced over his shoulder. Still she could not read what lay in his eyes. But a new, almost eager note, boyishly eager Terry thought in dismay, had burst into his voice:

"If he wants fight—by God, Terry Temple, I'm as much Packard as he is!"

She watched him wheel again and go. This time she did not call to him. Her little figure stiffened, her hands were down at her sides and clenched, her chin was lifted a little. The whole attitude was soldierlike.

"They are two of a kind," said Terry within herself. "They are men. They are Packards. I am proud and—and afraid—and— Oh, dear God! Dear God! Bring him back to me!"

She could hear Steve giving his brief orders crisply. Other figures loomed about him, coming out of the night and the shadows. There was young Yellow Barbee and Bandy Oliver; there was the Number Ten cowboy whom she knew only as "Spotty"; in a moment these and two or three other men were with Steve. Six or seven; possibly eight of them all told. And Barbee had said that there were about a dozen men with old man Packard.

"This is my fight, boys," Steve was saying. "Mine and my grandfather's. I want you fellows to keep out of it unless the boys with old man Packard mix in. If they do—"

"We're with you," said Yellow Barbee. "Huh, boys?"

And a little nervously and hurriedly they answered—

"Yes."

"Then," concluded Steve, "keep your eyes open. Hang back, now."

She saw him lean forward in the saddle, noted how the

horse leaped under him, took anxious stock of the manner in which he carried his rifle. Then suddenly there came back into Terry's cheeks the good hot blood, into her eyes the sparkle and shine, into her heart something akin to the sheer joy of battle. Had she a horse she would not have hung back for want of a rifle, but would have ridden after him, with him. As it was she cried out ringingly:

"God go with you, Steve Packard! I'm proud of you!"

She might not ride with him; at least she would not crouch and cringe and hide her eyes. She would watch him as he rode, watch him as he fought, watch him to the end even though he slipped from the saddle.

So she made her way hastily to a point of vantage, running the brief distance lying between the slight knoll on which she stood and the eastern edge of the valley where the rugged peaks rose abruptly. She scrambled up the first bit of slope, her heart beating wildly, expecting each second to hear the snap and crackle of rifle-fire. She turned and looked back; the floor of the valley was too uneven for her to have a sweeping view.

She began climbing again. Great boulders rose in her path; somehow she got on them and over them. Broken slabs of granite strewed the way; she made of them steps on which to mount higher and higher. Still no sound of a shot and at last, upon a narrow shelf of rock offering sufficient foothold, she stopped.

Here, with her back tight pressed to a rock, her hands gripping at irregularities on each side of her to steady her, she sent her questing gaze down into Drop Off Valley.

Now she understood why there had as yet been no rifle-fire. The day, coming on slowly, still offered more gloom than radiance, but she could pick out two figures clearly. One was that of Steve. He had ridden on ahead of his men, perhaps a hundred feet ahead, and was upon a bit of higher ground.

The other form, bulking big in the thin light, was indisputably that of old man Packard. Like Steve, he had ridden on in advance of his men. She could just make out a dull mass yonder behind him which might have been but a group of boulders had not the impatient stirring showed where his horsemen were waiting.

It was very still there on the uplands in the dim dawning. In breathless watchfulness a few men behind Steve watched; a few men behind old man Packard watched; a girl upon a granite peak watched. Down toward the lower end of the valley where the floor of the plateau dropped precipitously into the steep-walled canon the fire Terry had set was still burning fiercely. But the wind carried its fury away from them, so that it was only an evil whisper.

Here and there, elsewhere in the valley, the fires still burned on. There were wide stretches across which the flames had already swept so that now they were ink-black, burnt-out, smoking a little. Upon such an open space, still hot under their horses' hoofs, the two Packards, grandfather and grandson, came face to face. And they were stern, ominously set faces confronting each other.

At last they had pulled rein, both of them, looking grotesquely like clockwork mechanisms, being actuated by the same impulse at the same time. Some ten feet only were between their horses' tossing heads. They were almost opposite Terry's lookout and at no great distance. In the quiet pervading the valley their voices came to her. Not each word, but a word now and then, lifted above its fellows, and always the purport. For there was no mistaking the quality of the two voices.

Rage in old Packard was welcomed by wrath in young Packard. Heat and anger and explosive denunciation, these were to be looked for now. Never had it been the Packard way to temporize; always had it been the Packard way to leap in and strike. Few-worded always was the old man; as few-worded was the young man now.

"You are a damn' scoundrel, sir!"

"You will draw your men off. You will pay for the damage Blenham has done."

"By God, sir!"

There was little more said. That thunderous "By God, sir!" from the old man's lips carried to Terry where she stood tight pressed against her rock. And then all unexpectedly and from an unexpected quarter, came the first rifle-shot.

The first shot and the second, close together. The bullets passed between grandfather and grandson, kicking up little puffs of dust beyond them. Neither looked to see whence the shots came. The thought was in each mind:

"Is this a Packard I am dealing with? Setting one of his hired assassins to shooting from a blind?"

The old man's rifle was thrown up before him; Steve's rose with it. Over yonder old Packard's men squared themselves in their saddles and made ready for grim work. Yellow Barbee gave a signal all unneeded to his men; his own rifle in his eager hands, was ready, the trigger yielding to his calloused forefinger.

And then from the flinty spire of a peak rising between

them and a sun that was slowly wheeling into the clear sky, came scream after scream that echoed and billowed across the open lands as Terry Temple, seeing something of the truth, cried out in terrified desperation and warning.

A girl's voice screaming—Old man Packard turned sharply and stared in wonderment. Terry's voice—Steve swung about, his anger suddenly quenched in alarm, his eyes seeking everywhere for her.

It was Barbee who saw her first. Barbee called out, a strange note in his voice, and clapped his spurs to his horse's sides and went racing across the undulating lands toward her. Then Steve saw and old man Packard and the rest. Saw but at first could not understand: the sun was just behind her, winking into their eyes. There was some one with her, struggling with her.

"Blenham!" shouted Steve.

And he was racing wildly along after Barbee, yearning to shoot to kill and yet not daring to shoot at all. Blenham and Terry struggling upon the iron side of the mountain, Terry striking and striking at him frantically, Blenham with his arms about her, dragging her back toward a wide fissure in the rocks, the sun bright above them.

To Terry it seemed that the universe had come crashing down about her ears. A moment ago, tense and rigid and breathless, she had stood watching two men face each other threateningly. Then there had been the crack of the unexpected, unseen rifle; the dust struck up between them; the second shot. And the smoking rifle-barrel was not three feet from where Terry stood, Blenham's convulsed face laid against the stock, Blenham's one evil eye lining the sights.

Almost on the instant she guessed something of the truth.

Blenham in this light was not sure of hitting; he would be a fool to shoot and miss. Unless—and it was then that she screamed out her warning, then before he had so much as put out his hand toward her.

Unless Blenham, with all of the guile of him uppermost, knew that that shot fired between the two would send them flying at each other's throats, ending all parley and bringing about unthinkable tragedy. Blenham had his own reasons for what he did; certainly it would fit in with Blenham's plans to see the hand of a Packard set against a Packard.

But she had not thought to have him seize her. Now his great, calloused, soiled, hairy hands shut down upon her, gripping her shoulders, jerking her from her place into the crevice from which his face had emerged. She fought, seeking to get the revolver in her blouse.

Blenham must have known that she kept it there. He snatched it and threw it behind him and cursed her as he dragged her with him. As Barbee came on and Steve came just behind him, the figures of Blenham and Terry were both gone as though the mountain-side had split for them and closed after them.

"They've got in a hole," called out Barbee. "Them mountains is full of caves. They can't get away far."

As they went up the steep slope Barbee was still in the lead. He mounted to the shelf of rock on which Terry had been standing. He stepped into the crevice through which Blenham had dragged Terry.

"There's a split in the rocks here," called Barbee. "He went this way."

"Watch out for him!" warned Steve, now on the ledge close

to the boy. "Let me go ahead!"

Barbee laughed.

"Long ago I told him I'd get him!"

But Blenham was waiting in a little rock-rimmed hollow. He shot from the hip, using a heavy revolver. Barbee stood a moment looking foolishly at the sky as he slowly leaned back against the rock. Then he lurched and fell, twisting, spinning so that he lay half in the fissure, his rifle clattering to the ledge outside, his body falling so that his head and shoulders were across the rifle.

Steve stepped over Barbee's twitching body, alert, every nerve taut, his finger crooked to the trigger of his rifle. But again Blenham had withdrawn. In the little rudely circular hollow from which Blenham had fired point-blank at Yellow Barbee was Terry's hat, trodden underfoot. Again it was as though the mountain had swallowed the man and the girl he had taken with him.

But a moment later Steve saw and understood. Not ten steps from where he stood was the mouth of a cave. Into it Blenham had retreated. In there was Blenham now; Blenham and Terry with him. And the way, for the moment at least, was securely blocked. Evidently here was a hangout known before, previously employed. It had a door made of heavy cedar slabs. The door was shut, and, of course, barred from within.

"Terry!" called Steve.

Terry sought to answer; he heard her voice in inarticulate terror, little more than a gasp, choked back in her throat. Steve went dead white. He visualized Blenham's hands upon her.

He came on to the door, his rifle clubbed. There was but the one thing to do; smash down the door and so come at Blenham the shortest, quickest, only way.

Then Blenham called to him for the first time.

"Fool, are you, Steve Packard? Look at that door. Don't you know before you can batter it down I can pick you off! An' I can do more'n that!"

As though he had cruelly drawn it from her, there came again Terry's scream. Steve sprang forward and struck at the heavy cedar planks. And Blenham called out again:

"Maybe you can break your way in; there's enough of you. But you'll find her dead when the door falls!"

Steve had again lifted his rifle. Now he let it sink slowly so that the butt came to rest gently upon the rock at his feet. Blenham held the high hand; Blenham was unthinkably vile; Blenham was desperate. And Terry, his little Terry on whom Blenham had always looked with the eye of a brute and a beast, was in there, just beyond three inches of solid seasoned cedar planking.

"If you harm her in the least—" It was Steve's voice though certainly at first neither Blenham nor even Terry could have recognized it. "If you harm her in the least, Blenham, I'll kill you. Not all at once—just by inches!"

Blenham answered him coolly.

"I know when I've lost a trick, Steve Packard. This ain't the firs' one an' it ain't goin' to be the last. I've played 'em high an' I always knowed I took chances. But I'm playin' safe! Get me? Safe!"

Jackson Gregory

"Go ahead; what do you mean?"

"Ol' man Packard is down there. This girl's yellin' spoiled my play. By now he has learned a thing or two. All right; that's jus' the run of luck, rotten luck!"

Under the words the restraint was gone and his rage flared out briefly. But it was patent that Blenham's shrewdness was still with him. He continued almost calmly:

"You an' him can have two words together. Then come back here an' give me your promises, both of you, to let me go. Then I'll let her go. Otherwise, I'm as good as dead— an' so's she. I'll jam a gun to her head the las' thing an' blow her brains out. An', what's more, I'll get one or two of you besides before you drop me."

Into their parley, interrupting it, his eyes flaming, his face hot with anger, mounted old man Packard.

"Stephen," he said sternly, his eyes hard on his grandson's face, "tell me an' tell me the down-right truth, so help you God: Did you rent this pasture from Andy Sprague, thinkin' he owned it?"

Though he wondered, Steve answered briefly, to have this done with so that he could again turn to Blenham—

"Yes."

"An' the boys says you have been losin' stock an' blamin' it to me? An' that you've had stock poisoned an' shot? An' blamed it to me?"

"Yes," said Steve.

"So've I," said the old man heavily. "An' I've always blamed

it to you. An' I never sold to Andy Sprague. Him an'
Blenham—Blenham has played us both ways for suckers,
has stole enough cows from one an' another—"

His voice was swept up into the roar of rage which had
given him his name of the old mountain-lion of the north.
He came stepping over poor Barbee's body, thrusting by
Steve, towering over the door of the cave.

"Hold back," commanded Steve queerly. "He's in there. But
he's got it on us. We've got to promise to let him go!"

"Let him go!" shouted the old man, his big bulk seeming
actually to quiver with rage. "After all he's done, let him go?
By the Lord, Stephen Packard, if you're that sort of a
man—"

"She is in there with him," said Steve heavily. "Terry is in
there. Don't you see?"

"Terry? That Temple girl? What have we to do—"

"In the first place," cried Steve sharply, "she's a girl and he's
a brute. In the second place, she is the next Mrs. Packard
and I won't have Blenham pawing over her!"

His grandfather stared at him, long and keenly. Then he
turned away and called out commandingly—

"Blenham, come out of that!"

Blenham jeered at him.

"And be shot down like a dog? There's a girl in here,
Packard. Young Packard is gone on her; he wants to marry
her. An' unless you an' him give your word to let me go, I'm
goin' to jam a gun at her head an' blow her brains out. An'

I'll get him as I come out; an' I'll get you."

"Let him go!" called Terry faintly. "Let him go, Steve! Oh, dear God—if you love me—"

"Come out, Blenham!" shouted Steve. "I give you my word, so help me God, to let you go scot-free. Come out!"

"Not so fast," mocked Blenham, lingering over his high card. "You've got to promise for your men; you've got to send 'em across the valley. You've got to have a horse handy for me to ride. You've got to back down the valley yourse'f. An' ol' man Packard has got to do the same."

Old man Packard roared out his curses, but in the end, seeing nothing else to do, he went grumbling down the rocky slope, back to his horse and to his men. But first he had known perhaps the supreme humiliation of his life. He had said:

"Blenham, on my word of honor as a Packard an' a gentleman, I'll let you go. An' I'll make my men let you go."

And there were actually tears hanging to his lashes as he swung again into his saddle.

"He has not hurt you, Terry?" asked Steve before he too would go down the slope.

"No," cried Terry. "No, no! But, oh, hurry, hurry, Steve. I feel that I'll smother, I'll die!"

From down in the valley they watched, close to a score of hard-eyed, wrath-filled men, as Blenham stepped out of the crevice and on to the ledge. They saw how he jeered as he stepped over the body of the man he had shot.

"A fool was Barbee," he called. "A fool the Packards, ol' an' young!"

They saw him come down the slope, carrying himself with a swaggering air of braggadocio, but plainly watchful and suspicious. Terry had come out upon the ledge and she too watched him. He came down swiftly and swung up into the saddle of the horse they had left for him.

And now at last his suspicion was past. His triumph broke out like a streak of evil light.

"I was ready to go," he called, "any time!"

He swung his arm out toward the blue hills of Old Mexico.

"Down there—"

Barbee whom they had thought dead stirred a little where he lay. The rifle under him he thrust forward six inches.

"Blenham!" he called weakly.

Blenham swung about and fired, again from the hip. But he had fired hastily. Barbee's rifle, resting upon the rock, was steady. Between its muzzle and Blenham's broad chest there was but the brief distance of some fifty feet. The report of Barbee's rifle, the thin upcurling smoke under the new sun—these were the chief matters in all the world for their little fragment of time.

Then Blenham threw out his arms and pitched forward. His foot caught in the stirrup. The frightened horse was plunging, running, dragging a man whose body was whipped this way and that.

"I promised—a long time ago," whispered Barbee, "that I'd get you, Blenham."

CHAPTER XXVII

IN HONOR OF THE FAIRY QUEEN!

"Guy Little!"

The old man's voice boomed out mightily as the old man himself strode back and forth impatiently in the big barn-like library of his ranch home. Guy Little appeared with a promptness savoring either of magic or prepared expectancy.

"You rang, your majesty?"

"Rang, your foot!" shouted old Packard. "I hollered my ol' head off. What's the day of the week, Guy Little?"

"It's Wednesday, your—"

"An' what's the day of the month?"

"It's the nineteenth, your—"

"Then tell me, sir," and the old man's tone was angry and challenging to a remarkable degree, "why in the name of the devil my gran'son, Stephen, ain't showed up yet!"

Guy Little might have remarked that it was rather early to expect any one to show up. It was not yet six o'clock of a

Jackson Gregory

morning which promised to be one of the very finest mornings ever known. The old man had, as Guy Little expressed it, "been prancin' an' pawin' aroun'," for an hour.

Guy Little grinned like any cherub.

"He has showed up," he chuckled, though he had meant to hold back the tidings teasingly. "He come in late las' night. You was asleep an' sleepin' soun', so—"

"He did, did he?" bellowed the old man. "Crept in like a damn' thief in the night, did he? Well, where is he now? Sleepin' yet, I'll be bound. When he ought to be up an'— Why, when I was a young devil his age—"

"He's outside somewhere," said Guy Little. "He has been down to the crick for a mornin' dip, I'd guess, your majesty."

"Why would you guess that?"

"Because pretty near all he had on was a towel an' a—a sort of a—immodes' britch-cloth," explained Guy Little confidentially.

"An'," continued old man Packard, "where's—she?"

"Meanin' the Fairy Queen, your majesty?" Guy Little's voice was now a whisper.

"Meanin' her—the Fairy Queen," said the old man gently. "Sleepin', Guy Little? I won't have her woke!"

"Woke, your eyebrow!" chuckled Guy Little. "I'd say she's gone for a—a dip, too, your majesty. An'—an', between just the two of us ol' fellers, hers is purty near as immodes' as his! Fact, an' I don't care whose granddaughter she is. Blue, you know; an' not very much of it. An' a red cap. An'—I couldn't see very well through the curtains an' I dasn't let 'em know I was lookin'. Only don't you let her know we know; why, bless her little simple heart, she ain't got the least idea how pretty an'—an'—immodes'—"

Old man Packard fixed him with a knowing eye.

"Ain't she?" he demanded. "Ain't she, Guy Little? Why, if there's one thing in this world worth knowin' that my granddaughter don't know—Go order breakfas' ready in two shakes, Guy Little."

"I did," said Guy Little. "It's ready already. There they come. Happy-lookin', ain't they? Like a couple kids."

"An' see that them two new saddle-horses is ready right after breakfas' for 'em, Guy Little."

"They're ready now," chuckled Guy Little. "I remembered."

"An—an' she likes—"

"Flowers on the table? An' her grapefruit stacked high with sugar? An' the coffee with hot milk? Don't I know nothin' a-tall, Packard?"

Steve and Terry, dripping and laughing, breaking into a run as they came on across the meadow, spied the big man and the little at the window and shouted a joyous good morning and Terry threw them a kiss apiece. And old man Packard, his hands on his hips, a look of absolute, ineffable content in his eyes, said softly:

"I've made a mistake or two in my life, Guy Little. But ain't I lived long enough to squeeze in a blunder or so here an' there? An' I've made a mistake a time or two on a man."

"Blenham did fool you pretty slick," suggested Guy Little.

"But," went on the old man hurriedly, "I know a real, upstandin', thoroughbred—"

"Fairy Queen of a woman."

"Fairy Queen of a woman when I see her. An' that little thing out there, her eyes shinin' like I ain't seen a pair of eyes shine for more'n fifty year, Guy Little—why, sir, she's what I call a—Why, she's a Packard, man!"

Choose from Thousands of 1stWorldLibrary Classics By

A. M. Barnard
Ada Leverson
Adolphus William Ward
Aesop
Agatha Christie
Alexander Aaronsohn
Alexander Kielland
Alexandre Dumas
Alfred Gatty
Alfred Ollivant
Alice Duer Miller
Alice Turner Curtis
Alice Dunbar
Allen Chapman
Alleyne Ireland
Ambrose Bierce
Amelia E. Barr
Amory H. Bradford
Andrew Lang
Andrew McFarland Davis
Andy Adams
Angela Brazil
Anna Alice Chapin
Anna Sewell
Annie Besant
Annie Hamilton Donnell
Annie Payson Call
Annie Roe Carr
Annonaymous
Anton Chekhov
Archibald Lee Fletcher
Arnold Bennett
Arthur C. Benson
Arthur Conan Doyle
Arthur M. Winfield
Arthur Ransome
Arthur Schnitzler
Arthur Train
Atticus
B.H. Baden-Powell
B. M. Bower
B. C. Chatterjee
Baroness Emmuska Orczy
Baroness Orczy
Basil King
Bayard Taylor
Ben Macomber
Bertha Muzzy Bower
Bjornstjerne Bjornson

Booth Tarkington
Boyd Cable
Bram Stoker
C. Collodi
C. E. Orr
C. M. Ingleby
Carolyn Wells
Catherine Parr Traill
Charles A. Eastman
Charles Amory Beach
Charles Dickens
Charles Dudley Warner
Charles Farrar Browne
Charles Ives
Charles Kingsley
Charles Klein
Charles Hanson Towne
Charles Lathrop Pack
Charles Romyn Dake
Charles Whibley
Charles Willing Beale
Charlotte M. Braeme
Charlotte M. Yonge
Charlotte Perkins Stetson
Clair W. Hayes
Clarence Day Jr.
Clarence E. Mulford
Clemence Housman
Confucius
Coningsby Dawson
Cornelis DeWitt Wilcox
Cyril Burleigh
D. H. Lawrence
Daniel Defoe
David Garnett
Dinah Craik
Don Carlos Janes
Donald Keyhoe
Dorothy Kilner
Dougan Clark
Douglas Fairbanks
E. Nesbit
E. P. Roe
E. Phillips Oppenheim
E. S. Brooks
Earl Barnes
Edgar Rice Burroughs
Edith Van Dyne
Edith Wharton

Edward Everett Hale
Edward J. O'Biren
Edward S. Ellis
Edwin L. Arnold
Eleanor Atkins
Eleanor Hallowell Abbott
Eliot Gregory
Elizabeth Gaskell
Elizabeth McCracken
Elizabeth Von Arnim
Ellem Key
Emerson Hough
Emilie F. Carlen
Emily Bronte
Emily Dickinson
Enid Bagnold
Enilor Macartney Lane
Erasmus W. Jones
Ernie Howard Pie
Ethel May Dell
Ethel Turner
Ethel Watts Mumford
Eugene Sue
Eugenie Foa
Eugene Wood
Eustace Hale Ball
Evelyn Everett-green
Everard Cotes
F. H. Cheley
F. J. Cross
F. Marion Crawford
Fannie E. Newberry
Federick Austin Ogg
Ferdinand Ossendowski
Fergus Hume
Florence A. Kilpatrick
Fremont B. Deering
Francis Bacon
Francis Darwin
Frances Hodgson Burnett
Frances Parkinson Keyes
Frank Gee Patchin
Frank Harris
Frank Jewett Mather
Frank L. Packard
Frank V. Webster
Frederic Stewart Isham
Frederick Trevor Hill
Frederick Winslow Taylor